Crimson Minds

A C Janes

First published in 2025 by Blossom Spring Publishing
Crimson Minds © 2025 A C Janes
ISBN 978-1-917938-10-5
E: admin@blossomspringpublishing.com
W: www.blossomspringpublishing.com

Part 1: The Emergence of Darkness

Chapter 1: Shadow's Breath

Charlie Blake

The transition from the structured life of military service to the unpredictable world of the Metropolitan Police had not been easy for Charlie Blake. As a former military police investigator, he was accustomed to the rigidity and discipline that came with the territory—attributes that had defined his existence for the better part of his adult life. Now, standing under the muted glow of a street lamp on a damp London evening, Blake found himself reflecting on the journey that had led him here.

His time in the military had instilled in him a sense of duty and a commitment to justice that transcended the battlefields he had left behind. The skills he had honed— sharp analytical thinking, an eye for detail, and an unwavering moral compass—were now tools in his arsenal as he navigated the complex and shadowy world of criminal investigation.

The city around him breathed a life of its own, a stark contrast to the deserts and conflict zones that had been his previous posts. Yet, the darkness that lurked in the corners of London's streets was not unlike the enemies he had faced before. Here, though, the battle was not against an opposing force but against the very elements of human nature that veered into the abyss of criminality.

Blake's thoughts were interrupted by the sudden vibration of his phone, a silent herald of the night's unfolding events. He answered the call with a practised ease, his voice steady and calm, betraying none of the anticipation that flickered within. The details were sparse: a body found in an abandoned warehouse, circumstances suspicious and unsettling. It was a call to arms, a reminder of the oath he had taken to serve and protect, regardless of the battlefield.

As he made his way to the scene, Blake's mind was a whirlwind of possibilities and scenarios. The transition from military to police work had taught him to expect the unexpected, to read between the lines of the unsaid and unseen. It was a skill that had served him well, a testament to his past and a beacon for his future in this new arena of justice.

The streets passed in a blur as Blake considered the path that lay ahead. This case, like every one before it, was a puzzle waiting to be solved—a story waiting to be told. And as he stepped out of the car and into the night, Blake knew that he was ready to face whatever darkness awaited him. For in the heart of darkness, there lay the opportunity for light, and it was his mission to find it, to bring it forth into the shadows that threatened to engulf the city he now served.

*

The chill of the London night had seeped into the bones of Detective Charlie Blake as he approached the derelict warehouse, the scene of the latest crime that had pulled him from the semblance of warmth his flat offered. The dim glow of the street lights barely penetrated the fog, casting long shadows that seemed to dance around him. Beside him, Detective Sarah Jennings moved with a quiet efficiency, her presence a steady constant in the unpredictable world of criminal investigation.

As they breached the threshold of the warehouse, the beam from Blake's flashlight cut through the darkness, revealing a scene that would haunt the dreams of even the most seasoned officers. Centre stage, under the harsh glare of their torches, lay the body of a young woman. Her arms were outstretched, positioned with a deliberate care that spoke of a ritualistic significance. Around her, a circle of salt, bordered with symbols, seemed to pulsate with a malevolent energy under the artificial light.

"The staging..." Jennings muttered, her voice a mix of fascination and horror. "It's methodical. Symbolic."

Blake nodded; his gaze fixed on the scene before him. The killer had not just taken a life; they had left a message. Kneeling beside the victim, he noted the precision of the cuts, the careful arrangement of her hair, the way her eyes were left open, staring into the void.

"Photographs first," Blake instructed, his voice cutting through the heavy silence that had enveloped the team. "I want everything documented before we move her."

As the forensic photographer began their grim task, Mike Hanover, the digital forensics expert, approached Blake, holding up a bagged item. "Found this under her. Looks like a phone, but there's no SIM card. Could be our key to understanding the symbols."

Blake took the bag, examining the phone through the plastic: "Get what you can from it. Anything could be the break we need."

Turning back to the scene, Blake's thoughts raced. The ritualistic elements, the careful staging— it all pointed to a serial killer, one who revelled in the theatrics of their crimes. It was a statement, a challenge to the police, a game of cat and mouse where human lives were at stake.

As the team worked around him, Blake felt the weight of the case settle on his shoulders. This was more than a murder investigation: it was a descent into the mind of a killer who saw themselves as an artist of death. The thought left a bitter taste in his mouth.

"We'll catch him," Jennings said, her voice steady, pulling Blake from his thoughts. "We'll make him pay for what he's done."

Blake met her gaze, the determination in her eyes mirroring his own resolve. "Yes, we will," he replied. "But first, we need to understand him. And to do that, we need to dive into his world."

As the team continued to collect evidence, Blake's mind was already racing ahead, piecing together fragments of a puzzle that was as dark as it was complex. The game had begun, and Blake was determined to win, to bring justice for the victim who lay before him, her life cut tragically short by a shadow that had yet to reveal its face.

*

With the initial shock of the crime scene's gruesome tableau somewhat abated, Detective Charlie Blake and his team began the meticulous process of gathering evidence, aware that even the smallest detail could be the key to unlocking the identity of the killer. The warehouse, once a place of industry and productivity, now bore witness to a macabre display of human depravity.

Mike Hanover, the unit's digital forensics specialist, had set up a mobile workstation near the perimeter of the scene. His fingers danced across the keyboard with a fervour, sifting through the digital detritus that modern criminals often left in their wake. The phone found beneath the victim, devoid of its SIM card, presented a challenge that Mike relished.

"Anything on that phone yet, Mike?" Blake asked, his voice cutting through the low murmur of activity.

"Working on it," Mike replied, without looking up. "It's locked, but I've got some tricks up my sleeve. Give me an hour."

Blake nodded, turning his attention to the forensic pathologist, Dr Emily Saunders, who was kneeling beside the victim. The air around her was thick with the scent of death, a smell Blake knew all too well from his military days.

"What can you tell us, Emily?" Blake inquired, his gaze fixed on the victim.

Dr Saunders looked up, removing her gloves with a snap. "Female, early twenties. Cause of death appears to be exsanguination from the throat slit. But it's the post-mortem work that's fascinating..." She paused, gauging Blake's reaction. "The precision of the cuts, the removal of specific organs—it's ritualistic, possibly symbolic. We'll need to do a full autopsy to understand more."

Blake felt a chill at her words. The killer wasn't just murdering; they were sending a message, one written in blood and shrouded in darkness.

As the team continued their work, Blake stepped outside for a moment of respite. The night air was cool against his skin, a stark contrast to the warmth of the warehouse. It was here, amidst the solitude, that Sarah Jennings found him.

"We're dealing with a serial killer, aren't we?" she asked, her voice barely above a whisper.

"It looks that way," Blake admitted, the weight of the situation heavy on his shoulders. "The staging, the ritualistic elements... This isn't a one-off. He's done this before, and he plans to do it again."

Sarah nodded, her expression grim. "Then we need to catch him before he does."

Blake looked back at the warehouse, a silent sentinel in the night. "We will," he said, with a determination that bordered on a vow. "We'll catch him, and we'll make him pay for what he's done."

Returning to the crime scene, Blake felt a renewed sense of purpose. The first clues had been laid out before them, a twisted path through the mind of a killer. It was a path Blake and his team were now bound to follow, wherever it might lead. The game had begun: a game of life and death, played in the shadows of human psyche and depravity. And Blake was determined to win.

*

As the investigation into the chilling murder at the warehouse deepened, Detective Charlie Blake found himself drawn into a complex web of clues that seemed to hint at a deeper, more personal connection to the case than he had initially realised. The meticulous nature of the crime scene, the ritualistic symbols, and the eerie sense of familiarity all pointed to one name that Blake had hoped never to encounter again in his career: Alex Morgan.

Morgan, whose name resonated with a sinister echo in the annals of the Metropolitan Police's unsolved cases, was a ghost from Blake's past. A brilliant mind turned malevolent, Morgan had been the suspect in a series of intricate crimes that had baffled the police several years earlier. His ability to elude capture, to remain always one step ahead of the investigation, had made him something of a legend—a dark shadow that loomed over Blake's career.

The connection to Morgan was initially dismissed by Blake as coincidence, the product of an overactive imagination fuelled by the stress of the case. However, as he pored over the evidence, Blake couldn't shake the nagging suspicion that there was more to it. The killer's use of digital surveillance, the ritualistic staging of the victim, even the choice of location—it all bore the hallmarks of Morgan's modus operandi.

"Could Morgan be involved?" Sarah Jennings asked, breaking the silence of the late-night evidence review session. Her question hung in the air, a palpable presence that demanded consideration.

Blake sighed, rubbing the bridge of his nose. "It's a stretch, but we can't ignore the similarities. Morgan always did enjoy the game, the challenge of pitting his wits against the police."

"But he's been off the grid for years," Mike Hanover chimed in, his gaze never leaving the computer screen. "Why resurface now? And why *this*?"

"That's what we need to find out," Blake said, his voice firm. "We need to dig deeper into Morgan's past cases, look for patterns, connections, anything that might give us an edge."

The team agreed, each member acutely aware of the stakes. The possibility that Alex Morgan was involved added a new layer of urgency to the investigation. Blake knew that facing Morgan again would not only be a test of his investigative skills but also a confrontation with his own past failures.

As the team set to work, Blake couldn't help but feel that the game had truly begun—a deadly cat-and-mouse chase that would lead them through the darkest corners of the human psyche. Morgan, if it were him, would not go quietly into the night. He would revel in the chase, in the intellectual battle that lay ahead.

And so, with determination and a grim resolve, Blake

and his team prepared to delve into the abyss, ready to face whatever horrors lay in wait. The hint of Alex Morgan's involvement was a clarion call to battle, a challenge that Blake could not—would not—ignore. The hunt was on, and this time, Blake vowed, there would be no escape for the shadow that haunted his every step.

*

The investigation into the serial killer's pattern had intensified, with each team member of the Metropolitan Police's elite unit bringing their expertise to the fore. The warehouse had become a hive of activity, a nucleus of analysis and theory, where each clue was dissected and discussed. Amidst this orchestrated frenzy of forensic science and detective work, Sarah Jennings stood out, her insights piercing through the veil of mystery that shrouded the case.

Jennings, with her sharp analytical mind and background in criminal psychology, had a way of getting into the heads of the perpetrators. As she walked through the crime scene, her eyes absorbed every detail, her mind weaving the disparate strands of evidence into a coherent psychological profile.

"Notice the symbolism," Jennings pointed out to Blake as they stood over the victim's body. "The killer is not just taking lives; they're curating scenes. It's a perverted form of artistry. Each victim is a statement, a piece to a puzzle we're yet to understand."

Blake listened intently, his respect for Jennings's perspective evident in his focused gaze. "Do you believe the killer is evolving with each scene?" he asked, voicing the concern that had been gnawing at him.

"It's possible," she replied. "It's like they're refining their method, getting bolder. They're enjoying the game, Charlie. And they're far from done."

The conversation was interrupted by the crackle of Hanover's voice over the walkie-talkie. "Boss, you might want to take a look at this," he said, urgency lacing his tone.

In the makeshift command centre, Hanover presented his findings from the victim's phone. "I managed to bypass the lock. The last message sent from this device was a quote: 'The beauty of the natural world lies in the details.' It's from a book, but it's been modified. This isn't just about the kills; there's a philosophy behind it."

The pieces of the puzzle were slowly fitting together, revealing the silhouette of a shadow they were chasing— a shadow that was both a person and an idea. Jennings's and Blake's discussion resumed, this time with a newfound urgency.

"We need to anticipate their next move," Blake said, his mind racing. Jennings nodded, her eyes reflecting a steely resolve.

"Agreed," Jennings responded. "We need to get into their headspace, understand their narrative. They're communicating through the chaos they create. The quote, the staging—it's all part of their dialogue with us."

Her statement hung in the air, a sobering reminder of the psychological warfare they had been unwittingly drafted into. The killer was indeed communicating, not just with the victims or the public, but directly with the police. It was a chilling thought, a game of intellect and morbidity.

Blake paced the room, his mind a vortex of strategy and profiles. "Sarah, focus on the psychological angle; pore over every detail. Mike, I need you to trace the origin of that quote, find out what book, what author. It's a clue we can't afford to overlook."

Jennings nodded, her determination mirroring Blake's intensity. She turned to the evidence laid out before them, each item a macabre breadcrumb leading back to the twisted mind they sought to understand.

The dynamics within the team, under the pressure of the investigation, had solidified into a force of collective will. They were more than just colleagues; they were comrades in a battle against a darkness that threatened to engulf them all. Blake knew that it was their unity, their shared resolve, that would see them through the labyrinthine twists and turns of the case.

As the team dispersed, each to their given tasks, Blake lingered, his eyes once again on the crime scene photos. The killer had left them a trail, and it was their duty to follow it, to piece together the fragments of a shattered psyche.

Sarah Jennings's role had become clearer with each passing moment. She was the key to understanding the narrative the killer was constructing, the bridge between the evidence and the elusive truth. And as Blake watched her work, he knew that together, they were the killer's nemesis, the light in the darkness that the perpetrator sought to weave.

*

The quiet of the command centre was a stark contrast to the chaotic churn of Charlie Blake's thoughts. With the team dispersed, chasing down leads and piecing together the profile of a killer, Blake allowed himself a moment of solitude. The dim glow from the overhead lights cast long shadows across the room, mirroring the dark recesses of doubt and determination that battled within him.

He pulled out the chair at his desk, the screech of metal on concrete jarring in the silence and sat down heavily. Before him lay the open case files: a mosaic of horror and intrigue that told the story of a killer's twisted crusade against the world. Blake ran his hand over his face, the stubble scratching against his palm, a tactile reminder of the hours they had all sunk into this case.

His mind drifted, unbidden, to the past, to the faces of those he had been too late to save. The military had taught him to be stoic, to build a wall around his emotions, but policing—this raw, unfiltered dive into the depravity of humanity—tested that fortitude. Blake knew the danger of becoming too enmeshed in the darkness, of allowing it to consume him. Yet it was a risk inherent to the path he had chosen, a path he walked willingly for the sake of justice.

Blake's eyes landed on a photo: the first victim, her life extinguished before it had truly begun. A surge of resolve coursed through him, banishing the shadows of doubt. This killer, this embodiment of malevolence, would not continue to haunt the living. He owed it to the victims, to the city he had sworn to protect, to the very ideals he upheld.

The detective rose, his chair scraping back with a decisive clang. He reached for his coat, feeling the weight of the badge over his heart—a weight that was both a burden and a privilege. As he turned off the lights, the room plunged into darkness, a darkness that no longer felt oppressive but rather a canvas against which the light of truth would shine all the brighter.

Blake stepped out into the night, the dawn a mere whisper on the horizon. The city was still asleep, unaware of the monster that walked among them—but Blake was awake, and he would not rest. His reflection was a promise, a silent oath to the city, to the victims, to himself. Justice would prevail, and he would be its steadfast harbinger.

Chapter 2: Echoes of the Past

Flashback

The air was thick with the dust of the Afghan desert, the relentless sun a searing reminder of the harshness of the environment. Captain Charlie Blake, then a military police investigator, stood in the shadow of a tent, his figure outlined against the canvas as he observed the man before him—Alex Morgan, a fellow soldier and a trusted ally in the field.

"Something doesn't add up, Morgan," Blake said, his voice low, carrying the weight of suspicion. "The attack on the convoy, the missing weapons—it feels orchestrated."

Morgan's eyes, a mirror of the desert sky, held a glimmer that spoke of shared secrets and mutual understanding. "We've made enemies, Charlie. Both within and outside our ranks. Trust is a luxury we can't afford," he replied, his voice tinged with an edge that hinted at deeper currents.

Their conversation was cut short by the arrival of a messenger, a young private who saluted crisply before delivering a report. Blake took it, his eyes scanning the contents quickly, his expression darkening with each word.

"We've got a leak. Intel is being fed to the insurgents," Blake announced, the gravity of the situation settling like a stone in his stomach.

Morgan's response was swift, his strategic mind already running through potential suspects. "We need to root it out, Charlie. Before more lives are lost."

The flashback shifted, the scene morphing into the cacophony of an ambush. Explosions rocked the ground, and gunfire stitched the air. Blake and Morgan fought side by side, their camaraderie forged in the crucible of conflict. But it was the aftermath that would haunt Blake—the sight of fallen comrades, the bitter taste of betrayal.

As the memory faded, the weight of the past hung heavily on Blake's shoulders. The trust he had placed in Morgan, the betrayal he felt when it was revealed that Morgan himself was the leak—it was a wound that time had not healed. The connection between past and present was a tangled web, and Blake knew that the key to understanding Morgan's descent into darkness lay in the echoes of their shared history.

*

The sterile glow of the fluorescent lights in the incident room bathed the investigative team in a harsh, revealing light. The walls were papered with timelines and photographs that chronicled the depravity of their quarry. At the centre of this mausoleum of memories stood Detective Charlie Blake, his eyes tracing the invisible lines that connected past to present.

"This isn't just a series of killings: it's a sequence," Blake began, his voice a steady thrum that resonated with conviction. "The MO is too specific, the staging too familiar. These aren't just echoes of my past cases—they're continuations of them."

Sarah Jennings leaned over the desk, her finger hovering over the images of the crime scenes. "You're saying the killer is picking up where your old cases left off?" Her question hung in the air, both a challenge and a call for affirmation.

Blake nodded, the lines on his face deepening. "Exactly. It's as if they're finishing a story I started reading years ago. We need to reopen those old case files—anything that predates my time with the Met."

The suggestion was met with a low hum of agreement from the team. Mike Hanover, their tech guru, chimed in, "I can pull up the digital archives. Anything specific we're looking for?"

"Patterns," Blake replied, the single word a mantra for their mission. "Look for similar victim profiles, geographical anomalies, and any references to the symbology we've been seeing."

The room surged into action, a flurry of keystrokes and hushed conversations as Blake's past began to bleed into the present investigation. He watched as his team worked, a sense of pride battling with the undercurrent of fear that what they would uncover could be more personal than any of them were prepared for.

Blake's phone vibrated, a silent sentinel alerting him to a new message. The text was from Lieutenant Grace Hudson, a name that carried with it memories of military camaraderie and the burdens of command. Her message was succinct. "We need to talk. It's about Morgan."

As Blake stepped out into the corridor, the soundproofing of the incident room muffled the persistent buzz of activity behind him. His conversation with Hudson was brief but laden with implications. Morgan's shadow loomed large, a spectre that had haunted Blake's career in the military police and now, it seemed, reached out from the past to wield influence over the present.

Returning to the team, Blake's expression was a mask of resolve. "We may have a lead from the military side of things. I'm going to need everything we have on Morgan's last known associates and operations."

Jennings caught the shift in Blake's demeanour, a

tightening of the jaw that spoke volumes. "Charlie, what aren't you telling us?" she asked, her gaze piercing.

Blake met her eyes, a silent communique passing between them. "Just trust me, Sarah. This case... it's personal in ways I wish it weren't."

As the team delved into the depths of Blake's past investigations, the air in the room seemed to grow heavier, charged with the promise of revelations yet to come. Blake stood at the helm, a captain navigating the treacherous waters of a case that was as much about his own history as it was about the victims'.

*

The sterile light of the morgue flickered as Detective Charlie Blake stepped in, the sharp scent of disinfectant and a chilling undercurrent of death greeting him. At the centre of this clinical tableau stood Dr Emily Saunders, the forensic pathologist, her figure poised with a scalpel in hand over the latest victim. The stark white of her coat was a striking contrast against the grisly scene before her.

"Dr Saunders," Blake acknowledged, his voice echoing slightly off the cold tiled walls.

"Detective," Emily greeted without looking up from the body on the table. "I was just about to begin the Y-incision."

Blake nodded, the familiarity of the procedure not diminishing its gravity. "Anything I should see before you start?"

"Actually, yes." Emily pointed to a series of marks on the victim's torso. "These aren't post-mortem. They were inflicted while the victim was still alive, with what I presume to be a kind of ceremonial dagger. The precision indicates the killer has a steady hand, likely with surgical or anatomical knowledge."

Blake's brow furrowed as he considered the implications. "That narrows our suspect pool."

"It does," Emily agreed, her gaze finally meeting his. "And there's more. I found traces of a compound on her skin—uncommon, mainly used in preservation methods for biological specimens. It's not something you find at your local pharmacy."

Blake's mind raced, cataloguing the new information. "Could the killer have a medical background?"

"It's a possibility," she replied, her eyes reflecting the depths of her thoughts. "I'll know more after the autopsy."

Blake watched as Emily turned back to her task, her hands steady and her focus unwavering. In the morgue, surrounded by the silent witnesses of crimes past, Emily Saunders was a beacon of clinical detachment and scientific rigour. Her expertise had been instrumental in many cases, but this one, with its ritualistic overtones and eerie precision, seemed to draw upon her skills even more.

"Keep me posted, Emily. Every detail matters."

"Of course, Charlie." Her voice was the epitome of professional coolness, but Blake could detect the slightest edge of concern. This case was getting under their skin, leaving its mark on each of them.

As he left the morgue, the click of the door behind him felt like the sealing of a covenant. They were in this together—a team bound by the pursuit of justice, each playing their part in the hunt for a killer who was as methodical as he was monstrous.

Blake processed the new information and considered its impact on the investigation, each revelation a piece in a larger, more disturbing puzzle.

*

Detective Charlie Blake and Mike Hanover huddled over a multitude of screens, the soft glow casting an otherworldly hue across the makeshift digital forensics lab. The rhythmic tapping of keyboards provided a steady backdrop to their intense focus. Mike, with a furrowed brow, sifted through lines of code and digital footprints that criss-crossed the dark web like a spider's web.

"These patterns are no accidents," Mike murmured, more to himself than to Blake. "Our killer is sophisticated, using the net like his personal hunting ground, luring and taunting."

Blake—whose experience with digital intricacies wasn't as nuanced—relied on Mike's expertise. "Translate that for those of us less versed in the digital world," he said.

Mike swivelled in his chair to face Blake, pushing his glasses up the bridge of his nose. "He left traces deliberately, almost like digital breadcrumbs. It's a trail, yes, but it's convoluted, looping back on itself, leading to dead ends, encrypted sites, message boards. It's a maze meant to baffle, to delay."

Blake leaned in, his eyes scanning the constellation of data points on the screen. "But you've found something, haven't you?"

A slight grin tugged at the corner of Mike's mouth. "I might have. There's a pattern to the chaos. Look here." He pointed at a series of timestamps and IP addresses that appeared random but were highlighted in a distinct colour. "Every third day, at precisely 3.33 a.m., our killer accesses a site. It's a message board for the esoteric, the occult."

The detective's interest piqued; the timing seemed ritualistic, another piece of the killer's psychological puzzle. "What does he access?"

"Posts about myths, legends, riddles. But there's one consistent theme—transformation. The killer sees himself as an agent of change. Each victim is a chrysalis, each crime scene a cocoon."

Blake absorbed the information, his brain firing on all cylinders. "So, he's not just killing. He's metamorphosing the world according to his vision."

"Exactly. And he wants us to know it," Mike affirmed, his eyes not leaving the screen. "He's playing God in his digital Eden."

The revelation was profound, unsettling. This was no ordinary killer; this was someone with a manifesto, someone who saw murder as a means to an end. The digital breadcrumbs weren't just to taunt the police—they were an invitation to understand, to enter the mind of a killer who was as philosophical as he was lethal.

Blake stood up, the wheels turning in his head "Keep digging, Mike. Anything he's accessed, any interaction. We need to understand his philosophy if we're to predict his next move."

As Blake walked away, a sense of urgency propelled him. The case was evolving, unfolding into something that transcended their typical purview. They were no longer just hunting a killer; they were delving into a mind that sought to rewrite the very fabric of reality—one victim at a time.

*

The late afternoon sun cast a warm glow over Dr Helen Zhao's office, the soft light filtering through the blinds and creating a stark contrast with the darkness of the conversation within. Detective Charlie Blake sat across from Zhao, her profile silhouetted against the light, her features composed yet hinting at the undercurrent of intensity that her profession demanded.

Dr Zhao slid a file across the desk towards Blake. "The killer's motives are rooted deeper than his actions suggest," she began, her tone measured. "Each victim represents a concept, an ideal that he's fixated on. He's not just taking lives; he's making a statement."

Blake opened the file, his eyes scanning the pages. "A manifesto?" he questioned, looking up.

"Precisely," Zhao affirmed. "He sees himself as a purveyor of change, a catalyst for a transformation that goes beyond the physical. His actions are symbolic, an attempt to awaken society to his vision of truth."

The room was steeped in silence as Blake pondered her words. The profile was painting a picture of a killer not driven by the usual motives of greed or passion, but by a belief system that justified his heinous acts.

"Have you found any connections? Patterns in his choice of victims?" Blake asked, his mind racing with the implications of her analysis.

Zhao leaned forward, her fingers laced together. "There's a commonality linking the victims—each was at a crossroads, a pivotal moment in their life. It's as if he's choosing them when they're most vulnerable to change, to transformation."

Blake felt a chill despite the room's warmth. "He's playing god," he murmured.

Zhao nodded. "In his mind, yes. And he won't stop. Each act, each... ritual is an evolution. He's escalating, seeking a pinnacle in his narrative."

"What's his endgame?" Blake asked, the profiler's insights painting a grim picture of a killer with a complex psychological tapestry.

"That's the million-dollar question, Charlie," Zhao

replied. "But one thing is clear—he won't stop until he's completed his narrative. And we need to catch him before this story reaches its resolution."

Blake stood up, the weight of the file in his hand as heavy as the burden he carried in his heart. "Thank you, Dr Zhao. Your insights are, as always, invaluable."

He left the office with the setting sun casting long shadows behind him, a metaphor for the darkening path that lay ahead. The killer was more than a mere predator; he was a storyteller using death as his medium, and Blake knew that he had to intercept the tale before the final chapter could be written.

*

The atmosphere in the briefing room was charged with a palpable tension as Detective Charlie Blake prepared to share the insights gained from Dr Helen Zhao with his team. The walls, adorned with the macabre timeline of the killer's activities, served as a grim reminder of the stakes at hand.

Blake stood at the front, the weight of leadership pressing down on him. He looked over his team: a collection of the finest minds the Metropolitan Police had to offer, each member keenly aware of the race against time they were engaged in.

"Team," Blake began, his voice firm, "we're not just dealing with a killer. We're dealing with someone who believes they're enacting a grand narrative, someone who's using murder as a medium for their twisted message."

He paused, allowing his words sink in, before continuing. "Dr Zhao has provided us with a profile that paints our suspect as not only as a murderer but as a zealot committed to a cause only they understand. This isn't just about catching a killer; it's about interrupting a narrative before more lives are claimed."

Sarah Jennings, always perceptive, leaned forward. "So, how do we alter our approach?"

Blake met her gaze, appreciating the directness of her question. "We need to think like him, get ahead of his story. Mike, any digital breadcrumbs he's left, we use them to predict his next move. Emily, I need you to dive deeper into the forensic signature he's leaving behind. What he's communicating with his choice of victims and methods—it's all part of his narrative."

Turning to the rest of the team, Blake's demeanour underscored the urgency of their mission. "Everyone has a role to play. This killer is smart, but he's also arrogant. He believes he's untouchable, weaving his narrative in plain sight. We're going to use that arrogance against him."

The room was silent, each member of the team processing their part in the strategy laid out before them. Blake knew that the path ahead would be fraught with challenges, but the determination and skill of his team gave him hope.

"We end his story on our terms, not his," Blake concluded, a note of resolve in his voice. "Let's get to work."

As the team dispersed, Blake stayed back, reviewing the case files once more. The killer had indeed been playing a game, but now, armed with new insights and a renewed sense of purpose, Blake and his team were ready to change the rules. The next move was theirs to make, and Blake was determined to make it count.

Chapter 3: Web of Deceit

Undercover Shadows

Elena Martinez had always thrived under pressure, of the kind that would crush most. As she merged with the shadows of London's underbelly, her heart raced—not from fear, but from anticipation. Tonight was not just any operation; it was the culmination of months of meticulous planning, of becoming someone else entirely. Elena, now known as Ellie Mason in the criminal circuits, was about to infiltrate one of the city's most elusive drug rings, believed to be a front for the serial killer the Metropolitan Police was desperately hunting.

Her transformation for the undercover operation was more than skin deep. It wasn't just the dyed hair or the faux tattoos that lined her arms, symbols of a past she had fabricated overnight; it was in her eyes, the way she moved, spoke, and even thought. Elena had to become Ellie, someone with enough edge and history to blend in, yet not so much as to stand out. This duality was her armour and her weapon.

The rendezvous point was a nondescript warehouse on the outskirts, the same type of location that had become all too familiar to Detective Charlie Blake and his team. As Elena approached, her senses were heightened, every shadow a potential threat, every sound a signal. Inside, the air was thick with anticipation and something more sinister: a malaise that seemed to seep from the very walls.

She was met by a figure who matched the description of Adrian Flint, the ring's supposed leader. His eyes scanned her with a mix of suspicion and interest. "Ellie

Mason," he began, his voice smooth like oil, "you're a hard woman to find."

Elena kept her posture relaxed and her voice steady. "And you're a man who values discretion," she retorted, matching his tone. "I believe we have mutual interests."

The conversation that followed was a delicate dance, a negotiation not just of goods but of trust. Elena, as Ellie, had to sell her identity, to make Flint believe she was the ally he needed, all while gathering the information that Blake and the team so desperately required. It was a high-wire act without a net.

Meanwhile, Blake and his team were stationed discreetly nearby, ears glued to the listening devices, hearts racing with every word transmitted. This operation was a gamble, one that could lead them to the heart of the darkness they were seeking or plunge them deeper into mystery. Blake's trust in Elena was absolute, but the risk was palpable, the tension in the surveillance van almost tangible.

As the meeting concluded, Elena made her way back to the shadows from which she'd emerged, her mind racing with the information she had gleaned. Flint was cautious, but she had seen the flicker of something in his eyes, a hint of the web of deceit they were all entangled in.

Back at the command centre, the team debriefed, poring over every detail Elena had provided. It was clear they were on the right track, but the path forward was fraught with danger. Blake's gaze lingered on Elena, a silent acknowledgment of the line she had walked tonight, of the balance between light and darkness.

This operation had brought them one step closer to understanding the killer's motives and methods—but it also served as a stark reminder of the stakes. In the web of deceit, every thread they pulled could either lead them to salvation or become a noose around their necks.

As Elena recounted her interactions with Flint, her observations of the warehouse, and the subtle clues she had noticed, Blake knew that this was more than just an operation. It was a declaration of war against a shadow that had haunted London for too long. The game was indeed afoot, and they were all players, whether they chose to be or not. The question that remained was who would make the next move, and at what cost.

*

The operation had taken a toll on the team, but there was no time to rest. The next phase demanded their undivided attention. Blake, leveraging the intelligence gathered by Elena, devised a plan to intercept a key exchange between Flint's ring and another unknown player in this sinister game. This was their chance to cut one of the many threads in the web of deceit and possibly identify a direct link to the killer.

As night enveloped the city, the team positioned themselves around the designated exchange location, a derelict parking lot illuminated by the occasional flicker of a distant street lamp. The air was thick with tension, each member aware of the operation's stakes and the danger that lay in wait.

Elena, though not in the field this time, was instrumental in coordinating the operation from the command centre. Her insights into Flint's operations provided Blake and his team with the edge they needed to anticipate their adversary's moves. The operation was a symphony of precision, each member playing their part in a larger plan orchestrated by Blake's strategic mind.

The exchange began as a shadowy figure emerged from the darkness, moving towards Flint's envoy with a cautious yet determined gait. Blake, watching from a distance, signalled his team to hold their positions. Timing was everything.

Just as the transaction was about to conclude, Blake gave the signal, and the team moved in. The ensuing moments were a blur of motion and sound, a chaotic dance of light and shadow. The team worked with a well-practised efficiency, securing the area and apprehending Flint's men. However, the mysterious figure managed to escape in the confusion, leaving behind more questions than answers.

In the aftermath, Blake and his team examined the evidence seized during the operation. Among the items was a nondescript flash drive, its contents encrypted. It was a small piece of the puzzle, but Blake knew that it could be the key to unravelling the killer's identity.

The close call of the operation was a stark reminder of the dangers they faced. Blake, reflecting on the night's events, realised that they were dealing with an adversary who was always one step ahead, a mastermind who thrived in the shadows of London's criminal underworld.

As the team regrouped, the personal toll of the case became apparent. The long hours and constant danger were wearing on them, but the resolve to see justice served kept them going. Blake, seeing the fatigue in his team's eyes, knew that they needed a breakthrough, and soon.

The flash drive held the potential to be that breakthrough. As Mike Hanover began the arduous process of decrypting its contents, Blake and the rest of the team waited with bated breath. This could be the moment they had been working towards, the thread that, once pulled, would unravel the killer's web of deceit.

The operation had been a close call, but it had also brought them one step closer to their quarry. Blake knew that the path ahead would be fraught with more dangers, but he also knew that his team was ready to face whatever darkness lay in wait. Together, they would bring light to the shadows that had engulfed London, no matter the cost.

*

In the aftermath of the operation, the team regrouped under the weight of exhaustion and the thrill of a narrow escape. The flash drive, now decrypted, revealed a labyrinth of financial transactions, cryptic communications, and, most intriguingly, a set of coordinates.

Blake, standing at the head of the command centre, projected the decrypted files onto the screen. "This," he declared, pointing to the string of numbers and letters, "could be where our killer feels safest. It's time we step into his world."

Dan Brooks, the team's seasoned investigator known for his knack for non-digital clues, leaned forward. "Coordinates could mean anything—a meeting point, a drop site, or something more personal. We need to understand its significance beyond its geographical location."

The team decided on a two-pronged approach. While Mike continued to sift through the digital breadcrumbs for any more hidden messages, Dan would lead a reconnaissance mission to the coordinates, a seemingly abandoned warehouse district on the edge of the city.

As Dan and a select team prepared, Sarah Jennings approached Blake with a concern. "Charlie, we're stretching ourselves thin. This chase is becoming more than just catching a killer—it's consuming us."

Blake met her gaze, understanding the toll it was taking on them all. "I know, Sarah. But think of the lives we'll save if we end this. We're not just officers; we're guardians."

The reconnaissance was a silent affair, the team moving through the shadows to avoid detection. The warehouse was as nondescript as they come, but as Dan peered through his binoculars, he noticed something—a faint light flickering through a cracked window.

"Team, eyes on target. There's activity inside," Dan whispered into his radio, signalling for a cautious approach.

Inside, they found not the killer but a workshop of horrors: detailed plans of each crime scene, photos of potential victims, and a chilling diary outlining the killer's twisted philosophy. It was a gold mine of evidence, but the killer was nowhere to be found.

As they secured the site, Blake received a call. It was Simon Fraser, their liaison with the press. "Charlie, the media's catching wind of something big. They're asking questions, and I'm running out of ways to deflect."

Blake sighed, the weight of public scrutiny adding another layer of complexity. "Tell them we're making progress, Simon. But nothing more. We can't afford to spook him now."

The discovery at the warehouse was a breakthrough, but it also meant the killer knew they were closing in. The game was escalating, and Blake felt the pressure mounting. Yet, amidst the chaos, a resolve solidified within the team. They were closer than ever, the path forward illuminated by the clues left in the shadows.

As they left the warehouse, Blake looked back at the flickering light in the window, a beacon in the night. "He's watching," he murmured. "But so are we. And we're not afraid of the dark."

*

The dim light of dawn crept into the command centre, casting long shadows over the evidence sprawled across the tables. Blake stood at the helm, his team arrayed around him, their faces etched with determination and fatigue. The breakthrough at the warehouse had provided them with an abundance of new evidence, but the killer's identity remained shrouded in mystery.

"Let's start with what we know," Blake began, his voice steady, anchoring the weary team. "The warehouse was not just a storage unit; it was a staging ground. Our killer is meticulous, calculating."

Dan Brooks laid out photographs and documents seized from the site. "We've got maps, notes, and what appears to be a schedule of planned crimes. It's a roadmap to his madness."

Elena, still feeling the adrenaline from her undercover work, pointed to a series of photographs. "These aren't random. Each location has a specific significance to the killer, a piece of a larger puzzle we're only beginning to decipher."

Mike Hanover, eyes tired from hours in front of a screen, chimed in. "And there's something in the digital footprint we've overlooked. The encryption on these files was sophisticated, beyond anything we've seen. He's hiding something big."

The team leaned in as Sarah Jennings, her expertise in criminal psychology more crucial than ever, offered her insights. "It's not just the physical evidence. The diary, the notes—they're all expressions of a deeply disturbed mind, one that sees itself as above the law, above morality."

Blake nodded, absorbing each point. "We're dealing with someone who believes they're orchestrating a symphony of chaos, but they've left us the score. We need to get ahead of his next move."

Simon Fraser broke the intense focus. "The media's starting to ask questions. They know we're onto something. How much do we reveal?"

Blake considered this, the balance between transparency and operational security weighing heavily on him. "We give them enough to keep the public safe, nothing more. Our priority is to stop him, not to feed headlines."

As the meeting drew to a close, the personal toll of the investigation was palpable. Blake saw the exhaustion in his team's eyes, the strain of the case drawing tight. Yet, there was also resolve, a shared commitment to justice that no amount of darkness could diminish.

"We regroup in two hours," Blake concluded, his voice imbued with quiet strength. "Take this time to rest, to reset. We're close, and when we come back we're going to end this."

The team dispersed, each member lost in thought. The clue analysis had provided a path forward, through the shadows and into the light of understanding. Now, it was a race against time to prevent the next act in the killer's grim performance.

*

As the investigation into the serial killer intensifies, the Metropolitan Police find themselves under the glaring spotlight of public scrutiny. Simon Fraser, the press officer, is at the forefront, navigating the treacherous waters of media demands and the public's thirst for information. In a cramped office filled with ringing phones and flashing screens, Simon crafts statements that reveal just enough to satisfy the media's appetite without compromising the investigation's integrity.

Detective Charlie Blake, meanwhile, feels the pressure mounting. Each press conference is a tightrope walk, balancing the need for transparency with the imperative of maintaining operational secrecy. The relentless media attention not only strains the resources of the team but also puts additional stress on the victims' families, who are caught in the unforgiving gaze of public interest.

The team's morale is tested as every move, decision, and even personal moments become fodder for speculation and sensational headlines. Blake sees the toll it takes on his team, particularly on Sarah, whose insights into the killer's psyche have become a focal point for media intrigue. The boundaries between their professional duties and personal lives blur, leaving them exposed and vulnerable.

In an effort to shield his team from the brunt of public scrutiny, Blake takes a bold step. He decides to engage directly with the media, offering a carefully orchestrated interview that aims to refocus the narrative on the victims and the ongoing efforts to bring the killer to justice. This strategic move is not without risks, but Blake is determined to regain control of the story, to remind the public of the human cost of the killer's actions and to appeal for patience and trust.

The interview is tense, with Blake fielding difficult questions and navigating the minefield of public opinion. He speaks with a calm authority, his words a testament to the dedication of his team and their unwavering commitment to solving the case. For a moment, the relentless pace of the investigation slows, allowing Blake and his team a brief respite from the storm.

However, the reprieve is short-lived. As new evidence comes to light, the media frenzy reaches new heights, and the team is once again thrust into the whirlwind of public scrutiny. This time, however, they are not just fighting to catch a killer—they are also battling to maintain the trust of the city they serve, to keep the media at bay, and to protect the integrity of their investigation.

Through it all, Blake remains a steadfast leader, his resolve hardened by the challenges they face. He knows that the path to justice is fraught with obstacles, but he is prepared to lead his team through the darkness, guided by the light of their shared commitment to justice and the unwavering support of the community they are sworn to protect.

*

In the quiet aftermath of another long day, Detectives Charlie Blake and Sarah Jennings find a moment's respite in the dimly lit confines of the office. The weight of the investigation, compounded by the intense media scrutiny, begins to show in their weary expressions and slumped postures.

Blake breaks the silence, his voice low and tinged with fatigue. "How are you holding up, Sarah?" he asks, his concern genuine, reflecting the bond formed through countless hours of shared struggles and determination.

Sarah looks up, her eyes reflecting the toll of sleepless nights and the emotional burden of delving into the mind of a killer. "It's hard," she admits, allowing herself a moment of vulnerability. "Every clue, every profile—it feels like we're getting closer, yet he's always just out of reach."

Blake nods, understanding all too well. "It's like we're shadows chasing shadows," he muses, his gaze lost in the cluttered expanse of case files and evidence photos that cover the desk. "But we can't let it break us. We owe it to the victims and their families to see this through."

The room falls silent again, the only sound the faint hum of the fluorescent lights. It's a silence that speaks volumes, filled with unspoken fears and the daunting realisation of the journey still ahead.

Suddenly, Blake stands, his movement breaking the spell. "Come on," he says, with a determined look. "Let's get some fresh air." They step out into the cool night, the city sounds a distant backdrop to their solitude.

As they walk, the barriers of rank and protocol momentarily dissolve, allowing them to speak freely. "I've been thinking," Blake begins, his voice thoughtful, "about the killer's next move, the patterns we're seeing. We're missing something, something crucial."

Sarah, energised by the night air and the opportunity to brainstorm without the confines of the office walls, engages eagerly. "The ritualistic aspect, the locations— it's all part of a larger narrative he's creating. We need to disrupt his narrative, force him to make a mistake."

Blake stops, turning to face her. "Exactly," he says, a spark of resolve lighting his features. "We've been reactive; it's time to be *proactive*, to think two steps ahead."

Their conversation grows more animated as they walk, the burdens of the case momentarily lifted as they focus on the challenge of outsmarting their adversary. It's a moment of connection, of shared purpose that renews their resolve.

As they return to the station, the dawn begins to break,

casting a soft light over the city. The path ahead remains fraught with uncertainty, but for Blake and Sarah the journey is a testament to their dedication, their unwavering commitment to justice and the personal sacrifices they are willing to make.

Chapter 4: The Hunter and the Hunted

Chasing Shadows

The twilight cloaked London in a veil of obscurity as Detective Charlie Blake stood before the expansive glass pane of the incident room. The relentless rain drew long, jagged lines across the surface, distorting the city's pulsating lights into a chaotic dance of shadows and light. He watched, his mind as tempestuous as the squall that battered the streets below, thoughts churning with the tumultuous promise of the night ahead.

Blake turned from the window, his reflection a ghostly spectre upon the glass—a fitting metaphor for the elusive quarry they hunted. The room was alive with a nervous energy, each member of his team poised on the precipice of action. They gathered around the central table, which was strewn with maps and photographs, each a piece of the macabre puzzle they were desperate to solve.

The catalyst for the night's operation was an informant, codenamed "Raven", whose cryptic message had set the gears in motion. It spoke of a gathering, a shadowy congregation where the currency of trade was not in goods, but in grim secrets and sinister pacts. If the intelligence held true, they stood on the brink of ensnaring the city's most enigmatic predator.

The stakes towered over them, a monolith of consequence. Blake addressed his team, his voice a calm harbour in the storm of anticipation that swirled around them. "This is the moment we've been waiting for," he declared, locking eyes with each member in turn. "Tonight, we may have our only chance to draw the killer into the light."

The team's preparation was a silent ballet of efficiency: firearms checked with reverent precision and bulletproof vests strapped on with the solemnity of armour. The air was thick with the scent of oiled metal and determination. Blake paused beside the youngest detective, whose hands betrayed a tremble of adrenaline. With a firm grip on the detective's shoulder, Blake offered a nod of silent encouragement—a beacon of steadfastness in the uncertain night.

As the convoy of unmarked cars cut through the rain-soaked streets, they moved as phantoms, unnoticed by the city that never slept. They converged on the warehouse district, where the buildings stood like silent sentinels, guardians of the night's dark deeds.

The operation unfolded with military precision. Blake's team dispersed into the shadows, invisible watchers in the gloom. Their target was the derelict warehouse at the dock's edge, where the Thames whispered secrets to those who dared listen. Blake found his place, his back to the cold brick, his eyes fixed on the entrance shrouded in darkness.

Minutes stretched into eternities as they waited for the signal. Blake's heart beat a rhythm of controlled anticipation, the stillness around him so profound he could hear the whispers of his team across their radios, a lifeline in the void.

And then, as sudden as a lightning strike, a figure emerged from the shadows—a silhouette defined against the warehouse's dimly lit doorway. The team tensed, each member ready to spring the trap. But there was a pause, a hitch in the night's breath, and Blake felt the first gnaw of doubt—the prelude to a realisation that the hunter could very well become the hunted.

As the figure stepped into the scant light, the rain ceased its relentless assault, and the world held its breath, waiting for the mask of darkness to fall away.

*

The warehouse loomed large and spectral, an edifice of decay that seemed to resonate with the night's oppressive silence. Detective Charlie Blake's team lay in wait, every sense strained to the utmost, every nerve alight with the electric tension of anticipation. The figure at the door had vanished as abruptly as it appeared, swallowed by the shadows once more, leaving behind a chilling void.

In the heartbeat that followed, Blake's radio crackled to life, and Lieutenant Grace Hudson's voice cut through the static, a steel thread in the dark tapestry of the night. "Blake, I have something you need to hear," she said, urgency sharpening her words. Blake signalled to his team to maintain positions before stepping away into the deeper gloom, the handset pressed to his ear.

Grace's words were a torrent of military precision and keen insight. She spoke of recent intelligence gathered, connections made through painstaking analysis of encrypted communications, all roads leading back to one name—Alex Morgan. Blake felt the name like a cold finger down his spine, a ghost from his past now haunting his present.

"He's planning something big, Charlie. Something that goes beyond the city, beyond the usual play of shadows we're accustomed to," Grace warned, her voice a harbinger of dark tidings. "You need to brace for the possibility that tonight's operation might only be a precursor to the storm that's coming."

Blake absorbed her words, his mind racing as he pieced together the fragments she provided, each one a shard of a larger, more terrifying picture. "And the informant, Raven?" he asked, his voice steady despite the tumult within.

"There's more to Raven than meets the eye. Be careful who you trust, Blake. Shadows can hide more than just secrets; they can obscure the line between ally and enemy," Grace replied, the line going dead with a click that echoed the finality of her warning.

Returning to his team, Blake was the embodiment of composed leadership, but beneath the surface a maelstrom of thoughts raged. He knew that they were on the cusp of something monumental, a case that would test the limits of their resolve and the strength of their courage.

With Grace Hudson's insights burning in his mind, Blake considered their next move. The trap set for the killer was more than a mere ploy for capture; it was a gambit in a grander scheme that they were only beginning to comprehend. The game had shifted, the board had changed, and they were players in a narrative far greater than they had imagined.

The night whispered of caution, of eyes unseen and plans unknown. Blake knew that they must tread carefully, for in the pursuit of a hunter as cunning as Alex Morgan, any misstep could be their last. But as Grace's intelligence took root, Blake's resolve only deepened—a resolve that would lead them through the coming darkness, come what may.

*

In the labyrinthine heart of the Metropolitan Police headquarters, Detective Charlie Blake and his trusted team huddled around a sprawl of digital screens and paper maps, the walls of the room closing in with the weight of impending confrontation. The murmurs of strategy discussions formed a low hum, punctuated by the occasional sharp command as Blake orchestrated the formation of a trap intricate enough to ensnare a killer as elusive as smoke.

With Grace Hudson's intelligence as their guiding star, the team dissected every known habit, every preferred haunt, every cryptic message left by Alex Morgan. They crafted a plan that was as much a psychological snare as it was a physical one, targeting the very ego that drove Morgan's twisted crimes.

Blake stood at the head of the table, his fingers tracing the lines of the city on the map before him. "He thrives in chaos, in fear," Blake mused aloud, his team's eyes fixed upon him. "But we'll offer him a stage, a grand performance where he believes he holds the spotlight."

The trap was a high-stakes masquerade, a staged crime scene that would appeal to Morgan's vanity and his insatiable desire to outsmart the law. It would be held at an abandoned theatre, a grim nod to the dramatic flair with which Morgan imbued his macabre work. The bait would be a planted article, a challenge woven into the narrative the killer so dearly loved—a dare hidden within the lines of a seemingly innocuous local news story.

As the details of the operation were finessed, Sarah Jennings, whose expertise in criminal psychology was unparalleled, spoke up. "He won't be able to resist," she assured the room, her voice a lighthouse in the stormy sea of profiles and patterns. "Morgan sees himself as the director of his own twisted play, and we're offering him a climax that's too enticing to ignore."

Blake nodded, satisfaction mingling with the leaden weight of responsibility. The team was in agreement, each member acutely aware of the stakes. They were not merely laying a trap for a killer; they were weaving a narrative of their own, one that required precision and a deep understanding of the darkness they sought to overcome.

The plan was set into motion with the silent efficiency that had become their hallmark. The theatre was dressed as a crime scene, each prop a deliberate choice, each light a cue in the performance they crafted. The news article, masked as an exposé on the Metropolitan Police's progress, was laced with the bait—a quote from a fictitious detective that mirrored one of Morgan's own, a detail only he would recognise.

As the pieces fell into place, Blake stood in the shadows of the theatre's wings, watching as his team worked with silent determination. This was their gambit, their feint in the grand chess game against a foe who revelled in the darkness.

Tonight, the theatre would host a different kind of production, one where the boundary between hunter and hunted blurred, where the stakes were life and death, and where the final act was yet unwritten.

*

The abandoned theatre, once a bastion of laughter and applause, now stood silent, its grandeur faded into a sombre backdrop for the night's grim undertaking. In the shadows of the stage, Detective Charlie Blake and his team lay in wait, the air thick with the tension of a string drawn taut, ready to snap. The trap had been laid with meticulous care, every detail a crafted lure for a killer who was a connoisseur of death's drama.

Hours passed, the silence of the theatre stretching into an agonising void. Blake's eyes never strayed from the balcony, where they expected Morgan to appear, drawn by the irresistible bait they had planted. Sarah Jennings stood close, her profile etched in the dim light, a sentinel poised for the slightest sign.

Then, a disturbance—a soft creak of aged wood from the balcony. It was a sound that sent a ripple of movement through the team, a silent signal that the hunter had taken the bait. Blake signalled, and, like phantoms, they moved to surround the area.

But the figure that emerged from the darkness was not Alex Morgan. It was Raven, the informant, her face pale, her eyes wide with terror. "It's a trap," she gasped, her voice barely a whisper. "He knew. He's always known."

Before Blake could react, the night erupted into chaos. Explosions thundered through the theatre, a cacophony of destruction that sent plaster and dust raining from the ceiling. The stage erupted in flames, a pyrotechnic nightmare that turned their carefully laid plan into a death trap.

The team scrambled, disoriented by the blast's concussive force. Blake found himself on his knees, his ears ringing, his vision blurred. Around him, the theatre was a maelstrom of confusion, the team's voices lost in its roar.

"He's playing us," Blake realised, the truth a bitter pill. Morgan hadn't just anticipated their move; he had turned it against them. The theatre, the article, the informant— they were but pawns in a larger game, one where Morgan held dominion over life and death.

As the team fought to evacuate, Blake's mind reeled with the implications. This was more than a mere escape; it was a statement of dominance, a display of cunning that dwarfed their own. They had underestimated their foe, and the cost of that miscalculation was etched in the flames that now consumed the theatre.

The ambush had gone wrong, spectacularly so. As they emerged into the night, the theatre a roaring inferno behind them, Blake's resolve hardened into something steely and unyielding. They had been bested, but the battle was far from over. The game continued, and Blake knew that the rules had changed. Now, it was not just about justice—it was personal, and he would not rest until the scales were balanced.

*

In the aftermath of the thwarted ambush, with the charred remains of the theatre smouldering under the watchful eye of the dawn, Detective Charlie Blake stood amidst the ruins, a silent sentinel surveying the damage wrought by a mind as devious as the killer they pursued. The air was tinged with the acrid stench of smoke and failure, the bitter tang of it filling Blake's lungs as he inhaled the morning chill.

The team had survived, by fortune or fate, but the night had taken its toll. Blake watched as they tended to one another, their faces smeared with soot, their eyes reflecting the night's terror. Yet, amidst the desolation, a fierce determination burned in Blake's chest, a flame that the theatre's inferno could not match.

He had dedicated his life to the pursuit of justice, a journey that had led him through the heart of humanity's darkest corridors. The confrontation with Alex Morgan was not just a challenge to his skill as a detective; it had become a crucible, testing the very essence of his resolve.

"Blake," Sarah Jennings's voice called to him, her hand resting lightly on his arm. "We were lucky tonight."

Blake turned to her, his gaze steely. "Luck favours the

41

prepared, Sarah. We weren't prepared—not for this," he admitted, the words tasting of ash. "But we will be. Next time, we'll be the ones writing the script."

Sarah nodded, understanding the unspoken weight behind his words. They had been outmanoeuvred, outplayed in their own game, but the match was not over. Blake's resolve was the anchor that kept them grounded, the unwavering force that would guide them through the storm Morgan had unleashed.

As the first rays of sunlight pierced the veil of smoke, Blake's silhouette was a stark contrast against the lightening sky. He made a silent vow amidst the wreckage, a vow that was as unbreakable as the dawn was inevitable. They would regroup, reforge their strategy with the hardened steel of their shared ordeal.

The path ahead would be fraught with challenges, each step a potential misstep in the dance with a shadow as elusive as Morgan. But Blake's resolve had been steeled in the fire of the theatre, and he would not falter, nor would he allow the darkness to claim any more lives.

He turned his back on the smouldering remains and set his sights on the horizon. The light of the new day was a symbol, a reminder that no night—no matter how dark—lasted forever. And with each new day there came new opportunities to right the wrongs and to chase the darkness back into the corners from which it crept.

Blake's resolve was a beacon for his team, a promise of the justice that was to come. The chase would continue, and he would lead it, undeterred by the fear or the complexity of the web that Morgan wove. For in the heart of the true hunter, there was no room for doubt—only the relentless pursuit of the prey.

*

The world was still waking as Detective Charlie Blake led his team back to the station, the sun climbing higher and casting long shadows that seemed to mock their retreat. The quiet of the early hour was a stark contrast to the chaos of the night before. They moved through the motions: a debrief, a collection of reports, the routine punctuated by a weariness that no amount of caffeine could dispel.

Blake sat in his office, blinds drawn, the dim light conducive to his contemplative mood. The pieces of the puzzle were there—but the image they formed remained elusive, obscured by the cunning of a killer who defied all patterns they had come to rely on.

A knock on the doorframe pulled Blake from his reverie. He looked up to find Grace Hudson standing there, her posture rigid, her face a mask that barely contained a storm beneath. In her hand she held an evidence bag, its contents seemingly innocuous—a single, charred piece of paper, salvaged from the theatre's ashes.

"Charlie, you need to see this," Grace said as she handed him the bag. Blake took it, his fingers deftly unfolding the paper to reveal what was hidden within.

It was a photograph, its edges burned, the image blistered—but the figures captured in it were unmistakably clear. It was a younger Blake, standing side by side with Alex Morgan, both in military uniform, brothers-in-arms, with smiles that spoke of unshakeable bonds and shared secrets.

The revelation was a gut punch, a visceral reminder of a past Blake had compartmentalised, locked away behind the professionalism of his badge. But here it was, tangible proof of the connection he had to the man they hunted—a connection that Morgan was well aware of and was using to his advantage.

"Where did you find this?" Blake's voice was a low growl, his eyes not leaving the photograph.

"In the theatre, near the stage. It was placed where we would find it if we survived," Grace replied, her voice steady despite the implications.

Blake stood, the photograph in his hand a piece of evidence that redefined the chase. This was personal in a way he had not allowed himself to acknowledge. Morgan was not just a shadow from his military past; he was a spectre that haunted the present, a ghost Blake had to face.

The room felt suddenly claustrophobic; the walls, adorned with the maps and notes of their investigation, now felt like a mausoleum for the dead and the yet-to-fall. Blake knew that the game had changed, that this was Morgan's way of upping the stakes, of drawing him into a more intimate dance with death.

"We'll need to re-evaluate everything," Blake said, finally looking up at Grace. "Morgan isn't just taunting us; he's telling us that he knows us, that he's always one step ahead."

The revelation of the photograph was a turning point, a catalyst that would drive Blake with newfound fervour. The pursuit was no longer just about justice; it was about confronting the past, about the dissolution of a brotherhood that had turned into a deadly rivalry.

As Blake gathered his team, the photograph laid bare on the table before them, there was a collective intake of breath. The case had become more than any of them had bargained for, a personal crusade that would test their limits and force them to confront the demons that lurked in the shadows of their past.

The hunt for Alex Morgan was no longer just a manhunt; it was a journey into the heart of darkness that resided in the soul of their leader. And as Blake met the eyes of each team member, he knew that they would follow him into that darkness, for the bond they shared was as unbreakable as the dawn was inevitable.

The revelation was a clarion call, a declaration that the endgame was approaching. And, when it came, Charlie Blake would be ready to face it, with his team at his side and the ghosts of his past laid to rest.

Chapter 5: The Spiral Deepens

Victim Secrets

Detective Charlie Blake sat across from Lisa Hammond in the dim light of the interview room, her face illuminated by the gentle glow of a desk lamp. Lisa was the latest link in a chain that stretched into the darkness, a chain that Blake was desperate to follow to its end. Her connection to the victims was a thread Blake needed to unravel to understand the motives behind the killings.

Lisa was an archivist, her life dedicated to the preservation of stories, of histories, of secrets that the dead carried to their graves. She had been called in to assist with the latest victim's background, to delve into a life cut short by violence and to shed light on the shadow that was Alex Morgan.

"The victims weren't just random selections," Lisa began, her voice a tremor of contained emotion. "They were chosen for a reason, a purpose that we're only beginning to understand."

Blake leaned forward, his gaze intense and focused. "Tell me about them," he urged, his pen poised over his notebook, ready to capture every word.

Lisa spread out a series of documents, photos, and notes before her: a mosaic of lives that had intersected with a killer's dark path. "Each one of them was at a crossroads," she explained, pointing to a timeline she had constructed. "Significant changes were happening in their lives—career shifts, relationships ending, new beginnings."

Blake's mind raced as he absorbed her words. The victims' vulnerabilities were being exploited, their moments of transition seized upon by a predator who saw opportunity in their uncertainty.

"The killer," Blake mused aloud, "sees these crossroads as opportune moments to strike, to weave his narrative into the victims' stories."

Lisa nodded, her eyes reflecting the gravity of their task. "There's more," she said, drawing Blake's attention to a collection of letters and emails. "They were all connected, not just by their transitions, but by their secrets."

The room fell silent as the implication settled between them. The victims shared secrets that were now clues, breadcrumbs left on a path that led into the heart of a killer's psyche.

As the hours ticked by, Blake and Lisa delved deeper into the lives that had been silenced. They unearthed a network of hidden relationships, of quiet confessions and concealed truths that painted a portrait of the victims as pieces of a puzzle that, when assembled, would reveal the face of their killer.

Blake felt the weight of the task, the responsibility to give voice to the voiceless, to piece together the story that the dead could no longer tell. With each secret uncovered, with each connection made, the spiral deepened, drawing them closer to the heart of the darkness.

Lisa's role was more than just assistance; she was the key to understanding the labyrinth they navigated—a labyrinth that Blake knew would lead them to Alex Morgan.

As the clock struck midnight, Blake stood, stretching the stiffness from his limbs. "Thank you, Lisa," he said, his voice thick with fatigue. "You've given us a map to follow."

Lisa smiled faintly, a weary acknowledgment of the

journey still ahead. "Just following the stories, Detective," she replied. "Where they lead us, that's your domain."

Blake nodded, his resolve a silent oath. He would follow the stories, the secrets, the silent whispers of the victims, wherever they led. For in the tapestry of hidden lives and unspoken truths, he would find the threads that bound the killer to his prey.

The investigation had taken a turn, delving into the depths of the victims' lives to unearth the motives of a killer. And as Blake left the interview room, documents and notes in hand, he knew that the race against time had begun—a race that he could not afford to lose.

*

The digital age had turned every keystroke into a potential lead, and Detective Charlie Blake knew the value of a tech trail in the hunt for a killer as elusive as shadows. This is why he found himself in the cluttered, dimly lit office of Marcus Levine, the tech analyst whose prowess could unearth secrets buried in the digital ether.

Marcus, surrounded by a fortress of screens, tapped away at his keyboard with a rhythmic intensity. Blake watched, a silent observer, as lines of code cascaded down monitors, a digital waterfall of information that could mean everything—or nothing.

"Talk to me, Marcus. What have you found?" Blake's voice cut through the hum of machines, a beacon in the binary storm.

Marcus swivelled in his chair, his eyes alight with the thrill of the chase. "I've been tracking the victims' digital footprints, looking for anomalies, patterns, anything out of the ordinary," he explained, pulling up a series of graphs and data points on a screen.

Blake leaned in, his gaze tracing the lines that Marcus highlighted. "Here," Marcus pointed, "each victim received an email from a secure server exactly three days before their disappearance."

The revelation sent a jolt through Blake. An email—such a mundane thing, yet now a harbinger of doom. "Can you trace it?" Blake asked, his voice a mix of hope and urgency.

Marcus' fingers danced across the keyboard, commands entered with a precision that spoke of years spent in the digital trenches. "It's not easy. The server uses military-grade encryption, but..." he trailed off, his focus narrowing.

The anticipation hung heavy in the room, the air charged with the electricity of potential discovery. Then, a breakthrough—a series of IP addresses, a digital breadcrumb trail leading back to a physical location.

"Got it!" Marcus exclaimed, triumph lifting his voice. "The server is being accessed from multiple locations, but one recurs with a pattern. It's an abandoned industrial complex on the outskirts of the city."

Blake's mind raced with the implications. An industrial complex could mean anything—a base of operations, a meeting point, a place where secrets were traded in the shadows.

"Marcus, you're a genius," Blake said, a rare smile breaking through his stoic facade. "This could be the break we've been looking for."

As they prepared to investigate the lead, Blake knew the net was tightening. The tech trails, once whispers in the vastness of cyberspace, were now shouts that echoed in the silence of the killer's trail.

He left Marcus to his digital domain, stepping out into

the brisk night air, the pieces of the puzzle assembling in his mind with each step he took. The killer had used the anonymity of the internet to cloak his movements, but now they had a tangible lead, a place where digital ghosts became flesh and blood.

Blake's phone buzzed with a message from Sarah, a reminder of the web of community ties they would explore next. But for now the tech trails had provided a path, and Blake would follow it to the end.

*

The city was a vast network of lives intersecting, and in the heart of its bustling community Detective Charlie Blake found an invaluable resource in Anna Kowalski. As the team's community liaison, Anna's role was to bridge the gap between the investigation and the public—a crucial task in a city gripped by fear of a predator in its midst.

In a small, bustling cafe, Blake met with Anna, her presence a calming force in the midst of public unrest. She was a pillar in the community, her connections far-reaching, her ability to glean information from a scared populace unparalleled.

"Anna, we're dealing with more than just a killer. He's sowing terror, and we need to contain it," Blake said, the concern evident in his furrowed brow.

Anna nodded, her demeanour composed. "The community trusts me, Charlie. They're scared, yes, but they're also eyes and ears on the ground. They see things, hear things that we don't," she replied, sipping her coffee.

Blake leaned forward, his hands wrapped around his own mug for warmth. "Anything that can help us? Any whisper, any rumour could lead us to him."

Anna set her cup down, her eyes locking with Blake's.

"There's talk of a man, seen at odd hours, keeping to the shadows. They say he's always there, in the aftermath of each incident, watching from afar," she relayed, her voice low.

The description sent a shiver down Blake's spine. Morgan was known to revisit his crime scenes, a macabre spectator to the chaos he created. "We need to find him, Anna. If he's part of the community, even on its fringes, someone knows him, knows his habits."

Anna reached into her bag, pulling out a small notebook filled with scribbled notes and names. "I've been keeping track of the sightings, the patterns of behaviour. There's a network here, Charlie, and we're starting to see its outline."

The detective's eyes scanned the pages, each entry a potential lead, each name a thread in the tapestry of the community that could unravel Morgan's anonymity.

"We've got teams ready to follow up on these," Blake said, determination steeling his voice. "You've done incredible work, Anna."

She smiled, a modest acknowledgement of her role in the hunt. "I just want to help bring him in, Charlie. To stop the fear."

As Blake stepped out of the cafe, his mind buzzed with the information Anna had provided. The community's ties had woven a net that he hoped would catch a killer. Each person's insight, each shared suspicion was a piece of the puzzle that was slowly forming a clearer picture of Alex Morgan.

The city that Morgan terrorised would also be his downfall, Blake mused. For in its streets and its people, there lay the clues that would lead to his capture. It was a race against time, but with Anna's help they were a step closer.

Blake's phone buzzed—a message from Fiona Barrett, their legal advisor, waiting to discuss the boundaries they had to navigate in their pursuit. With a deep breath, he moved forward, knowing each step took them closer to the end.

*

Fiona Barrett's office was a stark contrast to the chaos of the city streets—a sanctuary of order amidst the uncertainty that gripped London. Detective Charlie Blake stepped in, greeted by walls lined with law books, their spines a testament to the rule of law he sought to uphold. Fiona, as legal advisor to the Metropolitan Police, was a bastion of judicial acumen, her counsel a compass in navigating the murky waters of criminal investigation.

"Charlie," Fiona greeted, her handshake firm, "we're walking a tightrope with this case. The eyes of the law—and the public—are on us."

Blake settled into the chair across from her, his mind a whirl of questions and concerns. "We're close, Fiona. But Morgan's clever. He leaves nothing to chance, and we need to be just as meticulous."

Fiona leaned back, her gaze assessing. "The warrants, the surveillance, the interrogations—they all need to be watertight. Any error, and he'll slip through our fingers," she warned, her words sharp with the gravity of their situation.

Blake nodded, a silent vow that he would not let bureaucracy hamstring their hunt. "We've got community tips leading to a potential suspect. I need to know how far we can push this, legally."

Fiona rifled through the papers on her desk, each document a building block in the fortress of their case. "You have probable cause," she began, her finger tracing the lines of legalese that could make or break their operation. "But remember, Morgan knows the system as well as we do. He'll be looking for any crack to exploit."

The conversation that followed was a dance of hypotheticals and legal strategy, Fiona outlining the parameters within which Blake and his team could operate. Surveillance had to be covert yet lawful, interviews conducted with precision, every piece of evidence collected with the utmost care for protocol.

"Every 'i' dotted, every 't' crossed," Fiona concluded, her voice a steady drumbeat to which Blake set the rhythm of his next moves.

As he left the office, the legal boundaries firmly etched in his mind, Blake felt a renewed sense of purpose. The law was a framework, a set of rules that governed the chaos of their pursuit, and he would use it as his sword and shield.

The next message on his phone was from Theo Wallace, an unexpected ally from the city's underbelly who claimed to have critical information. Blake's pulse quickened; the law had given him the boundaries, and now the streets were calling him back to the hunt.

The race against time took on a new urgency, the killer's timeline accelerating with each passing day. Blake's personal stakes were higher than ever, and he knew that to catch a man like Morgan, he would need to marshal all the resources at his disposal—legal, communal, and otherwise.

*

The underbelly of London was a place of shadows and half-truths, where information was currency and trust a commodity few could afford. Detective Charlie Blake, a man of the law, found himself in a dusky pub, a stone's throw from the river, where the city's pulse beat strongest in the veins of those who operated outside the system.

Theo Wallace's reputation preceded him—a man with fingers in many pies, whose allegiance to the law was tenuous at best. Yet it was he who reached out to Blake with the promise of information too critical to ignore. Blake, sitting in the pub's dimmest corner, watched as Theo approached, his gait casual, his eyes sharp and calculating.

"Theo," Blake greeted, his voice neutral, masking the scepticism within.

"Detective," Theo replied with a nod, sliding into the booth. "I hear you're hunting a ghost. Alex Morgan, is it?"

Blake's eyes narrowed. "I'm listening," he said simply.

Theo leaned forward, his voice low. "Morgan's been a spectre on my radar for a while. He's bad for business, bad for everyone. I have... let's call it an interest in seeing him taken care of."

Blake considered Theo's words, aware of the delicate dance between law enforcement and those who skirted its edges. "And what do you expect in return?"

Theo's lips quirked in a half-smile. "Consider it a community service," he said. "I like my city clean, Detective. Morgan is making a mess."

With a flick of his wrist, Theo produced a flash drive, sliding it across the table. "You'll find a list of properties there—places Morgan might be using. Some... less than legal surveillance might have been involved."

Blake pocketed the flash drive, his mind already turning over the possibilities. "This doesn't put us square," he said, meeting Theo's gaze. "But it's a start."

Theo's chuckle was a low rumble. "I don't expect to be

square, Detective. But perhaps a little less... tilted against me."

The conversation was brief, their alliance a temporary truce in a city at war with itself. As Blake left the pub, the weight of the flash drive in his pocket was a tangible reminder of the unconventional avenues his search for justice had taken.

Back at the station, Marcus Levine was already decrypting the data, his fingers flying across the keyboard. The list Theo provided opened new avenues, new doors behind which Morgan might be lurking. Each address was a piece of the puzzle, each surveillance feed a window into the world Morgan inhabited—a world they were closing in on with every passing hour.

As Blake prepared to dive into the intel, his phone rang with an urgency that set his heart racing. It was Sarah—there had been another incident, another life claimed. The race against time was not just a metaphor; it was a stark reality, and their window to stop Morgan was closing fast.

The unexpected ally had given them a lead, but it was up to Blake and his team to follow it to the end and to stem the tide of terror that Morgan had unleashed upon the city. The spiral was deepening, and Blake's resolve had never been firmer.

*

The sterile buzz of fluorescent lights filled the incident room where Detective Charlie Blake stood, a sentinel amidst a sea of activity. News of another victim had sent shockwaves through the station, a grim reminder of the killer's relentless pace. Time, once a steady march, now raced against them with a ferocity that matched the public's growing fear.

Blake's gaze shifted over the team, each member a study in controlled urgency, their faces set in grim determination. The latest victim—a young journalist with a penchant for stories that lurked in the city's darker corners—had been found with the same signature brutality that marked all of Morgan's work. Blake felt the personal stakes climbing with each life taken, a mounting debt he was determined to settle.

"Team," Blake's voice cut through the din, commanding attention. "We're not just tracking a killer. We're up against time itself. Morgan's escalating, and we must outpace him."

The room hushed, every eye fixed on the central table where the victim's files lay, a testament to the cost of their chase. Blake leaned over the table, his finger tracing the paths that led from each piece of evidence to the heart of their investigation—the list of properties provided by Theo Wallace.

"We follow every lead, chase down every shadow. No stone unturned," Blake declared, his words a rallying cry that galvanised his weary team.

Marcus Levine, his eyes tired from the glow of computer screens, nodded. "I've cross-referenced the properties with traffic and security cams. There are patterns, gaps in the feeds where someone's been careful to avoid detection."

Blake's eyes met Marcus's, a silent exchange of resolve passing between them. "That's where we start. We find the gaps, we find Morgan," Blake stated, with a certainty that belied the uncertainty of their task.

The room burst into a hive of activity as Blake's team set to work, the race against the killer's clock now a tangible presence in the room, driving them forward.

Blake himself pored over the journalist's articles, searching for the narrative that had made her a target, for the story that had signed her death warrant.

As he read, a pattern emerged, a thread of investigation the journalist had been pulling, one that drew too near to the truth Morgan sought to conceal. Blake felt the edges of the web they were untangling finally giving way, revealing glimpses of the predator they sought.

The phone calls that followed were terse, the orders clear. Teams dispatched to the gaps in the city's surveillance, to the shadows where Morgan lurked. Blake felt the weight of command, the responsibility for each life in his hands, for each decision that could mean the difference between life and death.

The race against time was more than a pursuit; it was a battle for the soul of the city, for the lives that hung in the balance. And as Blake led his team into the fray, his personal stakes became synonymous with the city's own. London's heartbeat was in his ears, its pulse the timer counting down, its breath the winds that propelled them onward.

Chapter 6: Shadows Cast

Breaking Point

Detective Charlie Blake stood in the ghostly glow of the moonlight streaming through the window of his office, the city's symphony a distant murmur against the glass. His reflection was a spectre of the man he once knew, the lines of his face etched with the toll of the hunt. The night was silent, but his mind was a cacophony of the case that consumed his every waking moment.

It was here, in the solitude of the night, that Blake's personal demons emerged from the shadows, a relentless tide that threatened to overwhelm him. Each victim's face was a reminder of the lives he hadn't saved, of promises broken under the weight of a badge heavy with expectation.

The door creaked open, and Sarah Jennings stepped in, her presence a beacon in the oppressive darkness of Blake's doubts. "You can't carry this alone, Charlie," she said, her voice a lifeline thrown across the churning waters of his thoughts.

Blake turned, his eyes meeting hers, and in them Sarah saw the conflict that waged within—a battle between the duty that called him and the fatigue that clawed at his resolve. "They look to me for answers, Sarah. But the deeper we go, the darker it gets, and the harder it becomes to see the way forward."

Sarah stepped closer, her hand finding his. "We trust you, Charlie. Your vision has led us this far," she reassured him, her loyalty to him unshaken by the tempest of the case.

Her words were a balm to the raw edges of Blake's

resolve. "This killer, he doesn't just take lives; he takes pieces of our soul with him. But I swear, we will stop him," Blake vowed, the steel in his voice a testament to the fire that still burned within him.

Together, they stood in silence, the bond between them a silent pact against the encroaching darkness. It was Sarah's unwavering support that fortified Blake's spirit, lending him the strength to confront the abyss without flinching.

As the first light of dawn crept into the sky, painting it with strokes of hope, Blake felt the weight of his demons lessen. The path ahead was treacherous, but he was not alone. With Sarah and his team, the shadows that cast over the city would be dispelled.

With a newfound determination, Blake turned from the window. It was time to face the day, to lead his team into the fray with the knowledge that their unity was their strength, and that together they would bring an end to the darkness that stalked the streets of London.

The first rays of sunlight pierced the horizon, casting long shadows that retreated with the night. Blake's silhouette was steadfast against the light, a symbol of the dedication that would see them through to the end—no matter the cost.

*

Blake's office had become a sanctuary of sorts, where the digital breadcrumbs of a killer were unravelled and laid bare. The room was filled with the low hum of machinery, a chorus accompanying the masterful keystrokes of Marcus Levine. His eyes, framed by the soft blue light of the screen, were focused, his concentration absolute as he sifted through the virtual detritus left in the wake of a digital ghost.

Detective Charlie Blake watched from a distance, his arms crossed, his patience a fortress holding back the siege of urgency that threatened to break at any moment. "Marcus, tell me we have something," he implored, his voice a rough whisper in the quiet of the room.

Marcus paused, a finger held up signalling for just one more moment, one more connection. Then, with a triumphant click, he spun the screen towards Blake. "This is it, Charlie. We've got him."

On the screen was a map, a constellation of data points that, to the untrained eye, would seem random. But to Blake, they were the notes of a symphony he had been desperate to hear. "This is his pattern," Marcus explained, his finger tracing the lines that connected the points. "Every victim, every location—it's all here. He's been communicating with someone, leaving a trail we were meant to find."

Blake leaned in, his eyes scanning the evidence that Mike had pieced together. "He's taunting us," Blake murmured, the realisation cold in his belly.

"Not just that," Marcus continued, tapping into a series of encrypted messages that had been intercepted. "He's planning something, a final act, and we've got the when and the where."

The breakthrough was a beacon, a signal flare in the dark. Blake felt the adrenaline surge, a current that galvanised his weary limbs. "We set up surveillance, tap every resource we have. This ends now," he commanded, the determination in his voice rallying the team around him.

The digital footprint was the clue they had been chasing, the pattern that had eluded them now clear and defined. Blake knew that they were on the brink of a confrontation that had been building since the first body was found, since the first shadow had been cast.

As the team mobilised, Blake felt the weight of command settle upon him. Each decision was a link in a chain that bound them to the outcome, each order a step closer to the killer they sought.

The race was on, the game afoot, and as they prepared to close the net around Alex Morgan, Blake knew that the digital trail they followed was but the first step into the labyrinth. But with Mike's breakthrough, the path was illuminated, and the shadows that had clouded their hunt began to dissipate.

The morning sun crept higher, casting a new light upon the city—a light that promised revelation and, with hope, resolution.

*

In the clinical sterility of the morgue, where the secrets of the dead were whispered on cold steel tables, Dr Emily Saunders was a custodian of the silent truths. The air was thick with the antiseptic tang of death's aftermath as Detective Charlie Blake entered, his steps measured, his mind braced for the revelation that awaited.

Emily stood over her latest subject: the journalist who had dared to probe too deeply into the darkness. Her tools were arrayed with precision, each instrument a key to unlocking the stories etched in flesh and blood.

Blake approached, his eyes sombre. "Emily, please tell me we have something," he implored, the weight of urgency a palpable presence between them.

Emily glanced up, her eyes meeting Blake's. "Charlie, the killer is evolving," she began, her voice steady despite the gravity of her findings. "This last one... it's different. The methodology, the precision—it's all changed."

Blake felt a shiver snake down his spine. Change meant adaptation, and adaptation meant they were dealing with an intelligence that refused to be static, a predator who altered his patterns to confound his pursuers.

"Show me," he said, steeling himself.

Emily directed his attention to the autopsy report, a digital display that catalogued the horror in stark, unflinching detail. "Here," she said, pointing to a section of the text, "the cuts are deeper, more deliberate. And there's something else."

She navigated to a microscopic image, a magnification of a wound that revealed a substance Blake had never seen before. "I found traces of a rare toxin, one that's not easy to come by. It's used in rituals in some cultures, a means to... communicate with the beyond."

Blake absorbed the information, the pieces clicking into place with a chilling clarity. Morgan wasn't just killing—he was performing a ceremony, each victim a message, each death a stanza in a poem written in blood.

"The killer's leaving us a trail, not just of bodies, but of symbols," Blake mused aloud, the profiler's insights from their previous cases echoing in his mind.

Emily nodded, her expression grim. "I've sent the toxin for further analysis, but I suspect it's more than just a means to an end. It's a signature, a part of the killer's identity."

The revelation sent Blake's thoughts racing. If they could trace the toxin, they could unravel the network that supplied Morgan, penetrate the veil he had drawn around his operations.

"Thank you, Emily," Blake said, his voice a low rumble of determination. "You've given us a new avenue to explore."

As he left the morgue, the fluorescent lights overhead seemed to flicker with the promise of discovery. The forensic revelations had provided a vital clue, a beacon that would guide them through the murk of uncertainty.

The team was waiting, their faces a tableau of expectation and resolve. Blake shared the findings, each word a piece of the puzzle they were desperately working to solve. The toxin was a thread, one that they would pull, unravelling the tapestry Morgan had woven with such meticulous care.

The race against time took on a new dimension, the stakes heightened by the knowledge that they were dealing with more than a killer—they were dealing with a man who saw himself as a messenger, an arbiter of life and death who wrote his creed in the language of the abyss.

As Blake marshalled his team, the commitment to the hunt was renewed, their dedication a fierce counterpoint to the doubt that had once shadowed their efforts. They would find this killer, this shadow that cast its pall over the city, and when they did, they would be ready.

*

The room was silent, save for the quiet hum of the station's air conditioning and the occasional rustle of papers as Dr Helen Zhao, the lead profiler, arranged her notes on the conference table. Detective Charlie Blake and his team encircled the table, a conclave convened to delve into the mind of the enigma that was Alex Morgan.

Dr Zhao, a woman whose insights into the human psyche were as sharp as a scalpel, began to speak, her voice the harbinger of a chilling realisation. "Morgan is not just a killer," she started, locking eyes with each member of the team in turn. "He is an artist in his own macabre gallery, each victim a masterpiece, each scene an exhibition of his work."

Blake listened, his hands clasped tightly in front of him, his jaw set. The profile that Dr Zhao constructed was more than a sketch of a suspect; it was a map of Morgan's twisted psychology.

"He sees the world as a canvas for his beliefs, his actions the brushstrokes of a larger vision," Dr Zhao continued, her fingers tracing the lines of a graph that displayed the escalation in Morgan's pattern. "Each crime scene is carefully selected, each act meticulously planned to convey a message we're meant to see."

The team absorbed her words, a grim understanding dawning in their eyes. Blake felt a cold knot in his stomach as he considered the implications. "You're saying he's communicating through his victims?" he asked, his voice a quiet force in the room.

"Exactly," Dr Zhao affirmed. "And his message is one of transformation. He believes he is changing the fabric of society, one life at a time."

The profile laid bare the profound depth of Morgan's delusion, a narrative written in the blood of innocents that spoke of a grandiose sense of destiny and power. It was this insight that sharpened the team's focus, each member now acutely aware of the stakes.

Blake stood, his resolve crystallised by Dr Zhao's revelations. "We need to intercept his message, disrupt his narrative," he said, a plan forming in his mind. "To anticipate his next move we need to understand his vision."

The team rallied around Blake's determination, the profiler's insights a beacon guiding their strategy. They were not just hunting a killer; they were dismantling a philosophy, a doctrine of death that had taken root in the darkest corners of a troubled mind.

As the meeting adjourned, Blake approached Dr Zhao, a silent acknowledgment passing between them. Her profile had provided the key to understanding the chaos that Morgan had unleashed upon the city. Now, it was up to Blake and his team to use that knowledge to end the cycle of violence.

The station buzzed with renewed energy as plans were drawn and resources marshalled. The hunt for Alex Morgan had reached a critical juncture, the shadows he cast now illuminated by the insights of a profiler who had stared into the abyss and mapped its contours.

Blake knew that the road ahead would be fraught with danger and moral ambiguity, but the path was clear. They would follow it to the end, wherever it led, whatever the cost. The shadows would be lifted, and the light of truth would expose the darkness for all to see.

*

The murmur of the city at dusk was a subtle prelude to the night's endeavour as Detective Charlie Blake briefed his team. They gathered around, their faces etched with the shadows of the coming operation, a tableau of tension and focus. Elena Martinez, their undercover specialist, stood ready, her eyes a mirror of the risk that lay ahead.

The operation was Blake's gambit, a calculated risk drawn from the playbook they were rewriting to catch a killer as elusive as the evening fog. Elena was to be the lure in a sting operation designed to draw Morgan out, based on the profile and patterns they'd painstakingly pieced together.

Blake addressed his team, his voice the calm before the storm. "We have one shot at this," he began, his gaze passing over each of his team members. "Elena will lead the operation on the ground. We'll be her eyes and ears, but once she's in, she's on her own until we can close the net."

Elena stepped forward, her posture radiating a quiet confidence that belied the danger of her task. "We know his patterns, his ego. He can't resist the challenge we present," she stated, accepting the operational earpiece and concealed firearm that would be her lifelines.

The plan was for Elena to simulate a scenario that Morgan couldn't ignore, one that would appeal to his twisted sense of artistry and control. She would pose as a journalist investigating a series of fictional underground events that mirrored the killer's modus operandi, baiting him with the prospect of a grand audience for his gruesome work.

As night cloaked the city, Elena made her way to the predetermined location, a derelict warehouse chosen for its seclusion and grim aesthetic, fitting for the scene they needed to set. Blake and his team monitored from a discreet distance, their surveillance equipment casting an electronic gaze over the area.

The operation was underway, the silence of anticipation as heavy as the darkness around them. Then, as Elena reached the heart of the warehouse, a flicker of movement—a shadow within shadows, a whisper of danger that set every nerve on edge.

Without warning, the operation spiraled into chaos. The surveillance feeds scrambled, a cacophony of static that blinded them to Elena's fate. Blake's voice crackled over the comm link, a commander rallying his forces amidst the fog of war. "Elena, report!"

But the line was dead, a suffocating silence that spoke

volumes. The trap they had set had been sprung upon themselves, the predator they hunted now the orchestrator of a trap far more cunning than their own.

The team sprang into action, a rush of motion and urgent commands as they breached the warehouse. Inside, the shadows loomed, a maze of uncertainty that closed around them like a vice.

It was Blake who found Elena, disarmed but unharmed, her capture a message from Morgan—a demonstration of his dominance and a challenge to the narrative they thought they controlled.

As they regrouped, the weight of the operation's failure was a tangible presence among them. Blake's jaw clenched with the knowledge that their operational risk had been countered with a move far more calculated and dangerous than they had anticipated.

The night's events were a stark reminder of the perilous game they were engaged in—a game where the rules were dictated by a killer's whim. But Blake's determination was a flame that the shadows could not extinguish. They would regroup, reassess, and respond. The hunt was far from over, and the next move was theirs to make.

*

The fallout from the operation's stark turn had settled over the station like a shroud. In the aftermath, questions arose like spectres, each one a pointed finger at the decisions that had led them here. At the centre stood Detective Charlie Blake, his leadership the eye of the storm, his choices both his armour and his albatross.

It was Victor Reynolds, a seasoned detective whose battle scars were etched in the lines of his face, who voiced the doubts that hung unspoken in the air. In the quiet confines of Blake's office, where the weight of command was a tangible presence, Reynolds's words were a challenge cast in concern.

"Charlie, you've led us through hell and back," Victor began, his tone a blend of respect and reproach. "But this... we were outplayed at our own game. How far will you push us?"

Blake stood by the window, his gaze on the city he swore to protect. "As far as it takes, Victor," he replied, his profile etched against the city lights. "I know the risks; I feel them every time we step out onto the wire. But if we don't push, more lives will be lost to the shadows."

Victor's frown was a testament to the burden they all bore, a shared load of moral complexity and duty. "And what of the team? Elena was nearly—"

"She wasn't," Blake cut in, turning to face Victor with a fire in his eyes that spoke of a resolve unbroken by doubt or fear. "And she won't be. I'll see to that personally."

The silence that followed was a chasm that stretched between duty and fear, bridged by the unspoken trust that had been the foundation of their bond. It was Sarah who broke the silence, her voice the rallying cry that had carried them this far.

"We believe in you, Charlie," she said, her hand on Victor's shoulder, a gesture of solidarity. "Your dedication has been our guiding light. We've all seen the darkness that we're fighting against."

Victor met Blake's gaze, the unspoken questions answered in the depths of his commander's eyes. "Then lead on," he said, the doubts dissipating like mist in the warmth of their shared dedication.

The team's unity was a beacon that shone all the brighter for the trials they had faced. Blake's leadership, questioned in the face of adversity, was ultimately reaffirmed by the very people who looked to him to navigate the tempest they were in.

As they left the office, the team's footsteps were a drumbeat of renewed purpose. The shadows cast by their quarry were long and deep, but they were cast by a light that Blake and his team carried—a light that would not be extinguished, not by fear, not by doubt, not by the darkness that sought to engulf them.

Chapter 7: The Face of Evil

Confrontation

The fluorescent glare of the interrogation room was a stark contrast to the dim pulsing heartbeat of the city that lay beyond. Detective Charlie Blake sat rigid, his hands folded before him, his eyes locked on the figure seated across the table. The suspect—a man whose features were as unremarkable as they were common—bore a striking resemblance to the sketches and descriptions of Alex Morgan.

The silence in the room was a tangible entity, thick with the anticipation of the coming verbal sparring. Blake had waited for this moment, for the opportunity to peel back the layers of deceit and come face to face with evil itself.

"You know why you're here," Blake began, his voice a measured cadence of control and authority.

The suspect nodded, a slight upturn of his lips hinting at a confidence Blake found unsettling. "I do, Detective," he replied, his voice a smooth baritone that belied the gravity of the situation. "But do *you*?"

Blake leaned forward, his motion deliberate and predatory. "You fit the profile. You were seen at the locations, and you have the knowledge and means to carry out the crimes."

The suspect's chuckle was a sound Blake imagined a snake would make if it could laugh. "Profiles are just educated guesses. And being seen? In a city of millions? That's hardly conclusive."

The dance of words had begun, Blake leading with the steps of logic and evidence, the suspect countering with deft manoeuvres of rhetoric and ambiguity. But Blake had not come unprepared. He laid out the photos from the crime scenes, the pattern of behaviour, the digital trails— all roads that led to this man.

With each piece of evidence presented, the suspect's facade began to crack, the edges of his composure fraying under the weight of undeniable truth. "What do you want?" Blake pressed, his voice a hammer seeking to shatter the remaining defences.

The suspect's eyes, a mirror to a soul as dark as the void, met Blake's. "To be understood, Detective. Isn't that what we all seek?"

Blake's fists clenched, a battle to maintain his composure against the twisted philosophy presented before him. "You seek to be understood through murder?" he demanded, the question sharp as a blade.

The suspect leaned back, the first sign of unease breaking through his confident exterior. "You see murder; I see... liberation. A release from the chains that bind us to a mundane existence."

The conversation spiralled, the suspect weaving a narrative of disillusionment and justification for the horrors he had wrought upon the city. Blake, a steadfast pillar of justice, dissected each word, searching for the crack, the inconsistency that would tear the whole sordid tale apart.

As the clock ticked on, the suspect's words became a labyrinth from which Blake meticulously emerged, with a clearer picture of the man before him—a man who could very well be the face of evil they had been chasing.

The confrontation ended with no confession, but Blake had gleaned more than the suspect realised. He stood, his resolve a hardened shell around the fury that burned within. "This is far from over," Blake vowed, his voice a quiet storm that promised retribution.

The suspect was taken away, back to the cell that awaited him, and Blake was left with the revelations that had unfolded. He knew that the interrogation was just the beginning. The real truths lay hidden beneath the suspect's words—and he would uncover them, no matter the cost.

The face of evil had been revealed, but the soul of it remained shrouded. Blake would strip away the shadows, he would cast light into the darkest corners, and he would find the truth.

*

The interrogation room was a crucible, the heat of inquiry pressing in on the walls, as Detective Charlie Blake sat once again opposite the man who might as well have been a ghost until now. The suspect's facade had begun to crumble, his veneer of confidence showing cracks through which Blake intended to shatter the mystery of Alex Morgan's motives.

"Let's talk about your past," Blake intoned, sliding a folder across the table, its contents a history of a life that paralleled Morgan's in a myriad of unsettling ways.

The suspect's eyes flitted towards the folder, a flicker of unease passing over his features. "My past is inconsequential," he dismissed—but Blake noted the quickened pulse at his throat, the tell-tale sign of a nerve struck.

"Inconsequential?" Blake challenged. "Or is it the foundation of your motives? This," he said, tapping the folder, "tells a story of abandonment, of resentment. It's a common theme in Morgan's choices, isn't it?"

Blake watched the suspect closely, each reaction a

paragraph, each evasion a chapter in the novel of his guilt. "Morgan targets those at the apex of change, moments when they are most vulnerable. Isn't that when you felt most abandoned, most resentful?"

The suspect leaned back, his mask slipping further, revealing a glint of the turmoil that roiled within. "You think you understand, but you're grasping at straws."

But Blake was relentless, the pieces of the puzzle coalescing into a clearer picture with each passing moment. "Am I?" he pressed on. "Or is it that I'm getting too close to the truth? The truth that you see yourself in each victim, each one a reflection of your own path not taken, of your own what-ifs and could-have-beens?"

The suspect's composure broke, then, like a dam yielding to the pressure of the waters it held back. "Yes!" he exploded, the word a gunshot in the quiet room. "Yes, they are me! They are all me!"

Blake remained calm—a lighthouse amidst the storm—as the suspect's revelations poured forth: a deluge of confession, of rationale twisted by pain and a distorted sense of justice.

"They *were* chosen not at random, but with purpose: each one a message, each one a piece of a larger truth I am unveiling," the suspect declared, the words tumbling from him in a frenzied rush.

Blake listened, his expression inscrutable, as the suspect detailed his connections to the victims, his justifications for his actions, his philosophies on life and the societal chains that bound people to mediocrity. It was a manifesto of madness, a treatise on the transformation he sought to inflict upon the world.

The interrogation stretched on, hours passing as Blake untangled the web of Morgan's psyche, the revelations unfolding like the petals of a dark flower, each one a different shade of the horror they faced.

As the suspect was led away, his words lingering like the echo of a death knell, Blake sat alone in the quiet aftermath. The revelations had indeed unfolded, unexpected truths laid bare, but they were truths that painted a larger, more complex portrait of the evil they were up against.

There was a tactical shift needed now, a new approach to the investigation. Blake's mind was already turning, already planning. He would adjust, adapt, and overcome. The game was changing, but so too was their strategy. Blake would see to that personally.

*

In the aftermath of the interrogation, the suspect remained a cipher, a shadow that danced just out of the light of clarity. Detective Charlie Blake sat in the quiet of his office, the files from the interrogation laid out before him like pieces of an unsolved puzzle. With each revelation that had unfolded, the image of Alex Morgan had become both clearer and more distorted.

It was in this solitude that Blake began to piece together a new approach. The interrogation had revealed unexpected truths about Morgan's motives, a narrative that wove through the tapestry of the crimes like a thread of a different colour. Morgan was not just executing a series of crimes; he was orchestrating a symphony of chaos that spoke to a deeper, more malevolent purpose.

Blake's eyes traced over the transcripts, the suspect's words echoing in his mind. "Liberation," he had said. It was a motive they had not considered, a philosophy that turned their understanding on its head.

With a newfound sense of direction, Blake gathered

his team, their faces a mosaic of expectation and weariness. "We've been thinking too small," he announced, the room hanging on his every word. "Morgan isn't just killing. He's trying to communicate a message—one we've been too blind to see."

The team listened intently as Blake outlined the suspect's testimony, the cryptic clues that now seemed so obvious. Morgan's targets were not random; they were carefully chosen symbols, each representing the pillars of a society he sought to dismantle.

"We need to shift our tactics," Blake continued, his strategy unfolding before them. "We can't just chase the man; we need to understand the ideology that drives him. We'll start with his targets—the victims. We need to discover what they represented to Morgan."

Sarah Jennings nodded, her resolve a reflection of Blake's own. "It's like he's trying to rewrite the narrative of the city, of our lives, with himself as the author," she mused.

Blake agreed. "And we're going to take back the pen," he declared, his voice a clarion call to action. "Mike, you'll continue to track the digital footprints, look for patterns in communications around the victims. Emily, re-examine the autopsies, focus on the symbolism of the wounds. And Victor, pull the case files on the victims. We need to know everything—associations, beliefs, their place in Morgan's twisted narrative."

The team dispersed, each member invigorated by the new direction. Blake's tactical shift had given them a fresh perspective, a new angle from which to hunt a killer who was more than just a shadow—they were hunting a man who believed he was the harbinger of a new order.

As the night deepened outside the station's walls,

Blake felt the familiar stir of the hunter within him. They were no longer just chasing a suspect; they were unravelling the manifesto of a madman. The chase had become a battle of ideologies, and Blake knew that the key to winning was to understand the mind behind the madness.

The team's resolve solidified, they delved deeper into the case, led by Blake's impassioned dedication to justice. The tactical shift was not just a new strategy; it was a new hope—a beacon that cut through the fog of uncertainty that had clouded their hunt for too long.

*

The incident room was a crucible, its walls lined with the spectral images of victims and maps crisscrossed with lines of inquiry—a stark reminder of the darkness they were fighting against. In the centre of it all stood Detective Charlie Blake, the embodiment of their collective resolve, ready to deliver the speech that would fortify their dedication to the cause.

His team, a patchwork of the city's finest minds and spirits, watched him with a mix of exhaustion and expectation. They had been through the wringer, their spirits tested and their limits pushed, but Blake knew that within each of them burned a flame that no darkness could extinguish.

"Each of you is here because you believe in justice," Blake began, his voice resonant in the hushed room. "We've seen too much to turn away now. We've felt the pain of loss, the sting of defeat, but we've also shared in the triumph of truth."

He paused, allowing his gaze to meet those of his team members, acknowledging their shared experiences. "Morgan thinks he's writing the story here, that we're just characters in his twisted narrative. But he's wrong. We are the authors of this tale, and we decide how it ends."

Blake moved to the map, his finger tracing the web of Morgan's influence. "We've been reactive, always one step behind. But that ends today. Today, we shift the paradigm and take control of this chase."

The room's energy shifted, a current of renewed purpose flowing through each member. Sarah Jennings, her insight into the criminal mind invaluable, nodded in agreement. "We need to stay ahead of him, anticipate his moves. We must think like him but never become him," she added, her voice a steel thread woven into the tapestry of their resolve.

Blake's eyes sparkled with a fierce determination. "Exactly, Sarah. We've been given a unique insight into Morgan's mind—his motives, his methods. We use this knowledge not just to catch him, but to halt his narrative, to rewrite the ending he doesn't expect."

He addressed the entire team now, his hands open in a gesture of unity. "We stand together, undivided, in the face of evil. Our resolve is our shield, our dedication our weapon. We will bring light to the shadows Morgan casts and justice to those who have suffered at his hands."

The team rose, their faces set with resolute lines, their posture embodying the very essence of their commitment. Mike Hanover, the tech analyst, spoke up, "We'll trace his digital shadow, pin him in the real world, and end this."

Emily Saunders, the forensic pathologist, added, "And I'll ensure that the stories of the victims are told, that their whispers from beyond become the roar that brings down this monster."

The room was alive with the energy of a newfound battle cry, each member invigorated by Blake's words, by the shared purpose that bound them. They dispersed to their respective tasks, each step a march towards a future where the darkness of Morgan's influence was a thing of the past.

Blake remained at the map, the lines and images blurring into a singular focus. His speech had been more than just words; it was a declaration of war against the chaos Morgan sought to sow. And as the team solidified their resolve, Blake knew they were more than just hunters—they were guardians standing firm against the face of evil.

*

The thrum of the newsroom was a symphony to Simon Fraser, the seasoned journalist whose pen had swayed public opinion more times than he could count. Sitting at his cluttered desk, framed by the relentless chaos of ringing phones and hurried conversations, Simon peered at the words sprawling across his computer screen. The story he was about to break would send ripples across London, and, perhaps, directly into the den of the beast they sought to cage—Alex Morgan.

Meanwhile, Detective Charlie Blake stood in the dim light of the station's briefing room, aware of the delicate dance between transparency and operational security. The balance had never been more critical, and the upcoming strategic leak to Simon Fraser was a testament to their desperate times.

"Simon, we need the public's eyes and ears, but we can't give away too much," Blake had said in their last meeting, his voice a low rumble of urgency. "We need to keep them informed, keep them safe, but Morgan... he thrives on the attention. It's part of his game."

Simon understood the assignment perfectly. With a

few well-chosen phrases, he could ignite the city's imagination and paranoia, all while concealing the vital details that would keep the investigation intact. His article would be a beacon, casting light on the darkness of Morgan's deeds, but it would also be a veil, masking the crucial moves of Blake's team from prying eyes—including Morgan's.

As the story went live, the city's pulse quickened. Simon's words painted a picture of a shadowy figure, a killer in their midst, and a police force on the brink of a breakthrough. The public's fascination turned to fervour, their fear a collective clamour for resolution and safety.

The article was a masterpiece of insinuation and urgency, a narrative that walked the tightrope between revelation and restraint. It was a call to arms for the people of London and a subliminal message to Morgan— the police were closing in, but the final act was yet to unfold.

Blake watched the city react from his office, the lights of the skyline flickering like the pulse of a living organism. Simon Fraser's leak had set the stage for the next phase of their operation, had stoked the fires of public interest, and placed pressure on all parties involved.

But it had also done something more: it had signalled to Morgan that his anonymity was slipping, that his control over the game was not as absolute as he believed. The message was clear: the hunter could become the hunted at any moment.

As day gave way to night, Blake felt the weight of the city's gaze, its hope and its fear resting upon his shoulders. The strategic leak was a gambit, a move in a grander strategy that he hoped would lead to Morgan's undoing. The pressure was immense, but so was their resolve.

The team, bolstered by the city's rallying cry, worked with renewed vigour. Every officer, every analyst, every member of the task force felt the eyes of London upon them, felt the stirrings of a story that they were a part of—a story that would end with justice, or with a pen still poised above a page awaiting a conclusion that Blake vowed would *not* be written by Alex Morgan.

*

The digital chime of his phone broke the silence of the evening, dragging Detective Charlie Blake away from his thoughts, back to the stark reality of the case that consumed him. The message was from an unknown number, but its contents sent a shiver down his spine—it was Morgan's unmistakable voice that spoke in the form of written words.

"You cannot grasp the nature of my work. But you will soon see the full picture. Await my signal."

The message, though cryptic, was a clear warning. Morgan was escalating the tension, making it personal. It was a psychological tactic, a way to unsettle Blake and assert control. But Blake, hardened by years of service and the twists of this very chase, felt a surge of adrenaline rather than fear. This was a sign that Morgan was feeling the pressure, that the strategic leaks and their relentless pursuit were getting to him.

Blake immediately convened a meeting with his team, the message projected on the screen at the front of the room for all to see. The atmosphere was thick with a mixture of anger and resolve.

"This," Blake pointed to the message, "is an act of desperation. He's trying to shake us, to make us afraid."

Sarah Jennings, eyes fixed on the screen, spoke up. "Or it's a challenge," she proposed. "He wants us to know he's still one step ahead."

Blake nodded in agreement. "Perhaps. But it also means he's watching our every move. We need to be cautious—but also more unpredictable. We change our patterns, our methods. We use this message to our advantage."

The team buzzed with renewed energy, discussing potential meanings behind the message and how they could twist this new development to their favour. Mike Hanover proposed a series of feints in their digital investigations to throw Morgan off their trail. Emily Saunders suggested revisiting the autopsies with a focus on any clues they might have missed, anything that could be a signal from Morgan.

As the meeting drew to a close, Blake's eyes returned to the message, and he realised that the words were not just a warning, but an invitation to a game of cat and mouse. Morgan wanted to be chased; he thrived on it. But Blake was determined to change the rules of the game.

The night was spent in a flurry of activity, the station alive with the sounds of a team working as one. The cryptic message had indeed escalated the tension, but it had also reaffirmed their purpose. They were closer than ever to bringing Morgan into the light, to ending the chaos he had sown.

Blake felt the weight of the chase, the burden of command, but also the unyielding desire to stop Morgan once and for all. The message was a catalyst, not just for the investigation, but for Blake himself. He would meet Morgan's challenge head-on—and he would not falter.

Blake, stood alone in the quiet of the early hours, the city of London sprawling before him. The message from Morgan lingered in his mind, a spectre that promised more darkness to come. But as dawn broke, casting a soft light over the city, Blake was reminded of the reason he took up the badge: to chase away the shadows, to protect the innocent, and to stand as a bulwark against the face of evil.

Chapter 8: Into the Abyss

Personal Sacrifice

Detective Charlie Blake sat in the dim light of his office, the glow from the city's skyline offering a stark contrast to the shadows that played across his face. The weight of the case was a tangible presence in the room, one that seemed to demand everything from him—his time, his thoughts, and, more often than not, pieces of his soul.

The door creaked open, and in the threshold stood Sarah Jennings, his partner and the closest thing Blake had to a confidante. Her gaze was laden with concern as she took in the sight of him: a silhouette carved out of determination and fatigue.

"Blake," she began, her voice cutting through the stillness, "you can't keep doing this to yourself. You've not been home in three days."

Blake's response was a mere tightening of his jaw. "Home won't bring us any closer to catching Morgan."

"It's not just about catching him," Sarah countered, stepping into the room. "It's about not losing yourself in the process. You need balance, Charlie, or there won't be anything left of you to come back to."

The mention of balance brought a wry, fleeting smile to Blake's lips. "Balance is a luxury we can't afford. Not with what's at stake."

"It's not a luxury, it's a necessity. And what about Emily? She's worried sick about you."

Blake's eyes flicked up to meet Sarah's, and for a moment, the facade cracked, revealing the strain. Emily Saunders had become more than just a colleague to him over the years. But admitting that to himself, let alone to her, was a line he wasn't ready to cross—not in the midst of this chaos.

"I'll manage," he said finally, the words almost a whisper. "I always do."

Sarah sighed, recognising the stubborn set of his shoulders, the unspoken resolve that marked his silhouette against the glass. "Just... don't forget that you're not alone in this, Blake. We're all here with you."

With a nod that felt heavier than it should, Blake watched as she left, the click of the door closing echoing like a period at the end of an unfinished sentence. He turned back to the array of screens and files before him, the ghost of her words lingering. But there was no time for personal demons—not when real ones roamed the streets.

Blake dove back into the abyss, the case his anchor in a sea of doubt and darkness, the personal sacrifice a silent scream only he could hear.

*

The relentless hum of fluorescent lights above provided a stark backdrop to the feverish atmosphere in the incident room. Detective Charlie Blake was a fixture in the corner, surrounded by monitors that cast an artificial day over the night's canvas. His focus was absolute, his eyes scanning lines of code and digital forensics reports that might as well have been in cipher to the untrained eye.

"Anything?" Sarah's voice cut through his concentration.

Blake didn't look up. "Just patterns. Patterns that don't make sense yet."

The room was thick with anticipation, each officer and analyst knowing that time was as much a commodity as the evidence they sifted through. Then, a junior analyst, a bright-eyed recruit named Tim, approached tentatively.

"Detective Blake, I think you need to see this." Tim's voice barely rose above a whisper, but it carried the weight of discovery.

Blake turned, and Tim handed him a printout. It was a log file from the latest batch of data from the killer's known digital footprint. At first glance, it looked like the hundreds they had already seen. But then, Blake's eyes narrowed. There was a pattern in the time stamps—a sequence that didn't fit the randomness of the rest.

He grabbed a pen, jotting down the sequence. "Every seventh entry," he muttered. "It's a countdown."

Sarah leaned in, her mind racing as Blake's findings dawned on her. "A countdown to what?"

Blake stood abruptly, the pieces falling into place like a chilling puzzle. "To the next victim."

The room fell silent, every pair of eyes fixed on Blake. His reputation for finding patterns where others saw chaos was legendary—but this was beyond.

"How can you be sure?" Tim asked, his initial excitement replaced by the gravity of the implication.

Blake pointed to the sequence. "It's not just the time stamps: the entries are all from locations around the city, each one closer to the heart of downtown. Our killer is sending us a message—he's telling us where he's going to strike next."

The revelation hung heavy in the air. They had a clue—an ingenious one that had been hiding in plain sight. The killer was toying with them, using their own tools against them.

Sarah stepped up, her resolve hardening. "We need to set up a perimeter, *now*."

Blake nodded, already moving to the map on the wall.

"I want eyes on every street camera, every traffic light, every piece of surveillance we have access to. We're not going to let this psychopath take another life."

As the team mobilised, Blake felt a surge of adrenaline. For the first time, they were not just reacting: they were *anticipating*. The hunter and the hunted, in a deadly dance of wits and wills.

But, in the back of his mind, a whisper of doubt remained. Was this clue a genuine opportunity, or just another layer of the labyrinth that Morgan had constructed around them? Only time would tell, and time was rapidly running out.

*Elena Martinez adjusted the wire beneath her blouse, feeling the cold metal against her skin—a stark reminder of the danger of her assignment. As an undercover agent, she had been the chameleon of the department, but tonight's operation was different. It was personal. The killer they were hunting had taken something from each of them, and for Elena, it was about justice.

She walked into the smoky haze of the underground gambling den, the air thick with the scent of vice and desperation. Here, amidst the clink of poker chips and the murmur of illicit deals, she was to find a man known only by his moniker: The Broker.

Elena's contact had set the meeting, a risky move given that nobody truly knew who The Broker was working for. But he was the key to a set of encrypted files that had been linked to their suspect, Morgan. Files that could potentially lead to the killer's identity.

Her heart thrummed in her chest, a staccato rhythm syncing with the blaring music as she approached the bar. A man with a serpent tattoo curling around his neck gave her a nod, the signal that she was in the right place.

"You Martinez?" His voice was a low growl, barely audible over the music.

She gave a subtle nod, not wanting to attract any unnecessary attention. "I'm here for the exchange."

The man eyed her for a long moment before motioning to a back room. "Follow me."

The corridor to the back room was lined with guarded doors and cameras that watched like silent sentinels. Elena's every instinct screamed that this was a trap, but she pushed forward.

Inside the room, The Broker waited—a shadowy figure with a reputation that preceded him. "You have the payment?" he asked, his voice devoid of any discernible emotion.

Elena handed over an envelope full of unmarked bills. "Now the files."

He slid a USB across the table towards her. "Everything you're looking for is in there. But be warned: some things can't be unseen."

She pocketed the USB and stood—but, as she turned to leave, the door burst open. Armed men flooded the room, guns raised.

"Police! Don't move!"

Elena froze, realising in an instant that her cover was blown. The sting operation had been compromised, and now she was in the line of fire, both figuratively and literally.

In the chaos, The Broker slipped away, a ghost in the turmoil. Elena dove for cover behind a steel desk as bullets ricocheted off the walls. The air was thick with shouts and gunfire, a cacophony of danger that she had walked into with eyes wide open.

When the smoke cleared, Elena emerged from her

cover, shaken but unscathed. The USB—the key to unlocking the next piece of the puzzle—was secure in her pocket. But the cost of obtaining it had been high. Trust within the team would be questioned, and her role as an undercover agent would never be the same.

Elena had walked into the abyss and emerged with a prize, but as she met Blake's gaze outside the den they both knew that the real peril lay ahead. The game had changed, and their enemy was always one step ahead.

*

In the deep silence of the lab, Dan Brooks stood motionless, his eyes fixed on the microscope's eyepiece. The lab's sterility was a stark contrast to the chaos of crime scenes he frequented. His heart raced as he scrutinised the samples—minute fibres that told of secrets shrouded in darkness.

The room was dim, save for the stark white light casting a halo on his workspace. It was here, amidst test tubes and petri dishes, that breakthroughs whispered quietly, away from the sirens and the relentless pace of the station. Dan was a man of few words, but his findings spoke volumes, shaping the path of justice with the precision of his analysis.

Blake entered the lab, his steps hesitant, knowing that whatever Dan had uncovered could steer their case into uncharted territories. "Dan, you said it was urgent?" he asked, the gravity of the moment weighing down his voice.

Without diverting his gaze, Dan replied, "It's the fibre sample from the latest crime scene. It's not just any fabric. It's a custom blend—very high-end, very unique." He finally looked up, locking eyes with Blake, ensuring the full weight of his words settled in. "It's the same material used in luxury car interiors, and there's only one dealership in the city that custom orders this fabric."

Blake's mind raced, connecting dots in a frenetic burst of synapses. This was no random thread—it was a deliberate trail left by the killer. He probed further, a sense of urgency propelling his words. "Do you have a make and model?"

Dan nodded, his hands already rifling through the printed analysis. "A 2018 Monteiro Luxe," he said, handing over the report. "And there's more. The dealership keeps detailed records. We could trace who purchased or serviced a car with this interior in the last two years."

A flurry of emotions swept over Blake: excitement, anticipation, but also the cold touch of fear. This could be the turning point, the moment where the hunter and the hunted edged closer, each aware of the other's presence.

"We need to move fast," Blake declared, his voice steady with resolve. "I'll get a warrant for those records. Whoever this car belongs to, they've just become our prime suspect."

As Dan nodded in silent agreement, Blake couldn't help but feel the tides of the investigation shifting beneath him. This forensic breakthrough could be the beacon they needed to navigate through the murky waters they found themselves in. The chase was on, and the predator was finally leaving tracks.

Exiting the lab, Blake felt the pulse of the station. It was alive with the buzz of activity, each officer playing a part in the symphony of law enforcement. But underneath it all was a new rhythm taking shape, a cadence dictated by the promise of discovery and the perilous dance between the law and those who dwelt in the shadows.

With the lab's door closing behind him, the sound echoed like a starting gun. The race to find the Monteiro Luxe's owner had begun, and with it a new chapter in their relentless pursuit of the killer known as Alex Morgan. Blake could feel the narrative of the investigation shifting, taking on a new direction towards an end none of them could yet see.

The hunt was narrowing, the focus sharpening. It was no longer a question of *if* they would catch the killer, but *when*. And as the pieces began to fall into place, Blake knew that they were moving closer to an encounter that would test the very limits of their resolve. The game had indeed changed, and they were all, unwittingly or not, players on a board set by a master of deception and death.

*

In the quiet confines of his office, Detective Charlie Blake sat with the weight of the world seemingly resting on his shoulders. Across from him sat Fiona Barrett, her sharp eyes softened with concern. The room felt suffocatingly small, packed with the gravity of their decisions.

Blake's fingers drummed an impatient rhythm on the desktop. "We're in uncharted territory, Fiona. Every step we take could be a minefield," he said, his voice strained with the burden of command.

Fiona's response was measured, her tone carrying the weight of legal and moral certitude. "It's the price of justice, Charlie. We navigate these waters with the compass of the law as our guide."

The recent breakthrough in the case had presented them with a dilemma. The evidence was compelling, but it skirted dangerously close to the line of entrapment. Blake's eyes flicked to the file on his desk, its contents a

Pandora's Box of moral complexity.

"Entrapment?" Blake echoed the term, its implications as heavy as a verdict. "If it's a choice between technicalities and stopping a killer, you know where I stand."

Fiona leaned forward, her hands folded neatly. "And if we step over that line, we become no better than vigilantes. The ends don't always justify the means, especially when those means could lead to a mistrial—or, worse, an acquittal."

Blake's gaze drifted to the cityscape beyond his window, the skyline a jagged graph charting the pulse of the metropolis. The same city that depended on him to keep its streets safe.

"We'll do it by the book then," Blake decided, his jaw setting with determination. "We'll use the evidence we've gathered legally. If he's as smart as we think he is, he'll slip up. They always do."

Fiona's expression relaxed slightly, a nod of approval at his decision. "We'll prepare airtight warrants and conduct our surveillance within the parameters of the law. Our case will be built on solid ground."

The conversation moved to the practicalities of their next steps. Fiona outlined the legal framework that would allow them to pursue their suspect aggressively yet ethically. Blake listened intently, his mind already racing ahead to the challenges they would face.

As Fiona left, Blake remained seated, the silence of the room echoing loudly. He pondered the razor's edge they walked between right and wrong, the delicate balance between justice and the law. It was a balance he had sworn to uphold, a vow he intended to keep, no matter how personal the cost.

The shadows lengthened as the day waned, and Blake

knew that time was running out. With each passing moment, the killer was out there, a spectre over the city. Blake stood, his resolve hardening. There was work to be done, a moral line to tread carefully, and a killer to catch.

He picked up the phone, dialling his team. "It's Blake. Get everyone ready. We move out first light. Remember, we do this right. We owe it to the city, to the victims, and to ourselves."

As he hung up, Blake felt the weight of the impending dawn. It was not just a new day approaching but the promise of a reckoning. Tomorrow, they would walk the fine line of moral dilemmas, guided by the law, towards the hope of capturing a shadow that had loomed over them for far too long.

*

The clatter of the station echoed in Blake's mind as he marched towards the interrogation room, a fortress of cold steel and harsh light. He paused at the door, the file under his arm a tangible symbol of the delicate alliance that had just been tested to its limits. Theo Wallace, a man whose name was whispered in the darkest corners of the city, was on the other side, brought in for questioning.

As Blake entered, Theo looked up, a sardonic smile playing on his lips. "Detective Blake," he greeted, his voice smooth as silk, but with an edge that could cut glass. "To what do I owe the pleasure?"

Blake took a seat opposite Theo, his gaze unyielding. "Cut the pleasantries, Theo. You know why you're here," Blake replied, opening the file. "This list of properties you gave us led to a dead end. Now, I want to know what you're playing at."

The smile vanished from Theo's face, replaced by a cold, hard stare. "I gave you what I had," he said flatly.

"If Morgan's not there, he's moved on. That's not my fault."

Blake leaned forward, the intensity of the moment filling the room. "Or maybe you're buying time for him. You've got a history, Theo. How do we know you're not playing both sides?"

The accusation hung in the air, a dangerous dance of trust and betrayal. Theo's eyes narrowed, and for a moment, Blake thought he had pushed too far. But then, Theo leaned back, a chuckle escaping his lips.

"Detective, if I *were* helping Morgan, you'd be the last to know," Theo said, his confidence unshaken. "I want him gone as much as you do. He's bad for business, and he's bad for the balance of the city. I gave you everything to get him off the streets."

Blake's resolve was unflinching, but Theo's words resonated with a ring of truth that he couldn't ignore. "Fine," Blake conceded. "But if I find out you're double-crossing us, there will be nowhere in this city for you to hide."

"Theo's smug smile returned as he rose to his feet, the officer at the door opening it for him. "You won't," he assured, then added with a glance back, "But, just in case, I've got a little insurance."

Blake frowned, watching as Theo sauntered out, the officer closing the door behind him. He flipped through the file once more, a single photograph falling out—a candid shot of Theo and Morgan in heated discussion, dated weeks prior.

It was the breakthrough they needed, a tangible link between Morgan and the city's underworld. Blake's mind raced with possibilities, the tension between him and Theo giving way to a grudging respect. The game was changing, the pieces moving rapidly, and this photo was the key to predicting Morgan's next move.

As Blake stood, his focus razor sharp. The alliance with Theo was fraught with risk, but it was yielding results. Now it was time to act, to use the information they had to corner Morgan before he could vanish into the shadows once again.

He grabbed his coat, heading out of the room with a new sense of purpose. The station, once a cacophony of noise and chaos, now seemed a symphony of potential. Every officer, every analyst, every piece of evidence was a note in the score that would lead to Morgan's capture.

And Blake, the conductor of this intricate orchestra, felt the weight of responsibility and the thrill of the hunt coursing through him. The alliance had been tested, but in the fires of suspicion a new weapon had been forged. The chase was on, and Blake was leading the charge.

Chapter 9: The Labyrinth

Complex Patterns

Detective Charlie Blake's eyes were gritty from lack of sleep, but his mind was ablaze with the frenetic energy of a breakthrough. The walls of his office were papered with maps and crime scene photos—red lines connecting dots only he seemed to see. The pattern was there, a sinister symphony of data points and victimology, waiting to be deciphered.

At his desk sat Dr Helen Zhao, a profiler who could read between the lines of what most would consider chaos. She was perusing a thick folder, her eyes moving rapidly over the pages. "I've seen this behaviour before," she murmured, not looking up. "It's not random; it's ritualistic. Your killer is evolving, Charlie."

Blake leaned in, his fatigue momentarily forgotten. "Evolving how?" he pressed.

Dr Zhao turned a page, tapping a passage with her finger. "Each crime scene is more elaborate than the last. It's as if he's perfecting his craft." She paused, then locked eyes with Blake. "And he's doing it all under our noses."

Blake's hands clenched into fists, frustration simmering beneath his steely exterior. "But what's his endgame, Helen?"

"That's the million-dollar question." Dr Zhao leaned back, her chair creaking under the shift. "But I think he's building up to something, some grand finale."

Blake felt a chill snake down his spine. Time was a luxury they didn't have, with each tick of the clock leading to—potentially—another victim in this macabre performance.

Suddenly, his computer pinged with an incoming message. It was from Natalie Chen, a junior detective with a knack for seeing what others overlooked. Her message was succinct: *Found something odd in the victim's financials. Might be worth a look.*

Blake opened the files attached to the message, and as he and Dr Zhao pored over them, a new layer of the pattern emerged. The victims had all made substantial, secretive contributions to a charity that didn't seem to exist. It was a front—but for what?

"The killer is using this charity as a way to select his victims," Blake hypothesised, his brain firing on all cylinders. "They're chosen not just for who they are but for what they can give him."

Dr Zhao nodded, her gaze returning to the folder. "He's not just taking lives; he's taking their secrets, their guilt. He's acting as judge and executioner."

Blake picked up his phone and dialled Natalie's number. "Good work, Chen. I need you to dig deeper into this charity. Find out where the money's going."

"On it, Detective," came the crisp reply.

The room felt smaller, the air charged with the electricity of the hunt. Blake stood up, stretching his back. He moved to the window, looking out at the city. Somewhere out there the killer was walking free, cloaked in the anonymity of the bustling metropolis.

Turning back to Dr Zhao, Blake's resolve was clear in his voice. "We're going to unravel this bastard's grand design, and when we do we'll be waiting to give him the finale he deserves."

The labyrinth they were navigating had just become more complex, but with each new discovery, they were drawing the map that would lead them through it. It was a game of cat and mouse, but Blake was determined to outplay the mastermind behind this twisted puzzle. The hunt was on, and the predator would soon become the prey.

*

The office was a hive of activity, the air ripe with the scent of coffee and the low hum of fervent discussion. At the heart of it all was Detective Natalie Chen, her eyes poring over the labyrinthine web of financial transactions that linked the victims to the elusive charity front. Her mind was alight with theories, each one a potential key to unlocking the killer's next move.

As Blake approached, he could see the intensity of Natalie's focus, the way her brows furrowed and her lips moved silently with the rhythm of her thoughts. "What have you got, Chen?" he asked, peering over her shoulder.

Natalie didn't look up, her finger tracing lines on the screen. "I think we've been looking at this all wrong," she said. "We assumed the contributions were a selection criterion, but what if they're a distraction? The amounts vary widely, too random for a killer as methodical as Morgan."

Blake's interest was piqued. "Go on," he prompted.

Natalie flipped through her notes, her voice steady with the thrill of discovery. "The dates, they align with significant events in financial markets—stock crashes, mergers, scandals. Morgan's background in finance... it can't be a coincidence."

Blake absorbed the information, a new angle emerging from the fog of data. "He's using the charity to launder money, but the victims... they're part of the message he's sending."

"Exactly," Natalie confirmed, finally looking up with a

fire in her eyes. "Each one played a part in these events, scapegoats or profiteers. Morgan is targeting the financial ecosystem that once was his domain."

The revelation sent a shiver down Blake's spine. Morgan wasn't just killing; he was dismantling a world he once belonged to, piece by piece. But why?

Natalie's next words were almost a whisper, a realisation that bordered on epiphany. "Retribution," she said. "For a fall from grace, a punishment for greed... his and theirs."

The pieces of the puzzle were beginning to coalesce into a clearer picture, a tapestry of revenge and corruption. Blake knew they were onto something. The financial angle offered a new avenue to predict Morgan's next move.

"Good work, Detective," Blake commended, a renewed sense of urgency fuelling his voice. "Get this information to Zhao and Brooks. See if they can find a pattern in the victims' histories that correlates with Morgan's career timeline."

Natalie nodded, already compiling the data. Blake watched her work, admiration mingling with the weight of responsibility. Natalie's insight had opened a new path in the labyrinth, and it was up to him to navigate it.

As Blake turned to leave, his phone buzzed with a message from Elena Martinez, their undercover specialist. "Found something. Meet me at the docks. Bring backup." The text read. A location Morgan was known to frequent in his heyday.

Blake felt the familiar rush of the chase. They were drawing closer to Morgan with every breakthrough, the hunt intensifying with each revelation. Natalie's insider's edge had given them a much-needed advantage, but

Blake knew that the real test was just beginning. They were stepping into Morgan's world, and they had to tread carefully lest they become prey in the killer's game.

*

The morning air was crisp, carrying the buzz of the city waking up to another day of uncertainty. Detective Charlie Blake stood by Anna Kowalski's side as she prepared to address the community at the local town hall. The worn brick building, usually a hub of local activity and joy, had taken on a sombre tone as the neighbourhood grappled with the terror instilled by Alex Morgan's actions.

Anna's voice, when she spoke, was a blend of warmth and firm resolve. "We understand your concerns," she began, her eyes scanning the crowd of anxious faces. "But I assure you, the Metropolitan Police are doing everything in our power to keep you safe and to catch the person responsible."

Blake watched as the crowd's rigid posture softened slightly. Anna's role was a delicate one; she was the conduit between the police and the public, a bearer of reassurance in a time where trust was as fragile as glass.

A hand rose from the crowd, a middle-aged man with the look of sleepless nights etched under his eyes. "How can we trust that we're not just waiting ducks for this... monster?" he asked, his voice barely hiding his fear.

Anna's response was immediate and confident. "We have our best detectives on the case, including Detective Blake here." She gestured to Blake, who gave a reassuring nod. "We've increased patrols, and we're following up on all leads. We're not just on the defensive; we're actively hunting this individual."

Blake stepped forward, his presence commanding yet

comforting. "We've made significant progress," he added, his voice carrying the weight of authority and the promise of protection. "Every piece of information helps, no matter how small. You know your community best; if you see something, say something."

The meeting continued with Anna and Blake fielding questions, providing as much information as they could without compromising the investigation. Blake could sense the tide of fear ebbing as Anna's words, backed by his assurances, fortified the community's resolve.

As the crowd dispersed, a woman approached Blake, her expression one of determination. "Detective, I may know something about Morgan," she whispered, glancing around nervously. "I've seen someone lurking around the old factory on my way home from work. It's probably nothing, but..."

"It could be everything," Blake finished for her, a spark of hope igniting in his eyes. "Thank you. We'll look into it immediately."

Anna watched the exchange, a small smile playing on her lips. "Good catch," she said, once the woman had left.

Blake looked at Anna, gratitude in his eyes. "No, good trust-building. This is how we'll catch him, Anna. With the community behind us."

They stepped out into the sunlight, the town hall's doors closing behind them. The Public Face of the investigation, Anna, had held strong, bridging the gap between the people and the police. And now, with a new lead in their hands, Blake felt the momentum of the case surge forward.

The labyrinth they navigated was intricate, but with Anna's help, they had found a new way through it. The trust she fostered within the community was their beacon, and it was leading them ever closer to Alex Morgan. As they walked back to the station, Blake knew that the trust of the people was as vital as any evidence; it could be the key that would unlock the labyrinth and bring Morgan into the light.

*

The digital forensics lab was a symphony of bleeps and keystrokes, a beacon of blue light in the dim station. Mike Hanover, fingers dancing over his keyboard, was the maestro, orchestrating a search through cyberspace with Marcus Levine, the tech analyst, his able second. They were in pursuit of Alex Morgan, whose digital shadow loomed large over the city.

"Any luck with those IP addresses?" Mike asked, without taking his eyes off the screen.

Marcus, surrounded by a fortress of monitors, was deep in concentration. "It's like chasing a ghost," he muttered. "But ghosts don't cover their tracks as well as Morgan does."

Blake stepped into the lab, feeling the electric tension of the digital duel. "Tell me you've got something," he said, hope and impatience lacing his tone.

Marcus pointed to a flurry of activity on one screen. "Here. We tracked the server Morgan used. It's been bouncing around, but we managed to isolate a pattern."

Mike interjected, "He's smart, leaving breadcrumbs through VPNs and proxies, but everyone makes mistakes." His screen displayed a map with lines converging on a single point. "He slipped here, accessed the server directly, just for a second, but it was enough."

Blake leaned over their shoulders, studying the map. The point was an old industrial sector, now mostly abandoned. "Could be a base of operations," he mused.

"We should move quickly," Marcus advised. "If he's as meticulous as we think, he won't stay in one place for long."

Mike nodded in agreement. "We've set up a honeypot. It's a trap, designed to look like a vulnerable server. If he bites, we'll have him."

Blake's gaze was steely. "Do it. Set the trap."

Hours passed, the room charged with silent anticipation. Then, a sudden spike in bandwidth—a flicker on the screen, a digital pulse.

"He took the bait!" Marcus exclaimed, triumph and adrenaline surging through his voice.

Mike's hands flew across the keyboard, tracking the connection. "I've got his location," he declared, a victorious glint in his eyes.

Blake's phone was already in his hand, dispatching units to the location. "Hanover, Levine, excellent work," he praised. "You've just outfoxed the fox."

The room erupted into controlled chaos as they prepared to act on the information. Blake knew this was a pivotal moment. The digital duel had given them a rare advantage over Morgan, and they needed to capitalise on it swiftly.

With the coordinates locked in, the hunt moved from cyberspace to the physical streets. Blake left the lab with renewed vigour, knowing that the collaboration between Mike and Marcus had brought them one step closer to ending Morgan's reign of terror. The digital battlefield had been theirs, but the real confrontation was just beginning.

*

The morgue was silent except for the hum of the refrigeration units, a cold and sterile symphony for the dead. Dr Emily Saunders, the lead forensic pathologist, preferred it this way; the quiet allowed her to think, to listen to what the silent could tell. She carefully arranged her instruments, each one cleaned to a mirror shine, ready to uncover the secrets held by the latest victim of Alex Morgan.

Detective Charlie Blake stood at the threshold, watching Emily as she worked. Her focus was unwavering, her hands steady as she performed the Y-incision with practised precision. The body before her was a canvas, and she was about to reveal the art of the killer's signature.

"Find anything?" Blake's voice was soft, not wanting to disrupt her concentration.

Emily didn't look up. "It's the same MO," she responded, her tone clinical. "Exsanguination. But there's something different about this one."

Blake moved closer, his eyes scanning the body. "Different how?"

Emily pointed with her scalpel to a series of markings that were almost imperceptible against the pale skin. "Do you see these?" she asked. "They're not random. Each one is precise, deliberate. They're symbols."

Blake felt a chill despite the room's chill. Symbols had become a horrifying language in Morgan's game. He leaned in, observing the symbols that seemed to dance in the harsh fluorescent light. "Can you decipher them?"

Emily shook her head. "Not yet. But I will." She was resolute, a detective in her own right, chasing the clues left in flesh rather than on the streets.

As she continued her meticulous work, Emily narrated her findings. The victim had been kept alive for the better part of the ordeal, the torture drawn out. It was a psychological component as much as it was physical—

Morgan was engaging with his victims on a level that went beyond the visceral act of killing.

Blake listened, his expression growing darker with each word. "He's evolving," he muttered. "This isn't just about killing anymore. It's a performance, and the city is his stage."

Emily paused, looking up at Blake. "There's more," she said, her voice steady. "I found traces of a rare botanical compound in the wounds. It's not native to this region; it's found only in a few remote areas."

"That's our signature," Blake said, the realisation hitting him like a wave. "If we can trace the source of that compound, we can start to map out his supply chain, get ahead of him."

Emily nodded in agreement. "I'll run a full tox screen, see what else I can find."

Blake placed a hand on her shoulder, a silent gesture of gratitude. "You're doing good work, Emily. Keep me posted."

He stepped out of the morgue, the click of the door marking his departure back into the living world. The information Emily had provided was a breakthrough. The symbols and the rare compound formed a pattern, a clue to the twisted psyche of Alex Morgan. It was a lead they desperately needed.

Back at the station, Blake convened a meeting with his team. The morgue's revelations had given them a new angle, a crack in the armour of their elusive adversary. Each piece of evidence, each symbol, each trace element was a breadcrumb leading them through the labyrinth.

"Morgan thinks he's untouchable, but he's mistaken," Blake declared to the room. "We're going to use his own signature against him."

The team set to work, cross-referencing the symbols with cultural databases and reaching out to botanists who might help them track the origin of the compound. Blake knew they were up against a formidable foe, a killer who revelled in the macabre theatre of his crimes. But now, they had a script of their own, a path that would lead them not only to Morgan's lair but into the dark heart of his madness.

As the team dispersed, Blake lingered over the crime scene photos, the symbols etched in flesh staring back at him. They were a message, and he was determined to decipher it. This was more than a puzzle; it was a declaration of war, one that Blake and his team were now fully equipped to wage.

The hunt for Alex Morgan was reaching its zenith, and the pathologist's puzzle had provided the map they needed to navigate the final twists and turns. Blake felt the weight of responsibility, the need for justice for the victims, their families, and the city that lived in fear. With Emily's analysis, they were one step closer to ending the nightmare, to unmasking the man behind the monster, and to restoring peace to the streets that Morgan had turned into a labyrinth of terror.

*

The task force room was abuzz with a sense of impending action, a crescendo of collected knowledge that had brought the team to the brink of an important breakthrough. Detective Charlie Blake, standing at the helm of a ship sailing through a storm of data and deduction, felt the weight of leadership heavy upon his shoulders.

Emily's analysis of the botanical toxin had opened up new avenues, while Mike and Marcus's digital snare had given them a glimpse into Morgan's operational patterns. Natalie's financial digging unearthed a network of transactions that painted a broader picture of Morgan's influence, and Anna's public liaison work had yielded a wealth of community intelligence. The disparate threads were weaving into a coherent narrative, a map that charted a course straight to Alex Morgan.

Blake surveyed the room, his eyes moving from face to face, each a specialist in their field, each holding a piece of the puzzle that was Alex Morgan. "We've got him on the back foot," Blake began, his voice firm. "He's been leading us through a labyrinth, but we've been picking up the breadcrumbs all along."

Sarah Jennings was the first to speak up. "He's smart, but his ego will be his downfall. He can't resist showing us how clever he thinks he is, and that's where we'll catch him."

Blake nodded, turning to the large map pinned to the wall, its surface a spider's web of connections. "Each victim, each crime scene, each movement he's made, has been a step in a dance he's choreographed. But now we're changing the music."

The room fell silent as Blake traced lines across the map, drawing connections with a red marker. "Here," he said, tapping on a cluster of markings, "is where we believe Morgan is hiding. It's secluded, hard to access, and right under our noses—the old industrial district."

Blake's team leaned in, their expressions a mix of concentration and resolve. Elena Martinez broke the silence. "We know his habits, his preferences. I can get in there, find the final piece we need to put this puzzle together."

Mike Hanover chimed in, his eyes tired but sharp.

"And we'll keep a digital eye on the area. Any electronic whisper, we'll hear it."

Blake looked at Fiona Barrett, who gave a small nod. "You have the green light. Everything's in place."

The team dispersed, moving with the kind of purpose that only comes when the endgame is in sight. Emily returned to her lab, Marcus to his bank of monitors and Natalie to her financial charts. Each knew that the culmination of their efforts was more than just a lead—it was the beacon that would guide them through the final dark.

As Blake prepared to leave, Dr Helen Zhao approached him. "Charlie, when you find him," she said, her voice low, "remember that he's not just a puzzle to be solved. He's dangerous."

Blake met her gaze, his eyes hard as flint. "I know. And we're going to stop him."

The pieces were in place, the team united by a single goal. The hunt for Alex Morgan was nearing its end, and the labyrinth that he had constructed was about to be dismantled, piece by piece, by the very people he had underestimated. The chase had led them here, and now it was time to close the net.

As Blake stepped out into the night, the city's soundscape a distant rumble, he felt the tide of the case turning. The culmination of their efforts was at hand, and soon they would face Morgan on their terms. The hunter was now the hunted, and justice was on the horizon.

Chapter 10: Edge of the Storm

Preparation for Confrontation

In the dim light of the early hours, the Metropolitan Police's Special Operations room was a flurry of controlled activity. Detective Charlie Blake stood at the centre, his silhouette stern and commanding against the backdrop of monitors and equipment. His team moved around him, each member a vital cog in the machinery of justice they were about to unleash.

Elena Martinez checked her gear with a methodical calm that belied the adrenaline coursing through her veins. Marcus Levine was engaged in a final sweep of their digital traps, ensuring no electronic stone was left unturned. Natalie Chen reviewed the financial trails one last time, searching for any missed thread that could unravel Morgan's web.

Blake watched them, a quiet pride swelling in his chest. They were more than a team: they were a battalion on the eve of battle, the air thick with the resolve of warriors who had traversed the abyss and now stood ready to face the storm.

He called them to gather, his voice the anchor in the tempest of preparation. "This is it," he began, his eyes meeting theirs. "Today, we end this. We know Morgan is dangerous, but we are ready. We know his methods, his madness, and we have the means to stop him."

The room settled into a hushed focus as Blake continued. "Remember, we're not just fighting for justice for those taken from us—we're fighting to prevent more darkness. Today, we bring light."

Mike Hanover approached with a laptop, the map of

the city splayed across the screen. "All surveillance drones are operational, and our intel suggests Morgan will be at the industrial site by dawn."

Blake nodded, his mind already turning the gears of strategy. "Good. Dan, Emily: make sure our forensic kits are ready. We may only get one chance to gather what we need from the scene."

Dan Brooks and Emily Saunders, a united front of scientific rigour, assured him with a nod. They understood the weight of evidence; they were the sentinels of truth in a world of shadows.

Blake then turned to Theo Wallace, the man whose allegiance had been a gamble but now stood as a testament to the complexities of the human psyche. "Theo, your insights into Morgan's network have been invaluable. Today, that knowledge could make all the difference."

Theo, once a figure from the underworld Blake had fought against, now nodded in acknowledgement, a wry smile hinting at the irony of their alliance. "You'll have everything you need, Detective. We all want Morgan in chains."

As the team dispersed to their respective tasks, Blake's gaze lingered on the empty chair at the end of the table. It belonged to Dr Helen Zhao, who had given them the psychological roadmap to Morgan's mind. Her insights had been instrumental, and though she couldn't be there in person her presence was felt.

Blake then turned to the window, watching the city stir awake. This was where the line was drawn, where the fight for the soul of the city would be won or lost. The storm was upon them, and they were the bulwark against the tide.

He turned back to his team, his voice cutting through the silence. "Gear up. We move out in thirty. Today, the labyrinth Morgan built will collapse, and we will be the ones to bring him out of the shadows."

The team moved with a renewed sense of purpose, donning bulletproof vests and checking sidearms. They were the shield against the coming storm, the edge of the blade that would restore balance.

As Blake strapped on his own vest, he felt the weight not just of the Kevlar but of the day ahead. It was a weight he was ready to bear, for himself, his team, and the city that had placed its trust in them.

Today, *they* were the storm—and Morgan would find no shelter from their resolve.

*

The day was breaking, a chorus of hues splattered across the London sky as Detective Charlie Blake sat in the dim glow of his office, the files from the previous night's operation spread out in front of him like a deconstructed mosaic. Each piece told a story, each detail a fragment of the psyche they were pursuing.

Blake's phone rang, the shrill tone a jarring contrast to the reflective silence. It was Theo Wallace, the informant whose criminal connections had proven invaluable. "Blake?" Theo's voice was a hushed whisper. "I've got something you need to know about Morgan."

The words cut through the morning calm, setting Blake's pulse on edge. "Go ahead," he said, bracing for the impact of Theo's revelation.

"It's about his sister," Theo continued, his voice tinged with the weight of significance. "You know the story— the car accident, the drunk driver who walked away scot-free because of a legal loophole?"

Blake's memory flickered to the case files he'd read, the tragedy that had struck Morgan's family years before. "Yes," he acknowledged, his mind racing to piece together the new angle.

"Morgan never forgave the system for that. He sees his actions as retribution, a balancing of scales that the law couldn't handle," Theo revealed, the picture becoming painfully clear.

The revelation was a punch to the gut, a key turning in the lock of understanding. Morgan's campaign of terror wasn't just a spree: it was a vendetta, a twisted quest for justice born from the deepest well of grief and fury.

Blake stood up, the detective in him awakening to the grim symmetry of the case. "The victims," he murmured, "they're not random. They're symbols, each representing a failure of the system that Morgan despises."

Theo's voice was grave. "Exactly. You're not just dealing with a killer; you're dealing with a crusader, and he won't stop until he's either dead or has razed the system to the ground."

The line went dead, leaving Blake in the quiet dawn of realisation. He looked out of the window at the city he'd sworn to protect, its beauty belying the darkness that lurked within.

Blake's team assembled, the room filling with the hum of anticipation as he shared the new insight. "Morgan is following a script, one written in the blood of his sister's memory. Each act is a scene in his play of vengeance."

Sarah Jennings nodded, her eyes reflecting the gravity of their task. "He's been leading us through the narrative of his pain, and we've been unwitting players on his stage," she said.

Blake leaned over the map, his finger tracing the

pattern of the crimes. "We've been reactive; it's time to be proactive. We need to disrupt his narrative, force him to the next act on *our* terms."

The team's eyes were fixed on Blake, their resolve mirroring his own. "We'll set a stage of our own," Blake declared, "one where Morgan's dark revelations will lead to his downfall."

The plan was set into motion, a trap laid with the bait of his own story. Blake knew they were stepping into the heart of the storm, where the darkest revelations awaited. But they were ready, armed with the truth of Morgan's pain and the resolve to end his vendetta.

As Blake and his team geared up, the city beyond remained oblivious to the drama that was about to unfold. But within the walls of the Metropolitan Police headquarters, the storm was brewing, and Blake was the eye: calm, focused, and ready to face the whirlwind of Alex Morgan's dark heart.

*

The morning light had yet to chase away the shadows of the station when Detective Charlie Blake, his face a map of sleepless nights, called for an impromptu meeting. The room was filled with a tangible tension, as Theo Wallace, a man more accustomed to the murky ethics of the underground, stood shoulder to shoulder with Marcus Levine, the team's digital sentinel.

"Theo, we need more," Blake began, his voice carrying a mix of urgency and reluctance. "Your connections, your... unconventional resources. Morgan's slippery, and we can't afford to play by the rules he's already rewriting."

Theo's gaze was steady, that a man who understood the language of need. "You know what it means to go down this road, Detective," he said, his voice low. "There's no turning back."

Marcus shifted uncomfortably, the glow from his laptop casting a ghostly pallor on his face. "And what of the law?" he interjected. "We're not vigilantes. There's a line we shouldn't cross."

Blake looked from Theo to Marcus, the moral dichotomy between the two as stark as day and night. "This isn't about crossing lines; it's about blurring them for the greater good. Morgan doesn't operate within our boundaries. We have to adapt."

Sarah Jennings spoke up. "It's a dangerous game, Charlie. Every step into the grey risks the integrity of the case, not to mention our own."

Blake nodded, acknowledging the weight of her words. "I know, but consider the stakes. Morgan is more than a killer; he's a spectre haunting this city, and if we don't stop him now the cost will be more than we can bear."

The room fell into a heavy silence, the team grappling with the necessity of their next move. Theo's network could provide them with the elusive edge they needed, but at what cost? Marcus's expertise had always been wielded within the confines of the law, yet now they faced an adversary who defied such confines.

Theo broke the silence. "I'll do what's needed," he affirmed, "but remember, the shadows are my territory. You all will have to live with what's found there."

Blake gave a curt nod. "We'll do what we must," he replied. "Marcus, I need you to work with Theo. Anything he brings in, I want it vetted, clean enough to hold up if it comes to light."

Marcus met Blake's gaze, a silent understanding

passing between them. "I'll make sure of it," he said, though the unease in his voice was palpable.

The meeting adjourned with the sunrise casting long shadows across the room. Blake pulled Theo aside, "Keep your methods out of the daylight," he instructed.

Theo's smirk was a flash of lightning in the dim room. "You just focus on catching Morgan. Leave the darkness to me."

Blake watched Theo leave, feeling the lines of the law and morality twist into a complex knot. He then turned to Marcus, who was already setting up digital filters and firewalls. "Keep me updated, every hour. If Theo dives too deep..."

"I'll pull him back," Marcus finished, his fingers already flying across the keyboard.

Blake left the digital hub, his mind a whirlwind of strategy and ethics. The alliance with Theo was necessary, albeit fraught with peril. Yet, the promise of stopping Morgan, of ending the nightmare that had gripped the city, made every strained alliance and every moral compromise seem a price worth paying.

As Blake stepped into the breaking day, the city coming alive around him, he carried the weight of their decisions. In the pursuit of justice, he and his team had entered a labyrinth of moral ambiguity, but with one shared beacon to guide them: to stop Alex Morgan, no matter the shadows they had to traverse.

*

In the sterile hum of the forensics lab, the air was thick with anticipation. Detective Charlie Blake stood shoulder to shoulder with Emily Saunders and Dan Brooks, their eyes fixed on the array of evidence spread before them. The room was silent, save for the soft clicks of the computer as images flickered on the screen—a silent testament to the gravity of their findings.

Emily broke the silence, her voice steady despite the storm brewing in her mind. "We've isolated the toxin found in the latest victims," she said, pointing to the digital chromatography results glowing on the monitor. "It's a derivative of a rare Amazonian plant, used by indigenous tribes for... spiritual cleansing."

Dan chimed in, his demeanour reflecting the seriousness of their breakthrough. "And we've tracked its source," he added, sliding a map across the table to Blake. "There's only one place in the city that cultivates such plants—the botanical conservatory."

Blake absorbed the information, the implications clear and dire. "So, Morgan's next move," he mused aloud. "He's taking us back to the beginning, to the root of his twisted journey."

The detectives exchanged a look, understanding dawning in their eyes. The conservatory was not just a place of beauty and tranquillity; it was a symbol of life and growth. But in Morgan's hands, it was poised to become the stage for his next act of horror.

Emily's fingers danced over the keyboard, cross-referencing the conservatory's visitor logs with the timeline of the crimes. "There's a pattern," she announced, her voice a blend of triumph and trepidation. "Morgan's visits increased in frequency leading up to the murders, always on nights when the conservatory held private events."

Blake leaned in, his gaze intense. "He was hiding in plain sight, masking his presence amidst the elite and the curious." His fist clenched involuntarily. "It's not just a pattern; it's a countdown."

Dan's attention was on the botanical database now, his brow furrowed. "The next private event at the conservatory is tonight," he said, the weight of urgency evident in his tone.

The revelation hit them like a physical force. The pieces of the puzzle were aligning, the image of Morgan's macabre plan becoming painfully clear. Blake's voice cut through the charged atmosphere. "We need to move— now. We have to stop him before he completes this cycle of violence."

Emily and Dan gathered the evidence, their movements swift and precise. The lab, once a sanctuary of science and discovery, was now the command centre of a race against time.

Blake's phone was already to his ear, calling in the alert. "All units, this is Blake. Suspect Alex Morgan's next target has been identified. Mobilise at the botanical conservatory immediately. We have one chance to end this."

As they left the lab, the trio moved with the cohesion of a single entity, their strides purposeful and determined. The forensic finality of Emily and Dan's findings had not only unveiled Morgan's next move but had also provided the catalyst for the final confrontation.

Tonight, the conservatory would not be a backdrop for the privileged few to admire nature's wonders. It would be the battleground where good and evil collided, where Blake and his team would face the storm head-on, armed with the power of science and the resolve to restore peace to a city held hostage by one man's madness.

*

The clock was edging towards midnight, and the normally bustling station had settled into an almost reverential hush. Detective Charlie Blake paced the floor of the operations room, where the hum of computers and the soft flicker of screen light were the only indicators of life. His team was out there in the shadows of the city, each member a moving piece in the intricate strategy that had been set into motion.

Then, the stillness shattered by the crackle of the radio. "Blake, it's Martinez," came the voice, urgent but controlled. "You need to see this."

Within minutes, Elena Martinez, the cornerstone of their undercover operations, was striding into the room, her demeanour a mix of triumph and gravity. In her hand was a USB drive—a small, seemingly innocuous piece of plastic and metal that held the weight of their entire case.

"We got him," Elena declared, her voice a whisper of steely resolve. "Morgan made a mistake, and we caught it on tape."

Blake's eyes narrowed, his focus absolute. "What kind of mistake?"

Elena slid the drive into the computer, and a video file popped up on the screen. There, in grainy clarity, was Alex Morgan, speaking fervently to an unseen companion. His words were brash, confident, but it was the backdrop that caught Blake's attention—a distinctive piece of graffiti that he recognised instantly. It was the mark of an underground artist known only as 'The Phantom', a signature that had appeared in one of the city's most dangerous and inaccessible areas.

"That's the old metro tunnels beneath the East End," Blake breathed, realisation dawning. "He's been using them to move around the city undetected."

Elena nodded, eyes locked on the screen. "He slipped up, bragging about his 'perfect hideaway'. Didn't realise we had the place under surveillance."

Blake watched the footage, every fibre of his being attuned to the man in the video. Morgan was unaware of the net closing in on him, his arrogance captured in high definition. But it was more than just a mistake; it was the final piece of the labyrinth that Morgan had built.

"Good work, Elena," Blake said, the pride in his team evident in his voice. "This is it. We now know where to find him."

The room erupted into activity, the quiet of moments earlier replaced with the urgent buzz of an imminent raid. Coordinates were confirmed, units were mobilised, and every available resource was directed towards the East End metro tunnels.

As the team prepared to move out, Blake paused, considering the gravity of what was about to unfold. The chase that had consumed them was reaching its climax, the final act in a deadly play that had been scripted by Morgan himself.

Elena's discovery had been the catalyst, the last clue in a series of intricate, dangerous moves. Blake knew the path ahead was fraught with peril, but the resolve in his team's eyes reflected his own. They were ready.

In the predawn darkness, as they descended into the bowels of the city, Blake felt the weight of the impending confrontation. This was where it would end, in the cold, forgotten tunnels that ran like arteries beneath the city's skin.

Morgan's final mistake was his undoing, and as Blake led his team through the labyrinthine underground, he knew that the hunter was about to become the hunted. The trap was set, the pieces in place, and justice was at their fingertips. The storm was about to break, and they were the tempest.

The abandoned theatre stood like a monolith of a bygone era, its hallowed halls resonating with the echoes of forgotten applause. Here, Detective Charlie Blake and his team were poised to set a trap for Alex Morgan, a man who had turned the city into a stage for his own macabre performance.

Blake could feel the pulse of the city, its nervous system electrified by the hunt that had consumed them all. In the depths of the theatre, Blake's team worked with silent precision, setting the stage for the final act. Every prop was a calculated placement, every light a potential spotlight for the grand deception they were orchestrating.

Sarah Jennings, her mind a library of criminal behaviour, watched the preparations unfold. "He's going to show," she whispered, her certainty a cold blade in the warm, dusty air. "He can't resist the chance to be the star of his own downfall."

Blake watched the scene, a mixture of pride and apprehension in his chest. He knew the dangers of the game they were playing. Morgan was a master of manipulation, a puppeteer who revelled in pulling the strings of law enforcement just as much as he did his victims. But this time, the strings would be pulled tight around him, binding him in a narrative of their own design.

The stage was set with a deliberate messiness, crafted to resemble the chaos Morgan left in his wake. The bait was laid out: a news article crafted with care, planted amongst the props. It was designed to catch Morgan's eye, a challenge interwoven with quotes that mirrored his twisted ideology. It was a taunt he would be unable to overlook.

"The article goes live in ten minutes," Mike Hanover confirmed, his eyes locked on the computer screen before him. "Once he sees it, it's only a matter of time."

Blake nodded, his eyes scanning the theatre's interior. "Everyone knows their role?" he asked, his voice cutting through the still air with a commander's authority.

Affirmations echoed back to him, a chorus of readiness from his team. They were scattered throughout the theatre, unseen guardians in the shadows, each prepared to close in at Blake's command.

The clock ticked down, the article went live, and the team held its collective breath. The minutes stretched, elongated by the tension that gripped the air.

And then, a notification. The digital trap they had set reported a hit. "He's seen it," Marcus announced, his voice a mixture of triumph and tension.

Blake moved to the wings of the stage, his place among the shadows chosen for the oversight it provided. From here, he could see the entire theatre and direct his team as needed. His hand rested on his sidearm, the cool metal a reminder of the reality of their situation.

The theatre, once a place of joy and entertainment, was now a battleground. The stakes were life and death, the audience an entire city that watched and waited, unknowingly holding its breath for the outcome of this drama.

Blake's earpiece crackled to life. "Movement at stage left," Elena's voice reported, her tone steady despite the adrenaline that coursed through them all.

"On my signal," Blake replied, his gaze fixed on the darkened entrance where a shadow had appeared—a shadow that moved with purpose and confidence.

As the figure stepped into the dim light, Blake's voice

was a calm storm. "Now."

The team converged as one, the theatre erupting into a cacophony of shouts and commands. The trap was sprung, the hunter now the hunted, the predator caught in a web of his own making.

But as the lights blazed on, illuminating the theatre with the harsh truth of reality, the figure on the stage froze. It was not Alex Morgan who stood in the spotlight, but a decoy—a pawn in a game that had just twisted anew.

Blake's mind raced. Morgan had anticipated their move, had manipulated them into revealing their hand. The realisation was a cold wash over him, but it only served to harden his resolve.

"We adapt," he spoke into the comm, his voice the rallying cry they needed. "This is just the beginning. He's close, and we're going to finish this."

The team regrouped, their determination a tangible force in the room. They had been outmanoeuvred, but not outplayed. The trap had been set, and the chase would continue. The storm was still on the horizon, and they were the ones who would weather it.

Blake's eyes were the last to leave the theatre, the final act yet unwritten. But as he stepped into the night, the city's heartbeat in sync with his own, he knew the final curtain would fall on their terms. The trap had been set, and the edge of the storm was now within their grasp.

Part 2: The Descent

Chapter 11: Echoes in Silence

Unravelling Secrets

Blake's gaze was unyielding, fixed on the myriad documents strewn across his desk. Each paper was a silent whisper from Alex Morgan's past, a mosaic of service records, psychological evaluations, and redacted mission details. The dim glow of the desk lamp cast long shadows, mirroring the dark recesses of Morgan's history he was about to traverse.

It began with the service records: commendations and medals that spoke of valour—but between the lines, there was a different narrative. Blake traced his fingers over a particular operation in Basra. The report was sanitised, the language sterile, but the subtext was clear. There were incidents, decisions that didn't align with the heroic image portrayed. His intuition, honed by years in the field, sensed the dissonance.

The psychological evaluations were more telling. Notes scribbled in haste by an overworked military psychologist hinted at volatility, a man grappling with his demons. Morgan's responses were guarded, often deflecting, but the strain was evident. There were sessions after Basra, the details omitted, but the outcomes were there in black and white: *fit for duty* yet *monitor closely*.

Blake's focus then shifted to a series of interviews conducted with Morgan's former comrades. They spoke of a man changed by war, someone who walked the edge of morality, whose clarity was obscured by the fog of combat. Yet, in every account, there was respect, a kind of wary admiration for his capabilities.

The deeper Blake dug, the more the image of Alex Morgan fragmented. He was no longer just a suspect; he was becoming an enigma, a man whose past was a patchwork of redactions and whispered rumours. Blake knew that to catch him he had to understand him, predict him. But with every secret uncovered, Morgan's psyche became more labyrinthine.

Blake leaned back, the weight of what he'd learned pressing upon him. The silence of the room was palpable, broken only by the soft ticking of the clock. Each tick was a reminder of the urgency of the case, of the lives still ensnared in Morgan's web of madness.

He gathered the papers, creating a chronological narrative of Morgan's descent. It was a descent that seemed inevitable, a trajectory towards darkness that perhaps began long before Basra. But there were gaps, moments unaccounted for, and Blake knew these voids held the key.

Just then, his phone vibrated, cutting through the quiet. He glanced at the screen—a message from Sarah: *We need to talk. It's about the case*. Blake felt a flicker of something stir within him—anticipation, or perhaps it was hope. They were fractured—both he and Sarah—but in this quest for truth there was a chance for mending, for unity.

He took a deep breath, steadying himself for the dive back into the abyss. There was more to unravel, more echoes in the silence of Alex Morgan's past to chase. And Detective Charlie Blake wouldn't stop until every last secret was laid bare.

*

The cafe was bustling with life, a stark contrast to the solemnity of Blake's office. He spotted Sarah at a corner table, her eyes scanning the room until they locked onto his. Blake approached, noting the tension in her posture, a wariness that hadn't been there before.

"Charlie," Sarah greeted, her voice a mix of relief and restraint as he took the seat opposite her.

"Sarah," he nodded, offering a small, earnest smile. "Thanks for meeting me."

They ordered coffee, a mundane act that served as a bridge over troubled waters. As the waitress left, Blake leaned forward, his eyes serious. "I've been going over Morgan's past. It's… convoluted."

Sarah's eyes mirrored his intensity. "I figured as much. I've been doing some digging of my own," she said, sliding a folder across the table. "I think it's time we pool our resources, Charlie. Our differences aside, we need to stop him."

The folder contained her own findings, a collection of interviews and statements from victims' families, insights that painted a broader picture of Morgan's possible motives. Blake felt a grudging respect for her dedication. He reached for the folder, but his hand hovered, hesitating.

"Sarah, about what happened—"

She lifted a hand, stopping him mid-sentence. "Not now, Charlie. Our focus has to be on the case. We can settle our personal scores later. Right now, Morgan is out there, and people are getting hurt."

Blake withdrew his hand, nodding slowly. "You're right," he conceded, the folder lying open between them. Together, they pored over the documents, their heads bent in concentration, their earlier discord giving way to a shared purpose. The cafe's ambient noise faded into the background as they entered their own world, one filled with the grim reality of their investigation.

As they discussed the connections between the victims, a pattern began to emerge. Blake found his analytical mind complemented by Sarah's empathetic approach. Where he saw facts and evidence, she saw the human element, the thread of pain that linked the seemingly random targets.

Their collaboration revealed a new angle on Morgan's activities, a possible link to an underground network that neither had considered. It was a breakthrough, one that could only have arisen from their combined efforts.

The hours slipped by unnoticed until the waitress gently reminded them of closing time. Blake and Sarah gathered their things—their relationship not repaired, but reinforced by a mutual goal. They stood outside the cafe, the chill of the evening air a sharp contrast to the warmth of their recent cooperation.

"We should do this more often," Blake said, a tentative offer of peace.

Sarah considered him for a moment, her features softening. "Yes, we should. Goodnight, Charlie."

"Goodnight, Sarah."

They parted ways, the night swallowing their solitary figures. But there was a shift in the air, a sense that the chasm between them had narrowed, if only slightly. Tomorrow, they would face the case again, but tonight, they had formed an alliance—one forged in the crucible of necessity.

*

The walls of Dr Helen Zhao's office were lined with bookshelves that seemed to sag under the weight of psychological treatises and medical journals. The air was thick with the scent of old paper and leather, a testament to the countless hours spent within these confines, dissecting the minds of those who perpetrated the unthinkable.

As Blake entered, Zhao looked up from her desk, her eyes reflecting a well of knowledge and a hint of weariness. "Charlie," she greeted, her voice steady, betraying none of the trepidation that the topic of their meeting warranted. "Please, sit."

Blake took the proffered chair across from her, his mind bracing for the psychological odyssey they were about to undertake. The desk between them was stark, save for a single manila folder—the epicentre of today's discussion.

"I've updated Morgan's profile," Dr Zhao began, her fingers poised over the folder. "This isn't your standard analysis. His pattern, his... methodology," she hesitated, searching for the right word, "it's evolving."

She opened the folder, revealing pages of notes, diagrams, and photos. "Look here." She pointed to a series of photos from the crime scenes. "His signatures, they're not just random acts of violence; they're communicative."

Blake leaned forward, absorbing every detail. The photos were gruesome, but to the trained eye they told a story. Symbols etched in blood, ritualistic placements of the victims' bodies—it was a narrative crafted in shadow and suffering.

"Morgan is not just killing. He is performing," Dr Zhao continued. "Each crime scene is a stage, and the horror inflicted is his script. He's not speaking to us, Charlie. He's speaking to someone else, or perhaps," she paused, considering her words, "to something within himself."

The notion sent a chill down Blake's spine. The idea that Morgan was enacting a personal, twisted play through his victims was a psychological leap that brought them into uncharted territory.

"His choices are becoming more... specific," Zhao explained. "Each victim now serves a purpose, represents an idea." Her finger traced a line connecting the victims. "Morgan is chasing a goal, a culmination of sorts."

Blake thought of the victims, of the pain they had endured. "Do we have any leads on who he might target next?" he asked, his voice edged with urgency.

Dr Zhao nodded, her expression grave. "I believe he's following a pattern, an escalation. Each victim is a step up a symbolic ladder. If we can decode the symbolism, we may predict his next move."

Blake absorbed the implications. "This is about more than anticipation," he realised. "It's about prevention."

"Yes," Zhao agreed. "And there's something else," she added, handing him a sheet with a psychological diagram. "Morgan's profile suggests that he is reaching a zenith, a point of no return. If we don't catch him soon..."

Her words hung in the air, the unfinished sentence as ominous as the silence that followed. Blake felt the weight of the moment, the race against time now more palpable than ever.

"Thank you, Helen," he said, standing. "This... insight is invaluable."

He left Zhao's office with a renewed sense of purpose, the profile tucked under his arm like a shield. The abyss that Morgan had created was deepening, its darkness spreading. But now, with Zhao's analysis, they had a light to guide them through it.

*

The rhythmic tapping of keys was the only sound in Mike Hanover's cramped workspace, cluttered with monitors that cast an artificial daybreak across his intent features. His eyes, shielded by thick-rimmed glasses, flicked back and forth with the data streams that flowed across the screens like digital rivers. Mike had been following the breadcrumbs of Alex Morgan's online presence, a shadowy trail that had thus far yielded more questions than answers.

Mike's dedication was more than professional; it was personal. Blake's impassioned pursuit of Morgan had resonated with him, imbuing his own work with a sense of urgency that transcended the usual call of duty. The digital realm was his battlefield, and he manoeuvred through it with the precision of a seasoned soldier.

As hours melded into the early morning, Mike's persistence began to fracture the carefully constructed obfuscation that Morgan had left in his wake. He had managed to track down an IP address that Morgan had used—a ghost signal that had bounced across the globe, a deliberate ploy to avoid detection. But Morgan had made a mistake, a singular moment of human error that Mike was all too human to exploit.

The breakthrough came in the form of a transaction: a small but unusual purchase that didn't align with Morgan's known patterns. It was a custom order from a niche tech company, a piece of equipment that had no place in the everyday. Mike cross-referenced the order with a list of known associates, a web of connections that Blake's team had been meticulously mapping.

One name stood out, a link that was faint but unmistakable. It wasn't direct—Morgan was too clever for that—but it was *something*. A middleman, a go-between who had been careful to stay in the shadows. Mike delved deeper, running algorithms that would make sense of the chaos, seeking the answer to the riddle that Morgan had posed.

The sun began to rise, casting a pale light that made the screens in front of Mike seem suddenly stark. He rubbed his eyes, fatigue clawing at his concentration. But the sight that greeted him upon his return was enough to jolt him back to full alertness. There, on the screen, was a pattern—a series of transactions that, when pieced together, formed a map. A digital map that led to a physical location, a place that Morgan had been using as a base of operations.

Mike's hands trembled as he compiled the data, aware of its significance. Blake needed to see this, needed to understand the implications. He grabbed his phone, the number already queued up from countless previous calls.

"Blake," Mike said, the moment the call connected, his voice an amalgam of excitement and exhaustion. "I've got something. It's big. It's the break we've been waiting for."

The words hung in the air, a promise of a turning tide. Mike Hanover had chased the digital spectre of Alex Morgan to a door that, once opened, could not be closed. The hunt was narrowing, and the line between predator and prey was becoming ever more blurred.

*

Elena Martinez slipped through the throng of bustling pedestrians with the ease of a shadow, her senses attuned to the pulse of the city around her. The air was heavy with the scent of rain on concrete, a fragrance that always seemed to make the world more tangible, more real. Her heart kept a steady rhythm, syncing with the mission that pulsed in her veins—to unravel the enigma of Alex Morgan.

Her destination was nondescript, a warehouse nestled within a lattice of back alleys and forgotten byways. It was the kind of place that thrived on anonymity, making it the perfect stitch in the fabric of the city for secrets to nestle. The tip had come from Mike's digital breakthrough, a location that was now a beacon in their search for Morgan.

Elena paused at the mouth of the alley, her gaze sweeping the area for signs of surveillance. Satisfied, she moved forward, her steps silent against the damp cobbles. She reached the warehouse, its facade a tapestry of peeling paint and rusted metal. The lock on the door was a mere formality, yielding to her skilled fingers with a soft click.

Inside, the warehouse was a cavernous space, its air stale with disuse. Pallets stacked with crates formed a maze that she navigated with cautious steps, her flashlight a solitary beam in the void. It was in the heart of this labyrinth that she found what they had been seeking—a shrine to Morgan's madness.

Photographs and articles peppered the walls, a constellation of faces and names that were connected by a web of string and pins. At the centre was a picture of Morgan, his eyes hollow, as if peering into a reality that only he could perceive. Below it: a map of the city with various locations marked in red, a pattern that spoke of a plan in motion.

Elena's breath caught in her throat as she took in the sight. It was more than evidence; it was a glimpse into Morgan's mind, a place of chaos and order entwined. She realised they were not just tracking a man; they were hunting a belief, a conviction that had rooted itself deep within Morgan's psyche.

Her fingers danced over her phone, capturing images of the space, the connections, the map. Each photo was a piece of the puzzle that was slowly coming into focus, a narrative that they could trace back to Morgan.

As she prepared to leave, a sound arrested her movement. A soft scuttle, a whisper of movement that was out of place in the stillness. Her hand moved instinctively to her side, gripping the comfort of her concealed weapon. Her eyes scanned the darkness, her every sense alert.

But it was only a rat, its eyes glinting momentarily in the light before it disappeared into the shadows once more. Elena exhaled, a wry smile touching her lips at the tension that had coiled within her.

She slipped out of the warehouse as silently as she had entered, the evidence secured in her phone, her mind already weaving through the implications of her discovery. The game was changing, the stakes escalating with every heartbeat. And Elena Martinez was at the heart of it, her own pulse a testament to the hunt that was only just beginning.

*

The morning light filtered through the blinds of Detective Blake's office, casting stripes across his weary face. He had been up most of the night, piecing together the information from Elena's discovery, when the shrill ring of his desk phone pierced the quiet.

"Blake," he answered curtly, the fatigue evident in his voice.

"Detective, have you seen the morning's news?" The voice on the other end was rushed, tinged with a mix of excitement and concern. It was Sarah.

He hadn't. He gestured towards the television remote,

switching it on. The screen came to life, revealing the fervent face of Simon Fraser, the journalist whose interest in the case had become a thorn in their side.

Fraser was outside the station, microphone in hand, reporting live: "—unconfirmed reports suggest that the police may be closing in on a suspect in what is being referred to as 'The Ritual Killings'."

Blake's hand tightened into a fist. This was the last thing they needed. Fraser was drawing connections out loud, speculating with an air of authority that was unwarranted and potentially dangerous. The case was sensitive, the investigation's integrity hinging on discretion, and now the media spotlight threatened to upend everything.

Sarah's voice brought him back. "It's all over the news, Charlie. He's speculating about the evidence, about Morgan. This could compromise our position."

Blake was silent, his mind racing. The media frenzy was like a wildfire, spreading chaos and distorting facts. It was a secondary adversary, one that played by different rules—sensationalism over accuracy, speculation over silence.

"We need to contain this," Blake finally spoke, resolve hardening in his tone. "Lockdown on information goes to full effect. No one talks to the press, no details get out, not until we have Morgan."

He hung up, his gaze returning to the screen where Fraser continued his discourse, painting a picture for the public that was equal parts truth and fiction. The detective knew that every word uttered on live television could be a potential lead for Morgan, a clue for him to stay one step ahead.

As he turned off the screen, Blake's thoughts went to

the victims, to the city that was now held in the grip of fear. The media circus would move on eventually, but the scars left behind would remain, etched into the lives of those affected by Morgan's actions.

Determined, Blake set out from his office, the weight of responsibility heavy on his shoulders. The battle lines had been redrawn, the investigation now a two-front war—one against a cunning adversary and the other against the onslaught of public scrutiny.

Blake stepped into the chaos, his resolve a steady flame amidst the frenzy. The hunt for Alex Morgan was reaching a critical juncture, and Detective Charlie Blake would need to navigate the treacherous waters of public opinion while keeping the trail hot on the heels of a ghost.

Chapter 12: The Puppet Master

Morgan's Manoeuvre

The city had always been a chessboard to Alex Morgan, its denizens unknowingly serving as pawns in a game only he seemed to understand. From his vantage point, hidden from the prying eyes of law and order, he watched his plans unfolding with the precision of a maestro conducting an orchestra.

The recent media frenzy was a calculated move, a deft stroke of manipulation that served to distract and diffuse the efforts of the police. As he had anticipated, the dissemination of half-truths and wild speculations had sent the investigation spiralling into chaos. It was in this confusion that Morgan thrived, a predator obscured by the fog of misinformation.

His hideout was an abandoned building that loomed over an array of alleyways like a sentinel. The walls, stripped of their past opulence, were now adorned with the tools of his trade—maps, articles, and an array of electronic devices that were his eyes and ears into the world he was toying with.

Morgan's mind was a fortress, impenetrable and dark, where plans were laid with meticulous care. The recent developments had forced him to adapt, to re-evaluate his approach. He knew the police were close, their steps echoing in the corridors of his intricate designs. Yet, he was not concerned. To him, it was just another variable in an equation he was destined to solve.

He perused the latest news, his fingers tracing the lines of text as he absorbed the information. Each word was a potential key, a means to further his agenda. His next move would need to be bold, a statement that would remind them all of the control he wielded.

As Morgan sat back in the shadows, the light from the monitor casting an eerie glow upon his face, he couldn't help but savour the moment. Detective Blake and his team were persistent—he'd give them that—but they were playing a game whose rules they didn't fully comprehend.

He had set the stage, and now it was time for the next act. With a few keystrokes, Morgan sent instructions to his unwitting agents, those ensnared by fear or loyalty. They would act, believing they had a choice, not realising they were puppets dancing on the strings of the puppet master.

The sun began to set, casting a crimson hue across the sky, mirroring the blood that had been shed and that which was yet to spill. Morgan's silhouette against the backdrop of the fading light was that of a man who had transcended his humanity, who had become the embodiment of the chaos he sought to create.

Tonight, the city would sleep uneasily, haunted by the echoes of his machinations. And Morgan, in his fortress of solitude, would plot, his mind a whirlwind of possibilities as he crafted the next chapter of his grand design.

*

The tension in the incident room was a presence that seemed to seep into the very walls. Detective Blake and his team were gathered around the central table, their faces etched with the fatigue of the long hours spent chasing the ghost of Alex Morgan. But it wasn't just weariness that weighed upon them; it was discord, a schism that threatened to fracture their unity.

Sarah Jennings, always the voice of reason, was the first to break the silence. "We're chasing our tails here," she said, her voice steady but her frustration clear. "Morgan's manipulating the media, and we're letting it direct our investigation. We need to refocus, get back to basics."

Dan Brooks, the youngest of the group, shifted uncomfortably. "But the public's perception is part of the case now. We can't just ignore it," he countered, his idealism clashing with the pragmatism of the job.

Blake watched the exchange, a slow-burning ire rising within him. He knew they were both right, that the path to Morgan was as much through the evidence as it was through the narrative being spun outside their walls. But the disagreement was a luxury they couldn't afford. Every moment spent in debate was a moment Morgan remained free.

"Enough!" he barked, the authority in his voice brooking no argument. "We do this my way. We keep to the facts, the evidence. The media circus is Morgan's stage, not ours."

Elena Martinez leaned back against the wall, her eyes scanning the room. The conflict was a reflection of the chaos Morgan had sown among them. She understood Blake's position, the need for a singular direction, but the rift was becoming a chasm—and in that divide Morgan would find his advantage.

Blake's gaze settled on each member of his team in turn, his eyes imploring them to see the necessity of cohesion. "Morgan wants us at each other's throats. He wants the doubt, the discord. We give him that, and we might as well hand him the next victim on a silver platter."

The room fell silent, the team members retreating into

their own thoughts, considering Blake's words. It was Emily Saunders, the forensic analyst, who finally spoke, her voice low but firm. "Charlie's right. We need to trust in the process, in each other. Our strength is in our unity."

The nodding heads that followed her statement were a silent accord, a reaffirmation of their commitment to the cause and to one another. The fracture was mended, not by avoidance, but by confronting it head-on—by acknowledging the difficulty of the task before them and the necessity of their alliance.

As the team dispersed, each to their own task, Blake remained at the table, his hands flat against the cold surface. The fracture had been a warning, a sign that Morgan's influence was reaching further than they had anticipated. It was a battle of wills, and Blake knew that the only way to win was to remain unbroken.

*

Amidst the ordered chaos of the forensic lab, Emily Saunders stood over her microscope, her mind as focused as the lens through which she peered. The lab was her domain, a place where the silent evidence spoke volumes, revealing secrets that were invisible to the naked eye. It was here, in the quietude of her scientific sanctuary, that Emily had uncovered a thread that could sew the disparate pieces of the investigation together.

The clue was microscopic, almost imperceptible—but to Emily's trained eye it was as glaring as a beacon. It was a unique compound, a residue that she had detected on the personal effects of the victims. This compound was not common: it was specialised, its use limited to certain industrial applications. It was the kind of detail easily overlooked, but Emily's meticulous nature had paid off.

Her hands, encased in the sterility of latex, handled the evidence with reverent precision. She had traced the compound to a defunct factory on the outskirts of the city, a place that had once thrived on the production of rare chemicals but had long since fallen into disuse. It was a place that matched the profile of Morgan's haunts, areas forgotten by time and progress, spaces where darkness could fester unseen.

With each victim, the compound's presence had been a constant, a signature that Morgan had unwittingly left behind. It was as if he had been taunting them, laying out a trail of breadcrumbs that he believed no one would discern. But Emily had—and, with this revelation, the investigation had a new vector to pursue.

The implications were manifold. This compound could lead them to locations Morgan frequented, to his methods of selecting and abducting victims. It was a forensic cornerstone upon which a case could be built, a testament to the truth that, no matter how careful a criminal might be, they always left something behind.

As she compiled her report, Emily's mind raced with the potential of her discovery. She knew Blake would understand its significance, the lifeline it represented in the murky waters of the case. With careful documentation and a few photographs of the microscopic evidence, she was ready to present her findings to the team.

The walk to Blake's office was short, but to Emily it felt like a pilgrimage, each step bringing them closer to the man who had cast such a long shadow over the city. She entered without knocking, her entrance a silent assertion of the urgency of her discovery.

Blake looked up, his expression one of weary anticipation. "What is it, Saunders?" he asked, his voice betraying a hint of hope.

Emily laid out her findings before him, the photographs and the report painting a picture that words alone could not convey. As Blake absorbed the information, his eyes lit with the fire of understanding. This was it; this was the break they had been desperately searching for.

"We move on this, fast and hard," Blake commanded, the wheels of action immediately set into motion.

As Emily left Blake's office, she couldn't shake the feeling that they were on the cusp of something monumental. The clue she had uncovered was the first real step into Morgan's world, a world they were now poised to infiltrate and dismantle. The game of cat and mouse had shifted, and they were finally gaining ground.

*

The weight of command had always been a familiar pressure for Detective Charlie Blake, but it had never felt as suffocating as it did in the silent hours of the predawn morning. As he sat alone in the dim light of his office, the lines between right and wrong blurred like the shadows that danced across his desk.

Blake knew that to catch a man like Morgan, one had to think like him, to step into the void and stare into the abyss. It was a perilous dance, one that threatened to consume one's own sense of self. The decision before him was the epitome of such a risk—a baiting strategy that employed one of their own as the lure.

The plan was unorthodox, to say the least. It involved Sarah Jennings going undercover, not in the traditional sense, but as a feigned dismissal from the force due to a 'leak' to the media—a ruse designed to attract Morgan's attention. The hope was that Morgan, believing her to be disgruntled and vulnerable, would see Sarah as a potential asset or, better yet, as bait to draw out Blake himself.

Blake had mulled over every other option, but time was a luxury they no longer possessed. Morgan was always two steps ahead, weaving through the city's underbelly like a spectre. This move was their chance to turn the tables, to create an opening in Morgan's meticulously crafted armour.

He picked up the phone and dialled Sarah's number, his finger hovering over the last digit. This call could very well fracture the trust he had built with his team. But as the seconds ticked by, the faces of Morgan's victims flashed before his eyes, their silent pleas for justice echoing in his mind.

With a deep breath, he pressed the final digit, and the line clicked as it connected. "Sarah, it's Charlie. I have a plan, but it's not without risk," he began, his voice steady despite the turmoil within.

As he outlined the strategy, Blake could hear the hesitation in Sarah's breath. She understood the danger, the potential fallout on a personal and professional level. Yet, beneath the concern, there was a steely resolve that Blake had come to admire.

"Let's do it," Sarah finally said, her commitment ringing clear through the line.

With that, the die was cast. The plan set into motion was akin to a gambit in chess, sacrificing safety for a greater advantage. Blake hung up the phone, aware that he had just asked one of his own to walk into the lion's den.

In the silence that followed, Blake's resolve hardened. He would protect Sarah at all costs, even if it meant crossing lines he had once drawn in the sand. Morgan had forced his hand, and now it was time to play their own game of shadows.

*

Dan Brooks sat in the hum of the fluorescent lights, the police department's records room a stark contrast to the vibrant chaos of the city outside. Before him lay a sprawl of documents, photographs, and old case files—each a fragment of the lives touched by the enigmatic Alex Morgan. Dan's task was Herculean: to find the invisible threads that connected these seemingly unrelated lives to the man who had made them his prey.

As a data analyst, Dan believed in the power of information—that within the chaos of data, patterns would emerge, telling stories that eyes alone might miss. His fingers danced across the keyboard, commands weaving through databases, cross-referencing names, dates, places. Hours slipped by unnoticed, the search narrowing, the connections beginning to materialise like stars in the night sky.

It was a series of financial transactions that first caught his eye, subtle anomalies that formed a pattern. Victims had made payments to various shell companies, all tracing back to one parent corporation. It was a front, a smokescreen that Morgan had thought impenetrable. But, under Dan's scrutiny, the facade began to crumble.

The more Dan dug, the clearer the picture became. These weren't random victims; they were chosen with purpose, each playing a role in Morgan's grand scheme. Some were unwitting financiers of his operations, others possessed knowledge or skills he required. Morgan had woven them into his narrative, a puppeteer pulling on their strings long before he cut them loose.

The realisation was a thunderclap in the quiet of the

records room. Dan leaned back in his chair, his mind racing. This was more than a breakthrough; it was a paradigm shift. The case wasn't just about catching a killer; it was about unravelling a conspiracy.

With a meticulously compiled dossier of connections, Dan left the records room, his steps quick with urgency. He found Blake in his office, the detective's eyes weary but alert.

"Blake," Dan said, the weight of his discovery lending gravity to his voice. "I think I've found something. It's not just who Morgan's victims *are*—it's why they were chosen."

He laid out the documents on Blake's desk, watching as the detective's eyes sharpened, the gears turning behind them. The connections were there, a spiderweb of motives and opportunities that Morgan had exploited.

Blake stood, a newfound energy in his posture. "This changes everything," he said. "We're not just hunting a killer; we're hunting a mastermind."

The two men pored over the dossier, the implications of Dan's findings dawning on them. They now had a map of Morgan's world, a guide to the minds and lives he had entangled in his dark tapestry.

As the night deepened outside, a resolve settled over them. They were closer now, the shadows that had obscured their path beginning to lift. With each connection Dan had uncovered, the puppet master's stage grew smaller, the strings more taut.

And, somewhere in the city's heart, Alex Morgan felt the first tremor of his empire beginning to shake.

*

The night had wrapped the city in its embrace, and in the solitude of his office Detective Charlie Blake was a lone figure against the backdrop of darkness. The recent revelations had brought them closer to Alex Morgan, but, as the web of deceit unravelled, Blake was left to grapple with the cost of their progress.

He had always seen the world in stark contrasts—right and wrong, good and evil, law and disorder. Yet, as the investigation delved deeper into the abyss Morgan had crafted, those lines had begun to blur. Decisions that once seemed so clear-cut now wavered in the shadows of ambiguity.

The plan involving Sarah Jennings was a gambit that carried with it a weight of uncertainty. He had made the call, but the echoes of doubt resounded with every beat of his heart. Was it right to use one of their own as bait? Could the ends ever truly justify the means?

Blake stepped to the window, his reflection a ghostly visage in the glass. He saw the fatigue etched in his features, the burden of command that bowed his shoulders. The city lights flickered below, a million lives oblivious to the silent war waged in their midst.

His thoughts turned to the victims, their lives snuffed out by a man who saw them as nothing more than pieces in a twisted game. It was for them that Blake walked this dark path, for the peace that seemed so elusive in the wake of such violence.

A knock at the door jolted him from his reverie. It was Dan Brooks, his presence a reminder of the team that stood behind him, that shared in the burden he bore.

"Charlie," Dan said, his voice soft, "we're with you, no matter what it takes. We trust your judgment."

The words were a balm to Blake's troubled soul, a tether that pulled him back from the edge of doubt. He nodded, a silent acknowledgment of the trust and unity that fortified them against the chaos.

As Dan left, Blake turned back to the darkness outside. The moral landscape of his world had shifted, but his resolve remained unyielded. The doubts would linger, a testament to his humanity in the face of such inhumanity. But he knew that in the battle for justice, some risks were necessary.

With a deep breath, Blake steeled himself for the road ahead. The choices he made might haunt him, but he would walk the path with the assurance that it was for the greater good. The darkness would not prevail.

Chapter 13: Reflections of Fear

A Victim's Plea

The day began with the kind of silence that preceded storms, heavy with the scent of a brewing tempest. The station was unnaturally still, a stark contrast to the chaos of the city that thrummed beyond its walls. Detective Charlie Blake sat in his office, the early morning light casting long shadows across his desk, when a sealed envelope landed softly beside his coffee cup. The handwriting on the front was delicate, yet fraught with urgency—its sender unknown.

Blake's fingers grazed the seal, an inexplicable chill crawling up his spine as he recognised the mark: a small embossed butterfly, the unofficial symbol among the victims' network—a silent fellowship bound by the trauma inflicted upon them by Alex Morgan. Swallowing the sudden tightness in his throat, he slit the envelope open and unfolded the letter within, his eyes scanning the first lines:

Dear Detective Blake,

You don't know me, but I know of you and your hunt for the monster that shadows our lives. I write to you not as a victim, but as a voice from the grave, echoing the cries of those who can no longer speak.

Blake leaned back, his heart pacing a little quicker. The letter was from Julia Stenson, a woman whose life had been claimed by Morgan's ruthless machinations two years prior—a case that had gone cold, leaving a void of justice in its wake. Her words, penned by a friend who had promised to deliver the message should the worst happen, were a haunting plea from beyond the grave.

145

I am one of many, a single note in a symphony of sorrow. But I refuse to be a silent victim in his cruel narrative. I've witnessed the darkness he carries, the perverse joy he derives from our pain. You must find him, not for vengeance, but to prevent the symphony from growing, from claiming another innocent life.

The letter continued, detailing moments of Julia's captivity, insights that painted a broader picture of Morgan's psyche—a man who viewed his victims as pawns in a grand, twisted game. She spoke of his meticulous methods, his cold, calculating eyes that showed no remorse, and his penchant for leaving a signature—a butterfly—on his victims as a mark of his 'artistry'.

Please, the letter concluded, *do not let my voice be drowned by the passage of time. Find him. Stop him. Look beyond the evidence; seek the patterns in the chaos. I've left you everything I know, every memory, every horror I've endured. It's all there, hidden within the lines of my life. Do not let it be in vain.*

Blake's hands trembled as he set the letter down, the victim's words igniting a fire within him. He had always carried the weight of the unsolved and the unresolved, but Julia's posthumous testimony was a clarion call that pierced through the numbness he had built around himself.

He rose, determination etching his features into a mask of resolve. He had a new piece of the puzzle, a secret whispered from the shadows. It was more than evidence; it was a sacred trust from someone who had suffered the ultimate price at Morgan's hands.

Today, the hunt took on a new edge, a personal testament that redefined the chase. Blake would not falter, not with Julia's silent plea echoing in his ears. Morgan's reflections of fear would come to an end, and it was Blake who would shatter the mirror he hid behind. The storm was coming, and justice was its harbinger.

*

As Detective Charlie Blake sat at the head of the dusty conference table, his team's eyes upon him, he felt the gravity of their gazes as much as the weight of the badge that lay against his chest. The room was silent, save for the low hum of the station outside the door, a muffled symphony of justice at work.

The letter from the past victim still lay open before him, its words a haunting plea from beyond the grave. Blake knew that each case was more than a file, more than a puzzle to be solved. They were stories of shattered lives, of pain echoing through time, demanding not just solutions, but understanding and closure.

He cleared his throat, breaking the spell of sombre reflections that had settled over the room. "We've been reactive for too long," he began, his voice a steady current against the tide of uncertainty. "It's time we change the game. Morgan thinks he's writing the story here, but it's time we grab the pen."

Elena Martinez, her eyes still carrying the shadows of her recent undercover perils, nodded. "So, what's the play, boss?" Her voice was gritty, a reflection of her unyielded resolve.

Blake stood, the chair scraping against the floor like a challenge flung at the feet of fate. "We've been trying to predict Morgan's moves, to think like him." He paused, his gaze scanning the room. "But we're not like him. We can't be. That's our strength."

Dan Brooks leaned in, interest piqued. "You're suggesting

we improvise, sir?"

"Not quite," Blake replied, a half-smile breaking through. "We're going to set a stage so tempting that not even Morgan can resist it. But this time, we'll write the script. He's been a step ahead because we've been playing by his rules on his board."

Sarah Jenning, her wisdom an anchor in the tumultuous sea of their task force, tilted her head. "And if he doesn't take the bait?"

Blake's smile widened, a hint of the old spark flickering in his eyes. "He will. Because we'll use what he craves most against him." He tapped the letter. "He wants to be seen, to be acknowledged. We'll give him an audience."

The team absorbed his words, the gears of their collective mind turning, crafting a new strategy. Blake could see the change in them, a reignition of purpose, the kindling of hope.

"Let's get to work," he said, the room already buzzing with the renewed energy of hunters no longer content to wait for the prey to come to them. They were the architects of the trap now, and Blake felt a surge of anticipation. The hunt was on, and the predator would soon find himself the prey.

*

Elena Martinez felt the adrenaline coursing through her veins like a fiery river, yet her expression was the model of placidity as she navigated the crowded casino floor. Each step was measured, every glance calculated; she was a shadow among silhouettes in this gilded den of iniquity.

The air was thick with the scent of desperation veiled by expensive perfumes and the sound of clinking chips was a staccato rhythm to the heartbeats of the hopeful. Elena, however, was not swayed by the siren's call of easy riches that the casino promised. Her eyes were searching, ever vigilant, for the familiar face of the dealer who wasn't just dealing cards.

Her contact, a woman known only by the alias "Madame Rouge", was her key to the underground network Blake believed was connected to Alex Morgan. Elena had seen her only once before, when the briefest exchange of glances had confirmed her next move. Now, she was about to delve deeper into the web of Morgan's making, a place where trust was currency, and betrayal was the only certainty.

As she approached the high-stakes tables, she spotted Madame Rouge, her red dress a deliberate cliché that served as the perfect cover. The dealer's eyes met hers, and the corner of Rouge's lips lifted in a cryptic smile. It was a silent invitation, one that Elena accepted by joining the game.

The cards were dealt, and with each round, Elena's pile of chips grew, attracting quiet murmurs from the onlookers. But the real game was not on the green felt table; it was the subtle exchange of coded words, the discreet passing of information, that was the true gambit. Elena played her part flawlessly, her wins a smokescreen for the dangerous liaison unfolding under the watchful eyes of the casino's silent sentinels.

Rouge's voice was a velvet threat as she leaned in. "You're playing with fire, my dear."

Elena's response was just as soft, but with a steel edge. "Some of us are born from the flames."

Their conversation continued in this manner, a dangerous tango of veiled threats and covert intelligence.

Elena gleaned bits of information about Morgan's activities—cryptic as they were, they were pieces to a puzzle only Blake's team could complete. But as the night wore on the risk grew. Rouge's bodyguard, a mountain of a man with eyes that missed nothing, began to hover closer, his suspicions aroused by the length of their game.

Elena knew her time was running short. With a final, calculated risk, she pushed all her chips forward, betting on the turn of a single card. As the queen of hearts revealed itself, a card that now seemed grimly appropriate, she collected her winnings and stood, her message from Rouge securely tucked away in her mind.

"I hope to see you again," Rouge said, a warning woven into her farewell.

"Fortune willing," Elena replied, her steady walk away from the table belying the pounding of her heart. She had entered the lion's den and emerged with crucial information—but the night had only just begun. The true peril lay in what came after, in the darkness that awaited outside the casino's false daylight.

As she slipped through the service entrance, the cool night air hit her face, and she allowed herself a moment to breathe. Her mind raced with the intelligence she had gathered, each piece a deadly stepping stone toward their quarry. But as she disappeared into the labyrinth of the city, she knew that every shadow could hold a knife, every whisper could be a death sentence. Elena had become a player in Morgan's game, and the stakes were life itself.

*

The air was thick with tension in the dimly lit room where Detective Charlie Blake faced the enigma, Alex Morgan, across a battered chessboard that had become their battleground. Each piece between them was more than wood; they were proxies for their psychological duel, a shadow game mirroring their real-life cat and mouse chase.

Blake moved his knight, the click of its landing a punctuation in the silence. "You're not just a killer," he began, his voice steady as he stared into Morgan's eyes, a mix of icy blue and the grey of storm clouds. "You fancy yourself an artist, a director of your narratives. But what you call art is nothing but madness and murder."

Morgan leaned back in his chair, a slight smile playing at the corners of his lips, his gaze never leaving the board. "Detective, you misunderstand the nature of art. It is an expression of the deepest human experiences, our fears, our desires. I merely bring those to the surface."

Blake's hand paused over his queen. He knew this game was dangerous, every word laden with double meaning, every move a potential revelation of his strategy. "And the lives you take? What of their experiences, their fears, their desires?"

"They are my chorus," Morgan replied, his voice a whisper of silk over sandpaper. "Each voice a note in a grand symphony I conduct. You aim to silence them, but in doing so, you fail to understand the music."

Blake moved his queen, taking Morgan's bishop. "Then consider this a dissonance in your composition.'

Morgan chuckled, a sound that sent shivers down Blake's spine. He countered swiftly, taking one of Blake's pawns. "A temporary setback, nothing more. I am many moves ahead, Detective. This game, our game, is far from over."

The chessboard between them was a map of their conflict, each piece a decision, a life, a moment in the twisted narrative Morgan had constructed. Blake knew he was being drawn deeper into Morgan's world, a place where morality was malleable, and every truth had its shadow.

Blake's next move was bold, a sacrifice that could cost him but one that had the potential to turn the tide. "Your vision is flawed, Morgan. You see patterns where there is only chaos, connections where there is only coincidence."

Morgan's eyes narrowed, the facade of control slipping. He leaned forward, his move aggressive, capturing Blake's rook. "Chaos is a pattern unrecognised, Detective. And you are close, so very close to seeing the whole picture."

Blake felt the edges of the abyss beckoning, the darkness that Morgan inhabited, that he tempted Blake to enter. It was a place where the light of Blake's badge didn't reach, where the line between hunter and hunted blurred.

"You may believe you are the puppet master, but even you can't control everything," Blake said, his voice low. "You're no god, Morgan. You're just a man, and every man has his limits, his end."

Morgan's smile was gone now, replaced by a look of contemplation. He studied the board, his next move critical. "We shall see, Detective. We shall see which of us reaches their end first."

The game continued, each move a testament to their wills, each piece taken a silent victory or defeat. Outside the room, the city continued its rhythm, unaware of the battle waged in its underbelly, a battle that would determine its safety, its very soul.

And as the clock ticked on, Blake knew that this mental tug of war with Morgan was more than a mere game of chess. It was a dance with darkness itself, a test of his resolve against the chaos Morgan sought to unleash. The battle lines were drawn not just on the board but in the streets, in the lives touched by tragedy, and in the hearts of those who fought to keep the darkness at bay.

Blake made his move, the path ahead fraught with peril, but his resolve was clear. This was a war he intended to win, for the chorus silenced by Morgan's hand, for the city he vowed to protect, and for the order he would restore in the face of the chaos that threatened to consume them all.

*

The office was a hive of frenetic energy as Blake's team operated like the many arms of a singular, driven entity. Yet amidst the orchestrated chaos, there was an undercurrent of something amiss, a dissonance in the symphony of their collective endeavour. Blake could feel it, an intangible thread out of place in the tapestry of trust they had woven.

He had felt the first stirrings of this unease when the latest round of reports came in, their contents an echo of information he hadn't yet disclosed, strategies he had barely formulated in his own mind. The sense of betrayal, initially a whisper, was now a roar in his ears as he called his team together.

The room fell silent as Blake stepped in, his countenance a blend of stoic resolve and the simmering turmoil of a storm yet to break. "We have a leak," he announced, his voice betraying none of the betrayal that churned within him. The team exchanged uneasy glances, the weight of suspicion settling like a shroud over the room.

Blake continued, "And not just any leak—an artery. Our movements, our plans, even our hunches seem to find their way to Morgan's ears." The implications were clear to all: there was a traitor in their midst.

Sarah Jennings, whose intuition was as sharp as her analytical skills, spoke up. "It has to be someone with deep access, someone who's been with us through every twist and turn." Her voice was calm, but the accusation hung in the air, an unspoken suspicion that had now been given voice.

The team's unity began to fray as trust, the very cornerstone of their bond, was called into question. Dan Brooks, the youngest member, his face a mask of disbelief, shook his head. "But we're a family. Who would do this?" His question, so full of the betrayal he felt, echoed the sentiment of all present.

Blake, whose experience in the force had taught him the painful lesson that loyalty was a currency not everyone valued, looked at his team. "I don't know," he admitted, "but I intend to find out."

The investigation that followed was meticulous and covert, as Blake quietly pulled records, cross-referenced access logs, and conducted discreet interviews. The breakthrough came with a small, almost insignificant piece of evidence—a logged access code to the communications room that did not align with the shift rosters.

With a heavy heart, Blake traced the code back to its owner, finding the trail leading to a trusted ally. Victor Reynolds, a seasoned detective whose salt-and-pepper hair was a testament to his years of service, sat across from Blake, the evidence laid bare between them.

Victor's face, usually an open book of honesty, was

closed off, his eyes averted. "Why, Victor?" Blake's voice was a low rumble, the hurt evident in his eyes.

Victor's response was quiet, filled with resignation. "It's not what you think, Charlie. It's not black and white. I had to protect my family—they were threatened. Morgan... he's got eyes and ears everywhere."

The revelation was a gut punch, the kind that knocked the wind out of Blake and left him reeling. Betrayal for the sake of protection, a decision made under duress, was a narrative as old as time, and yet it stung with fresh pain.

Blake knew that the consequences would be severe. Trust within the team had been compromised, and the road to rebuild it would be a long one. But first, they had to contain the damage.

"Victor, you should have come to me," Blake said, the betrayal now mixed with a profound sadness. The breach in their ranks would need to be addressed—but first, they had to deal with the immediate threat. Morgan was still out there, and now more than ever they needed to be a united front.

As Victor was escorted away, a silence descended on the team. It was a silence filled with introspection, of unspoken fears and doubts about the nature of trust and the price of loyalty. But it was also a silence that preceded the rallying cry that would soon come.

Blake, his resolve hardened by the sting of betrayal, addressed his team. "We will not let this divide us. We are stronger than the sum of our parts, and we will close this breach in our ranks." His voice, firm and sure, left no room for doubt. "We will catch Morgan, and we will do it together."

The team, shaken but not shattered, nodded in agreement. The road ahead was uncertain, but their determination was unyielding. They would rise from this trial by fire, tempered and more resilient. The hunt for Morgan would continue, but now with a keener edge, honed by the pain of betrayal and the unassailable strength of a bond reforged in the crucible of truth.

*

The fluorescent lights of the incident room buzzed like an anxious swarm as Detective Charlie Blake's team clustered around the central table, their faces etched with the urgency of their task. The room was thick with the scent of coffee and the undercurrent of tension that always accompanied the countdown of a race against time.

Blake's eyes, usually a clear signal of intent, now flickered with the flame of desperation. The betrayal within their ranks had been a blow, but it was the ticking clock that weighed heaviest on his mind. Morgan was out there, a spectre in the night, his next move a mystery wrapped in the shadows of his twisted game.

He addressed the team, his voice steady despite the storm raging inside him. "We have a window, small, but it's all we have. Morgan's pattern is escalating, and if we don't intercept him now, the cost will be higher than any of us are willing to pay."

The team's focus sharpened, their movements brisk and purposeful. Dan Brooks manned the digital forensics station, his fingers dancing over the keyboard as he sifted through the sea of data for any anomaly. Sarah Jennings, her eyes scanning over the case files, was a picture of concentration, her quick mind piecing together the fragments of a horrifying puzzle.

Elena Martinez, fresh from her undercover ordeal, still carried the fire of her close encounter in her eyes. She leaned in. "We're not just looking for a pattern, we're looking for a break in it. Something he didn't plan for."

Blake nodded, acknowledging her insight. "Exactly. Morgan thrives on control, on orchestrating every detail. Any deviation from his plan, that's where we'll find him."

The clock on the wall seemed to tick louder, each second a drumbeat to the urgency of their mission. Blake could feel the pulse of the city outside, millions of lives moving obliviously through the night, unaware of the danger that lurked in the darkness.

Suddenly, the room stilled as Dan called out, "Got something. A deviation in the traffic cams near the last crime scene. It's subtle, but it's there. A blind spot that shouldn't exist."

Blake moved to Dan's side, his gaze following the young detective's pointed finger on the screen. A map of the city, a web of electronic eyes, and there, a dark patch. It was a clue—small, but significant.

He turned to the team, his directive clear. "We have our lead. I want teams A and B to canvas the area. Look for anything out of place, any sign of Morgan. We move fast and silent. No sirens, no noise, just eyes and ears on the ground."

The team dispersed, a flurry of activity as they prepared to move out. Blake stayed back for a moment, his hand resting on the map, his mind racing with the possibilities. This was it, the moment before the storm, the prelude to the encounter they had all been dreading and longing for in equal measure.

As the teams filed out, Blake took a deep breath, the weight of command a familiar cloak around his shoulders. He glanced once more at the map, at the city that lay beyond the walls of the station. The city he had sworn to protect.

"Let's end this," he whispered to the silent room before turning to join his team. The race was on, and they were running headlong into the maw of an unknown beast. But they were ready, each carrying the determination and the hope that this night, the shadows they chased would finally give way to the light of justice.

Chapter 14: The Chameleon

Morgan's Disguise

The streets were bustling with the usual cacophony of urban life, pedestrians weaving through the foot traffic with the practiced indifference of city dwellers. In the sea of faces, one stood out by not standing out at all. Alex Morgan moved with the flow of the crowd, his every gesture measured to mimic the average, the forgettable. Today, he was no one; he was everyone.

A baseball cap pulled low over his brow, glasses perched on his nose, not quite fashionable, not quite outmoded, Morgan's choice of attire was deliberate. It was the costume of anonymity, the uniform of the urban chameleon. In his pocket, a newspaper folded to the obituaries—a grim nod to his handiwork, and a signal to those in the know.

As Morgan strolled past a series of cafes and boutiques, his gaze was keen, taking in the minute details around him. To the untrained eye, he was just another commuter on his way to a nondescript job. But beneath the facade, his mind was alight with the dance of manipulation and control. He had the unique talent to orchestrate chaos while standing in its eye, serene and indifferent.

He slipped into a cafe, the bell above the door jingling an innocuous welcome. The barista greeted him with a nod, the same nod given to a hundred other faces that morning. Morgan ordered a coffee: black, no sugar—simple, unremarkable. As he waited, his eyes flicked to the door, watching, calculating. It was not paranoia but prudence; the predator's instinct to know every exit, every threat.

Taking his coffee, Morgan found a seat at the back, his back to the wall, his view encompassing the entire establishment. He sipped slowly, savouring the bitterness, a sensory echo to his nature. He unfolded the newspaper, scanning the headlines with feigned interest, but his attention was on the reflection in the window, the world behind him playing out in reverse.

This was his stage, and he was both director and lead, the master of puppets in a play where the strings were pulled with such finesse that the puppets believed themselves to be dancing freely. It was here, in these moments of public solitude, that Morgan planned his next steps.

As the morning waned, Morgan rose, leaving a few crumpled bills on the table. He stepped back into the stream of humanity, his presence dissolving into the multitude. He was the chameleon, and the city was his jungle—a place where he could be predator and prey, seen and unseen, a ghost in the flesh.

Today, he had been a man enjoying his coffee, reading the paper. Tomorrow, he could be anyone. The thought brought a twisted smile to his lips as he melted away, a whisper in the roar of the city, a shadow sliding through the light, ever elusive, ever dangerous.

*

Elena Martinez's breath came in ragged gasps as she darted through the narrow alley, her footsteps echoing off the grimy walls. The city had transformed from a familiar urban landscape into a maze of shadows and dangers, each corner potentially concealing her demise. Her mind raced as fast as her heart, the crucial information she had obtained was a heavy burden—the key to Blake's next move against Morgan, and possibly her own death warrant.

She risked a glance over her shoulder. Her pursuers were faceless adversaries, but she knew they were Morgan's hounds, unleashed with the sole purpose of retrieving what she had taken. She clutched the small USB drive in her pocket, its contents more valuable than gold, more dangerous than poison.

As she burst onto a busier street, the anonymity of the crowd embraced her, and for a moment, she allowed herself to be swept along by the tide of bodies. But her relief was short-lived: she caught sight of a familiar menacing figure cutting through the crowd, his eyes locked on her. Her breath hitched, and she ducked into a nearby store, a desperate attempt to blend in.

The shop was a riot of colours and scents, a gift boutique filled with trinkets and souvenirs. Elena weaved through the aisles, her senses on high alert. She could hear her pursuer's footsteps—a measured tread that seemed in no rush, confident in its hunt.

She reached the back of the shop where a group of tourists was clustered around a display. With no time to hesitate, she slipped a wide-brimmed hat and sunglasses from a rack onto her head and face, mingling with the crowd, becoming just another face in the sea of anonymity.

The hunter entered the shop, his gaze sweeping over the patrons, the predator searching for its prey. Elena held her breath, her disguise as thin as the air she dared not draw too loudly. He was close enough for her to see the cold intent in his eyes, the danger that clung to him like a second skin.

He paused, his eyes scanning her disguised form, and, for a split second, their gazes met. Time stood still, a silent stand-off in the midst of oblivious onlookers. Then, he moved on, his confidence in his mission unshaken, his search thorough but ultimately fruitless.

Elena didn't wait for him to double back. She made her way to the front, purchased the hat and sunglasses with shaky hands and slipped out onto the street, melting into the crowd once more. The USB drive pressed against her skin was a reminder of the stakes—they were as high as they could get.

She needed to get to Blake, to deliver the information that could turn the tide. But, more importantly, she needed to survive. Morgan had shown he could reach out and touch them at any time, anywhere. The narrow escape was a testament to his reach and her vulnerability.

As Elena put distance between herself and the shop, she knew that every step was a victory, however small. The information she carried was a beacon in the darkness, a hope that they could outmanoeuvre Morgan at last. But as the city swallowed her up, Elena knew that the game was far from over, and survival was a daily gamble in the shadow of the chameleon.

*

Back at the station, the atmosphere was saturated with a palpable sense of urgency. Blake's team huddled around a cluttered array of monitors, the glow casting an otherworldly light on their determined faces. But as the hours passed with no word from Elena, the tension escalated into a silent alarm that rang in every heartbeat, every nervous glance.

Finally, the door swung open, and Elena strode in, her usual poised demeanour replaced with the sheen of someone who had sprinted through the gauntlet of fear and emerged victorious—yet not unscathed. She held up the USB drive—a talisman of hope—and the room let out a collective breath they hadn't realised they'd been holding.

Blake was the first to reach her, his eyes searching hers for the ordeal she had endured. "You're safe now," he said, his voice a low anchor in the stormy sea of their mission.

Elena nodded, her relief at being back in the sanctuary of her team almost overwhelming. "I've got it. It wasn't easy, but I've got it," she managed to say, her breath still catching up with her calm facade.

The information was immediately plugged into the mainframe, and the team watched as data cascaded down the screens, encrypted messages slowly unravelling to reveal their secrets. It was a process that under any other circumstances would have elicited excitement, but now it was a grim task, each byte of data a potential clue, a potential danger.

Blake observed the operation, his mind racing with the possibilities this new intelligence could open up. Yet, as the leader, he also recognised the toll their relentless pursuit was taking on his team. The fatigue that shadowed their eyes, the lines of tension etching their faces—they were all signs that could not be ignored.

"Team." Blake's voice cut through the hum of machinery, commanding the attention of the room. "We've been on this chase non-stop, and you've all given it everything. But we're no good to anyone burned out."

The team shifted uneasily, their dedication a tangible thing, almost resistant to the idea of a respite.

Blake continued, "We're going to take a step back, regroup, and reassess our approach. We have new data now, thanks to Elena, and we need to be sharp to use it effectively."

Sarah Jennings, her analytical mind always processing,

finally nodded in agreement. "You're right, Blake. We need to be tactical, not just tenacious."

The team began to power down their stations, the glow from the monitors fading as a symbolic gesture to their tactical retreat. It was a necessary pause, a moment to breathe, to plan, and to steel themselves for the next phase of their operation.

As the room emptied, Blake lingered, his gaze on the darkened screens that held the key to Morgan's next move. This retreat was not an admission of defeat, but a strategic withdrawal. They were down but not out, and Blake knew that the battle of wits against the chameleon was just entering a new, more critical phase.

They would return, rested and ready to face Morgan's next ploy with a renewed vigour and a sharpened focus. The game was evolving, and so were they. Blake turned off the last of the lights and stepped out into the cool night air, the city's pulse a backdrop to his thoughts. Tomorrow, they would begin anew—and this time, *they* would be the predators, with Morgan as their quarry.

*

Detective Charlie Blake sat alone in the dim light of his office, the station's usual nocturnal symphony of distant sirens and muffled voices serving as a sombre soundtrack to his thoughts. Before him lay the remnants of a past long buried, now resurfaced: a collection of faded photographs, dog-eared reports, and military memorabilia from a chapter of his life he had compartmentalised like a file tucked away in the recesses of his mind.

His fingers traced a worn photo, the edges frayed, the image a tableau of young soldiers in desert fatigues, their faces a mixture of bravado and naivety. One face, in particular, drew his gaze—a younger version of Alex

164

Morgan, his features not yet hardened by the life that would lead him down the path of a chameleon in a world of black and white.

Blake's reverie was interrupted by the soft click of his office door. Dr Zhao, the team's forensic psychologist, stepped in, her presence a silent question. Blake gestured to the seat opposite his desk as he shuffled the photos into a semblance of order.

"You found something," Dr Zhao stated more than asked, her keen eyes taking in the spread of Blake's history laid bare on the desk.

Blake nodded, his hand coming to rest on a particularly weathered report. "Operation Silent Echo," he began, his voice taking on the cadence of a story told from memory, each word a piece of the past. "We were young, idealistic, and trained for scenarios we hoped never to face. Morgan was different even then—calm, calculated, always a step ahead. I never knew how much so until now."

Dr Zhao listened, her analytical mind already piecing together the fragments of Blake's tale with the profile she had been building of Morgan. "You think there's a link to what he's doing now?"

Blake's eyes met hers, a spark of something—a blend of fury and determination—flaring within them. "More than a link. A blueprint. Morgan's tactics, his need to manipulate and control, I've seen it before. He's using the same strategies, but this time, we're the enemy."

He handed her the report, his fingers lingering on the paper. "Silent Echo was about disrupting the enemy's communications, sewing misinformation, creating phantoms where there were none. Morgan was a maestro even then. He's playing the same game, but the stakes are higher, the audience unwilling."

Dr Zhao absorbed the information, her mind racing. "And you think there's something in this operation that could help us predict his next move?"

"It's more than that," Blake replied, his gaze returning to the photographs. "It's understanding his mindset. We know he's always a step ahead because he's always been the architect. But what if we can change the foundation of what he's built?"

The room was silent as the gravity of Blake's words settled between them. If they could decipher the origins of Morgan's methods, they might anticipate his manoeuvres, predict the unpredictable.

Dr Zhao stood, the report now in her hands. "I'll get started. Maybe between the man he was and the man he's become, we'll find our advantage."

Blake nodded, his eyes not leaving the photo. The man in the picture was a ghost of Alex Morgan, but the essence was the same. It was time to confront the ghost, to delve into the past to secure the future.

As Dr Zhao left, Blake leaned back in his chair, the gears of his mind turning with renewed purpose. The clue to unravelling Morgan's web lay in the threads of history, in the echoes of an operation that had shaped them both. The chameleon was adept at changing his skin—but, underneath, the skeleton remained the same.

With the past as his guide, Blake would trace the line from then to now, from soldier to nemesis, from comrade to chameleon. And somewhere in that journey, he would find the weakness, the flaw in the armour of the man who had become the phantom in their midst.

Blake stood, his resolve a tangible force in the room. He would delve into the depths of his own history, into the annals of military strategy, to find the key to stopping Morgan. The game was complex, but the next move was clear. It was time to confront the past to change the course of the present.

*

In the quiet confines of her office, Dr Helen Zhao, the forensic psychologist, sat surrounded by her notes on Alex Morgan. The walls, usually a comforting enclosure for thought, now seemed to echo with the complexities of the human mind she was trying to unravel. The case files had spilled their secrets, and now it was her turn to weave them into a coherent narrative that could give Detective Blake and his team the edge they needed.

Her eyes were drawn to the whiteboard before her, a constellation of facts, theories, and psychological profiles that charted the dark universe of Morgan's psyche. With a steady hand, she added new elements from Blake's military operation, connecting dots that formed a more ominous picture of Morgan's behavioural patterns.

She was deep in thought when Blake knocked and entered, his presence a silent testament to the weight of their shared burden.

"Any insights?" Blake asked, his voice betraying his hope for a breakthrough.

Dr Zhao leaned back, her gaze sweeping over the whiteboard. "Morgan's patterns are evolving, becoming more complex. It's as if he's challenging us to keep up, testing our limits," she explained, her tone clinical yet tinged with a note of concern.

Blake's brow furrowed. "Is he escalating?"

"Yes, but not in the traditional sense. He's not just intensifying his actions; he's diversifying them, becoming more unpredictable. It's a psychological escalation." Dr

Zhao turned to face Blake, her eyes locking onto his. "He's a chameleon not just in disguise but in his mind. He adapts his behaviour to throw us off, to keep us guessing, and in doing so, maintains control."

Blake considered her words, the implications clear and disturbing. "So, he's not just reacting to us; he's staying ahead by changing the game itself."

"Exactly." Dr Zhao walked over to a bookshelf and retrieved a thick tome on criminal psychology, flipping it open to a bookmarked page. "Here," she said, pointing to a passage about behavioural adaptation. "Morgan's profile fits this pattern. He's not just a step ahead in planning; he's a step ahead in thinking. To catch him, we'll have to think not just outside the box, but as if there is no box."

Blake absorbed the information, a new kind of determination setting in. "We've been trying to profile him based on what he's done, but we should be profiling him based on what he's capable of doing *next*, considering his psychological adaptability."

Dr Zhao nodded. "We need to anticipate not just his moves but his potential to change those moves mid-stream."

The two stood in silence, the enormity of their task dawning upon them. Morgan was more than a criminal; he was a force of nature, his mind a labyrinth with ever-shifting walls.

Blake broke the silence, his voice resolute. "Then we adapt too. We stay fluid, ready to change our approach at a moment's notice."

Dr Zhao smiled, a rare moment of levity in the gravity of their situation. "Just like a chameleon."

Blake returned the smile, then turned to leave. "Keep me updated on any new insights, Dr Zhao. We're going to need all the help we can get."

As Blake left, Dr Zhao turned back to her whiteboard, the marker in her hand poised to chart the new course of their hunt. The depths of Morgan's psychological profile were profound, but so was her determination to plumb them. For Blake, for the team, and for the justice that seemed just beyond their grasp, she would delve as deep as necessary.

The chameleon had many colours, but so did the light that sought to reveal them.

*

The digital clock on the wall read 3.17 a.m. when the ping of an incoming message cut through the silence of the otherwise deserted incident room. Detective Charlie Blake, who had been poring over the array of evidence from Operation Silent Echo, looked up, his fatigue momentarily forgotten. He approached the main console where the message flickered, its subject line stark against the dim glow of the monitors: *Urgent Lead—Potential Breakthrough.*

With a cautious yet decisive click, Blake opened the message. It was from an informant known only by the codename "Whisper", whose reliability had been proven in past cases. The message was terse: a location, a time, and a simple instruction: *Come alone. It's about Morgan.*

Blake felt the familiar surge of adrenaline, the same rush that came with the scent of a fresh trail. This could be it—the breakthrough they desperately needed. However, *come alone* was a dangerous preposition, especially given Morgan's known propensity for traps. But the potential gain was too alluring to ignore.

He stood up, his mind already weighing the risks against the rewards. If this lead proved genuine it could pivot the entire investigation, giving them the leverage they needed to finally capture the chameleon who had blended into the fabric of their city, eluding capture with infuriating ease.

Blake grabbed his coat, the decision made. This was a gambit he was willing to take. As he headed for the door, he typed a quick message to Sarah Jennings, the most senior detective on his team, informing her of the meeting but leaving out the details. If something went wrong, he needed someone to know where he was.

The streets were deserted as Blake's car sliced through the night. The city that never slept seemed to be taking a rare breath, the calm before the storm of dawn. He parked a block away from the specified location—an abandoned warehouse that loomed like a sentinel of bygone industry.

Blake checked his weapon before stepping out of the car, his senses heightened. The night was still, the only sound his footsteps on the pavement. He reached the warehouse entrance, the metal door ajar as if awaiting his arrival.

Inside, the vast space was a cathedral of shadows, the remnants of machinery casting strange, elongated shapes on the walls. Whisper was already there, a silhouette against the far wall. Blake approached, every instinct on alert.

Whisper's voice was a rasp, a sound barely above the threshold of hearing. "Morgan's planning something big. Something that will shake the city to its core. He's got a mole in the department—someone close to you."

Blake's pulse quickened. They had suspected as much after the betrayal of Victor Reynolds, but this was confirmation that there was still a threat within. "Do you have a name?" he asked, his voice controlled despite the thundering implications of Whisper's words.

"Not yet," Whisper replied, "but I know where you can find the evidence. Morgan's gotten sloppy, overconfident."

The informant handed Blake a slip of paper with an address scrawled on it. "You didn't get this from me," Whisper said, before blending back into the darkness from which they had emerged.

Blake pocketed the paper, his mind racing. This was the lead they needed, but it came with the bitter knowledge of another traitor in their midst. As he left the warehouse, the first light of dawn was touching the horizon, painting the sky with the hues of fire.

The city was waking up, oblivious to the storm that was brewing within its heart. Blake felt the weight of the coming day, a day that promised revelations and confrontations. The chameleon had left a trail, and now it was time to follow it to the end.

Chapter 15: The Gathering Storm

Preparations

The predawn hours at the station found Detective Charlie Blake's team in a state of intense activity, the urgency of their mission pulsating through the room like a live current. Maps were spread out across tables, dotted with markers and notes, digital screens flickered with surveillance feeds, and the air buzzed with the crackle of police radios in a symphony of impending action.

Blake stood at the helm, his eyes scanning over the preparations, the weight of command heavy on his shoulders. This was it—the culmination of all their efforts, the operation that would either bring Morgan into the light or slip through their fingers like shadows at daybreak.

"Check your gear, go over the plan one more time, and be ready to move on my mark," Blake instructed, his voice cutting through the noise with the authority of experience. The team members nodded, their movements precise and deliberate. They were a machine of many parts, but a single purpose: the capture of Alex Morgan.

As the team readied themselves, Blake pulled Elena Martinez aside. Her intelligence had led them to this point, the discovery of one of Morgan's lairs, a break in the case that had rekindled their hope.

"Your work has been exceptional," Blake said, meeting her eyes with a gratitude that went beyond words. "But this is where it gets dangerous. Morgan will be desperate, and that makes him unpredictable."

Elena's nod was resolute, her stance unyielding. "I know the risks. We all do. Let's just bring this guy in and end this nightmare."

Their exchange was cut short as Sarah Jennings approached, her hand clasped around a radio. "We've got eyes on the target location. All teams are in position and waiting for the green light."

Blake took a deep breath, his gaze sweeping over his team, his city's protectors, each braced for the storm that was about to break. This was more than a police operation; it was a battle for justice, a strike against the darkness that had taken root in the heart of their city.

"Give the signal," Blake said, his voice steady. "It's time to bring the storm to Morgan's door."

As the radio crackled with the confirmation of his order, the team moved out, a fluid force of determination and duty. The station emptied, leaving behind a silence that was both a respite and a harbinger of the chaos to come.

Blake was the last to leave, his hand resting momentarily on the map that charted their course. The path was drawn, the players set, and the storm was upon them. They were ready, each carrying the hope and the will to see the dawn break on a city cleansed of its hidden predator.

The door shut behind him with the finality of a vault sealing, the quiet click a punctuation to the moment. Outside, the sky was beginning to bruise with the light of morning, the city unaware of the forces moving in its shadows, of the gathering storm that would soon break upon its streets.

*

In the solitude of his office, with the relentless tick of the clock marking the passage of time, Detective Charlie Blake contemplated the sea of evidence spread before him. Each piece told a story; each clue was a breadcrumb on the trail leading to Alex Morgan. Yet amidst the growing storm, a seed of doubt took root in Blake's mind, threatening to sprout into a choking vine.

He'd been through this before, the sleepless nights, the relentless pursuit, the weight of command. But this time, it was different. The lines between right and wrong blurred with each revelation, each piece of the puzzle that was Morgan. The adversary he hunted was not just a criminal but a spectre, an idea, a vendetta against a system that Blake had dedicated his life to uphold.

The detective's eyes fell upon a single photograph amongst the files—a candid shot of Morgan, taken years back. In it, Morgan's eyes bore a depth of understanding and pain that Blake had seen in his own reflection countless times. It was the look of a man who had been to hell and back, a man who had seen the system fail those it was supposed to protect. In that moment, Blake couldn't help but wonder if the difference between him and Morgan was merely a matter of circumstance.

A knock at the door snapped Blake out of his introspection. It was Sarah Jennings, her keen eyes quick to read the room. "You okay, Charlie?" she asked, her voice grounding Blake back to the present.

Blake sighed, the weight of his thoughts momentarily lifting. "I'm fine," he lied, not wanting to burden his team with his crisis of conscience. "Just ready to put an end to this."

Sarah approached and placed a firm hand on his shoulder, offering silent support. "We all are," she said. "But don't lose yourself in this storm, Charlie. We need you to lead us through it, not get swept away by it."

Her words echoed in Blake's mind as he gazed back at

the evidence. He had always prided himself on being the beacon for his team, the unwavering point of reference in their search for justice. But in the darkness that Morgan had cast over the city, even the brightest lights could flicker.

With a deep breath, Blake stood up, his resolve hardening once more. This moment of doubt was just that—a moment. He wouldn't let it derail him from the mission at hand. They were close now, closer than ever to ending Morgan's reign of terror, and Blake would not falter when his team, his city, needed him most.

"Let's get to work," Blake declared, his voice now a bastion of renewed determination. He would face this storm head-on, with his team beside him, and together they would weather whatever Morgan had in store for them.

The doubts might never fully dissipate, but Blake understood now that they were a part of the burden he carried, a testament to his humanity in the face of the inhumanity they sought to vanquish. With the team's trust as his armour, he was ready to lead them into the fray, into the very eye of the storm.

*

With the light of dawn painting a soft palette across the sky, Detective Charlie Blake's team gathered in the shadow of an abandoned warehouse, the location provided by Elena's crucial intel. This was one of Morgan's hideouts, a place that reeked of abandonment and decay but might hold the key to his undoing.

Elena, despite the exhaustion etched on her features from her recent narrow escape, was the embodiment of focus. She had changed out of her undercover attire into tactical gear, but the intensity in her eyes was the same.

"According to the blueprints and my sources, Morgan uses the basement for... something. He's cautious, never brings anyone with him," she briefed the team.

Blake nodded, processing the information. "If he's been using it regularly, he might have gotten comfortable. That's when mistakes happen," he mused. His eyes swept over the team. "We go in quiet, no surprises. We're looking for anything—papers, drives, anything he might have left behind."

Sarah Jennings, always ready with her kit, added, "We'll sweep for prints and DNA. Anything Morgan has touched, we'll find it."

The team split into pairs, methodically making their entry into the building. The interior was a maze of corridors and deserted rooms, the air stale with the mustiness of neglect. The silence was oppressive, the sense of desolation palpable.

Blake and Elena led the way to the basement, the beam from their flashlights slicing through the darkness. The stairs creaked under their weight, a discordant symphony to the tension that clung to the air like cobwebs.

The basement was vast, the darkness more profound, a black so absolute it seemed to swallow the beams of their flashlights. The walls were lined with shelves, and it didn't take long for Elena to find what they were looking for—a series of binders and stacks of papers that seemed out of place in the derelict gloom.

As Blake thumbed through the pages, the dim light revealed maps of the city, photographs of various locations, and myriad notes written in a hand that was meticulous and obsessive. "This is it. This is his planning room," Blake whispered, a chill running down his spine.

The realisation hit him: they were standing in the nerve centre of Morgan's operations.

The find was significant, a treasure trove of evidence and insight into the mind of their quarry. As the team collected every scrap of paper and photographed every inch of the room, Blake felt a sense of momentum building. This was a turning point, a shift in the wind that could very well lead to the storm they were eager to bring upon Morgan.

As they emerged from the warehouse, the first rays of the sun crested the horizon, casting long shadows behind them. Blake looked back at the building, its secrets now exposed to the light. They had uncovered one of Morgan's lairs, but the man himself remained a spectre, his presence felt but not seen.

But the day was young, and Blake's resolve was steel. "He's been hiding in plain sight, but not anymore. We're closing in," he said to his team, their faces lit by the dawn of a new day, a day that promised progress and peril in equal measure.

*

The mood in the makeshift command centre was electric with silent tension. Each member of Detective Charlie Blake's team was acutely aware of the mission's gravity. The walls, plastered with maps and photos, seemed to close in on them, a physical manifestation of the pressure they all felt.

Blake noted the subtle shifts in body language, the uncharacteristic quietness of his normally talkative team. They were on the precipice, the edge of a momentous operation, and the air was thick with the weight of unspoken anxieties. They were not just colleagues; they were comrades, bound by a common goal, yet each harboured their personal tempests.

Elena, who had been instrumental in discovering Morgan's lair, now seemed distant, her eyes occasionally flitting to the exit as if contemplating the escape route. Sarah Jennings, ever the voice of reason, had a crease of concern between her brows that had deepened over the past hours.

Blake cleared his throat, ready to address the elephant in the room. "I know what you're all thinking," he began, his tone more subdued than usual. "We're closer than we've ever been to Morgan, and it's natural to feel the strain. But we must trust in the strength of our alliance, in the bond that we have built."

Marcus, the tech expert, broke the silence. "It's not just about catching Morgan anymore," he said, pushing a tangle of wires aside with a frustrated hand. "It's about making it through this together."

Theo Wallace, once an adversary and now an ally, leaned against a wall, his arms folded. "In my world, trust is a rare commodity," he offered in a gravelly voice. "But I trust this team. We've got different methods, but we share the same goal. We'll get Morgan, together or not at all."

Blake nodded, acknowledging the unorthodox partnership that had formed. Theo's connections in the underbelly of the city had proven invaluable, even if they walked a moral tightrope.

Sarah chimed in, her analytical mind always looking to soothe tensions. "We have a unity that Morgan can't understand. He relies on fear and manipulation, but we have trust and collaboration. It's our advantage."

As the team members exchanged nods and murmurs of agreement, Blake felt the alliance solidifying. The tensions, though present, were overshadowed by a collective resolve.

It was Dan Brooks, the youngest member, whose voice cut through the renewed sense of purpose. "We might have our differences," he said, his hands steady on the keyboard in front of him, "but Morgan has no idea who he's up against. He's not facing one of us; he's facing all of us."

Blake allowed a small smile to break through. "Exactly. We are the storm he didn't plan for," he said, his gaze sweeping across the room, meeting the eyes of each team member. "Now, let's show Morgan the power of a united front."

As the team dispersed to finalise their preparations, the command centre hummed back to life, the silence replaced by the sound of determination. They were a diverse group, each with their skills and secrets, but they had a common thread binding them together: the pursuit of justice. It was a tense alliance, yes, but it was also their greatest strength.

*

The remnants of the night hung heavily over the industrial district as Detective Charlie Blake's team positioned themselves around the perimeter of what they believed to be Morgan's latest hideout. The building was an old textile mill, its windows like darkened eyes and its façade a tapestry of brick and grime. It stood as a silent testament to the decay of the area, a perfect haven for someone looking to operate from the shadows.

Blake surveyed the area, his eyes sharp, his mind running through every possible scenario. "Eyes up, everyone. This is it," he whispered into the comm, his voice a calm in the brewing storm. "We're in the eye of it now."

The team acknowledged with a series of clicks in their earpieces, a Morse code of readiness. Blake gave the nod, and the breach began. They entered the mill with a practised stealth, every step a measured tread, every breath controlled.

Inside, the mill was a labyrinth of old machinery and towering stacks of fabric, a derelict maze that played tricks on the eyes. The air was thick with dust, the only sound their synchronised movements and the distant drip of water echoing through the vast emptiness.

The team split up, flanking the central space where they expected to find Morgan. Blake led one group, with Elena on point. Her earlier reconnaissance had been invaluable, and now she moved with a silent grace, a ghost slipping through the gears of the past.

As they approached the heart of the mill, Blake's pulse quickened. Every shadow seemed to move, every noise a potential threat. They were in Morgan's domain now, and his traps could be anywhere.

The trap sprung without warning. The floor beneath two team members gave way, a hidden pit claiming them with a suddenness that turned the stomach. Blake's voice was a sharp command. "Man down! Secure ropes!"

The team acted with precision, securing the area as Blake and another officer carefully rappelled into the pit. The fallen detectives were alive but injured, caught in a web of old cabling that had cushioned their fall. As they were hoisted up, Blake's mind raced. Morgan was turning their hunt into a house of horrors, each step potentially their last.

Back on the main floor, they regrouped, the tension now a palpable entity that clung to their sweaty skin. Blake's mind was a whirlwind. Morgan's traps were not just physical; they were psychological warfare designed to fray nerves and induce fear.

They pressed on, clearing each section with meticulous care, but the mill was silent save for the echoes of their own movement. It was as if Morgan had vanished, a wraith in the wind.

It was then that the building itself seemed to turn against them. A sudden cacophony of noise erupted as machines whirred to life, the clatter of looms and spindles a disorienting din that filled the space with an industrial symphony of terror.

Blake's team staggered under the assault of sound, their comms rendered useless. Through the chaos, Blake caught a glimpse of a figure moving with impossible speed and agility through the machines, a shadow among shadows. Morgan.

He pursued, his team following his lead, their training overcoming their fear. But as they closed in, the figure vanished once more, leaving them grasping at phantoms.

The operation was a storm, and they were in its midst— but Blake knew storms could be weathered. They regrouped once more, their resolve unbroken, their determination a beacon that cut through the pandemonium.

As the noise ceased as abruptly as it had begun, Blake and his team stood amidst the silence, the eye of the storm passing over them. They were battered but not beaten. They had survived Morgan's traps, but the cost was yet to be tallied.

Blake's voice, when he spoke, was a steel blade cutting through the uncertainty. "We move forward. Morgan wants to break us, but we will not bend. We end this today."

*

181

The operation had reached its zenith; Detective Charlie Blake and his team were about to close the net on Alex Morgan. Each member was in position, their eyes were a matrix of vigilance surrounding the perimeter of an old, decrepit factory that intel suggested was Morgan's current hideout.

Blake's voice was a whisper through the comms. "Steady... on my mark." The team held their collective breath, every muscle tensed for action. The building stood, ominously quiet, the calm before the proverbial storm.

But the storm came from an unexpected quarter. The screech of tires shattered the silence, and a van hurtled toward the factory's main entrance. The team tensed, preparing for a breach, but instead of crashing through the door, the van came to an abrupt halt, and its back doors flew open.

From the van's dark interior, a figure was roughly thrown onto the ground—it was Elena Martinez, looking battered but alive. The van sped away, leaving a cloud of exhaust and a clear message from Morgan: he was always one step ahead.

Blake was first to reach Elena, his concern etched deeply into his face. "Report!" he demanded, even as he checked her for injuries.

Elena's voice was shaky but determined as she pushed herself to her feet. As Blake thumbed through the pages, the dim light revealed maps of the city, photographs of various locations, and myriad notes written in a hand that was meticulous and obsessive. Blake's mind raced. This was more than a failed operation; it was a statement. Morgan wasn't just evading them; he was challenging the very foundation of their pursuit.

The incident room was a frenzy of activity as the team regrouped, their screens a flurry of data as they attempted to track the van. But it was like chasing a ghost—no license plates, no identifiable marks. Morgan had covered his tracks with precision.

As Blake directed the search, his phone buzzed with an incoming message. The sender was unknown, but the content struck like a bolt of lightning—a video feed, live from inside the factory. It showed a room filled with monitors, each one displaying a different location around the city, and in the centre, a single chair.

Blake's heart stopped as he recognised the figure now taking a seat in the chair. It was Morgan, his face revealed in the harsh artificial light as he looked directly into the camera, directly at Blake.

Morgan's voice filled the room, emanating from the phone's speaker. "I wanted you to see, Detective. See the extent of my reach, the futility of your efforts." He gestured, and the screens behind him shifted to show live footage of various team members, including shots of Blake's own home.

The message was clear—Morgan wasn't just a step ahead; he was ensnaring them in a web that extended to their personal lives. The line between hunter and hunted was no longer discernible.

Blake's fist clenched, his nails digging into his palm. The video feed cut off, leaving the room in stunned silence. It was a declaration of war, one that had become personal and perilous.

As the team absorbed the gravity of the situation, Blake's resolve crystallised. This wasn't the end; it was an escalation, a pivot to a new battlefield where the rules were written by a madman.

"We regroup," Blake said, his voice steady, "We protect our own, and then we end this. He wants a war? He'll get one."

The team rallied around him, their faces set in grim determination. They were a unit, bound together not just by duty, but by a shared vulnerability. Morgan had struck at the heart of their team, but in doing so he had only strengthened their resolve.

The team's resolve galvanised, their strategy evolving. They would have to become the storm Morgan so relished creating—unpredictable, unyielding, and relentless.

Chapter 16: Into the Fire

Direct Confrontation

The stale air of the derelict building hung heavy as Detective Charlie Blake stepped through the shattered doorway, the echo of his footsteps a sombre drumbeat in the silence. He had been here before, a place of faded memories and lost souls, but tonight it held the promise of a long-awaited reckoning.

Alex Morgan's silhouette was barely discernible in the dim light, a spectre from the past materialising before him. "Blake," Morgan's voice resonated in the hollow space, a taunt wrapped in the familiarity of a shared history.

Blake's hand rested on his weapon, a reassurance of reality in the phantasmal stand-off. "Morgan," he replied, his voice a sharp edge in the quiet. "This ends tonight."

The two men were opposites cast from the same mould, once brothers in arms, now adversaries in a game that had spiralled beyond the confines of law and morality. The air crackled with the intensity of their shared gaze, two forces of will clashing without a word.

Morgan stepped forward, the light casting his face in stark relief, revealing the lines etched by years of a twisted journey. "You always had a hero complex, Charlie. But this isn't a story of good and evil. It's about the shades in between."

Blake's grip tightened, his resolve a steel framework amidst the storm of emotions. "You crossed the line, Alex. You made this personal when you made the city your hunting ground."

A laugh, humourless and cold, escaped Morgan. "The

city is a jungle, and I am merely a predator. Survival is the only morality that matters."

Blake could hear the team outside, a distant storm brewing, ready to descend upon Morgan's position. But this moment, this confrontation, was theirs alone—a culmination of a chase that had consumed Blake's life.

"Your survival ends with justice," Blake declared, the words a vow he intended to keep.

Morgan's eyes narrowed, a dark amusement flickering within. "Justice? Your justice is as flawed as the system you serve. I am the true arbiter."

The stand-off was a frozen tableau, a moment in time where the past and present collided with the inevitability of the future. Blake knew that Morgan would not be taken easily, that the man before him was a manifestation of chaos and cunning.

The silence shattered like glass as the team breached the building, their shouts a distant echo to the explosion of movement. Morgan lunged, not towards Blake but towards the shadows, where his intricate web of escape routes lay.

Blake pursued, his training a honed instinct that carried him through the melee. Bullets flew, a hailstorm in the enclosed space, but Blake's focus was singular— Morgan.

They collided with the force of history between them, the physical struggle a mere extension of their mental chess game. Blake's determination was a match for Morgan's desperation, the fight a savage dance of survival.

As the struggle continued, Blake realised this was more than just a capture; it was an exorcism of demons that had haunted him, the physical manifestation of a journey that had started years ago in the deserts of far-off lands.

The confrontation was brutal and swift—Blake's resolve versus Morgan's anarchy. And as reinforcements swarmed the space, pulling the two men apart, Blake's gaze locked with Morgan's, a silent communication that spoke of the endgame now set in motion.

This was the direct confrontation that had been inevitable since the beginning, the fire they both had walked into. And as Morgan was led away in cuffs, Blake knew that the flames of this fire would either cleanse or consume.

*

The sterile white of the hospital's emergency room was a stark contrast to the grim shadows of the textile mill where Detective Charlie Blake's team had faced off against Alex Morgan's traps. Now, under the fluorescent lights, the cost of their pursuit was laid bare in the bruised and battered bodies of his officers.

Blake paced the corridor, his hands clenched into fists at his sides, the sound of his footsteps a metronome to his troubled thoughts. Every so often, he glanced through the windows into the treatment rooms, where his team was being tended to by a flurry of medical staff.

Elena had a bandage wrapped around her head, a stark red spot blooming against the white gauze. Marcus— always the stoic one—had his arm in a sling, his face pale but his jaw set in a grim line of endurance. Each member of his team bore the marks of the night's chaos, a physical manifestation of their collective ordeal.

Blake's heart clenched as he took in the scene, the guilt gnawing at him. They were here because of him, because of the path he had led them down in his unwavering pursuit of justice. The weight of command was a heavy mantle, and, in moments like these, it felt suffocating.

Dr Helen Zhao approached him, her face a mask of professionalism, but her eyes betrayed her concern. "They'll make it, Charlie. They're strong," she said, placing a hand on his shoulder in a gesture meant to ground him.

He nodded, the tightness in his chest easing ever so slightly at her words. "I know. But it's not just the physical wounds. It's what this chase is doing to us, to our spirits. Morgan is taking a toll on us all."

Zhao understood. The psychological scars often ran deeper and healed slower than flesh. "We'll get through this," she assured him. "We'll heal, and we'll become stronger for it. Morgan can't break what he doesn't understand, and he doesn't understand the bond this team has."

Blake allowed himself a moment of vulnerability, the facade of the unbreakable leader slipping. "I just hope the price isn't too high in the end," he murmured, his gaze returning to his wounded team.

As the morning shifted into afternoon, reports came in, updates on the conditions of the injured and the status of the operation. Blake listened, absorbed the information, and with each passing hour, his resolve solidified once again.

They had paid a price, yes, but the cost of justice was never cheap. The wounds would become badges of honour, the pain a testament to their dedication. And as each member of his team was released, their expressions determined, Blake knew that they would not be deterred.

The team had walked through the fire and emerged

scorched but alive, their resolve unshaken. Morgan had intended to weaken them, but Blake saw a new strength in their eyes, a new depth to their determination.

They would need time to recover, but they would not retreat. The battle was far from over, and as they regrouped, their unity became their shield, their shared purpose their weapon. The storm had gathered, had broken over them, but they stood firm. And together they would face the fires of their pursuit until justice was served.

*

Detective Charlie Blake leaned over the cluttered desk, piecing together the fragments of information that formed the mosaic of Alex Morgan's motivations. The criminal network he was uncovering was far more intricate than they had initially suspected. Every new thread they pulled seemed to unravel another layer, exposing a deeper darkness beneath the already murky waters of Morgan's operations.

Elena's breakthrough had led them here, to the core of Morgan's hideout, now a crime scene bustling with forensic teams methodically cataloguing every item. The walls were lined with maps, photographs, and strings connecting points like a web spun by a meticulous spider. In the centre, a series of monitors remained, some still flickering with the ghostly after-images of the surveillance feeds Morgan had so carefully curated.

Blake's eyes were drawn to a collection of files, each meticulously labelled. The contents were chilling—a ledger of crimes, each entry a life affected by Morgan's influence. It was the work of a man who saw himself not just as a criminal but as a maestro conducting an orchestra of chaos.

"This was his hub," Blake murmured, his voice barely above a whisper. The realisation was a heavy stone in his gut. Morgan wasn't just perpetrating crimes; he was nurturing them, cultivating a network of darkness that spread across the city like a cancer.

Sarah joined him, her gaze following his. "It's a franchise of fear," she observed, her analytical mind already racing ahead. "He's not just a solitary actor. He's franchised his brand of terror, outsourcing to other criminals while maintaining control."

The implications were staggering. It wasn't just a matter of bringing in a single man anymore. They were up against an entire syndicate that operated in the shadows, a hydra with Morgan as its head.

Blake felt a cold anger settling in his bones. "He's been using the city as a chessboard, and we've been playing checkers," he said, his hands forming into fists.

Elena approached, her expression grim. "It's more than that, Charlie. Look at this." She handed him a photograph. It was a snapshot of a younger Morgan in military uniform, standing with a man whose face had been crossed out. "That's our mole," she said.

Blake's pulse quickened as he studied the image. "We need to find out who this is, how deep they're in, and what they know."

The discovery of Morgan's motivations and the deeper criminal network was a pivot point in the investigation. It was no longer just a manhunt; it was a war against a legion of shadows, with the city's very soul at stake.

As the team worked into the night, Blake knew they were only beginning to grasp the full extent of the threat. They had uncovered the heart of Morgan's darkness, but the battle was far from over. It was a sobering thought that as they delved deeper into Morgan's world, they might find themselves looking into the abyss, and Blake wondered, not for the first time, what would be looking back.

*

The station was alive with a low murmur, the soft clicking of keyboards, and the rustle of paper as Detective Charlie Blake's team regathered in the incident room. The walls, once a pristine white, now held the layered textures of the city's secrets, charts, and photographs—the vestiges of the night's revelations, each a piece in the dark mosaic of Alex Morgan's criminal empire.

Blake, his face a mask of contemplation, watched his team, their faces a myriad of resolve and weariness. The recent discoveries had forced them into a new understanding of the breadth and depth of Morgan's influence. It was time to reforge their strategy with the hardened steel of their shared ordeal.

"Alright, listen up," Blake commanded, his voice cutting through the murmur, rallying his team's scattered focus. "We've been knocked down, but we're far from broken. We've discovered more in the last twenty-four hours than we have in weeks. Morgan's reach is extensive, but it's not infinite."

Elena, her wounds a testament to their recent brush with Morgan's traps, stepped closer to the map that dominated one wall. "We've mapped his hideouts, his possible escape routes, and his network. It's time we use this to our advantage."

The team's eyes were fixed on Blake as he began to outline their next steps. "We know he's watching, always watching. But now, so are we," Blake said with a steely determination that bolstered the resolve of his weary team.

Sarah Jennings, her analytical mind already processing the information, joined in. "We've been reactive, but that changes now. We anticipate, we set the traps, and we end this—on our terms."

Blake nodded in agreement. "Exactly. We've been playing checkers while Morgan's been playing chess. But now we know the board, and we know our pieces. It's time we make a move he won't expect."

The team leaned in, drawn by Blake's unwavering confidence. Marcus Levine, the tech analyst, tapped at his keyboard, bringing up a series of surveillance feeds. "We'll keep an eye on known associates, tap into street cams, anything that gives us an edge."

Emily Saunders, the forensic pathologist, spoke up, her voice steady. "And I'll go over everything we've collected from his lairs again. There *has* to be something we've missed, some clue as to where he'll strike next."

Theo Wallace, once a figure from the underworld they had fought against, now stood with them. "Morgan's arrogant; he'll slip up, and when he does, we'll be there."

Blake surveyed his team, their dedication a tangible force in the room. "This is a war, not just of bodies, but of minds. We've seen what Morgan is capable of, but he has yet to see what we can do when we're united, when we're driven, not just by the pursuit of justice, but by the defence of our city, our people."

As the team dispersed to their respective tasks, the incident room hummed with renewed purpose. They were more than colleagues; they were guardians standing between the city and the chaos Morgan threatened to unleash. With Blake at the helm, they regrouped, not as a team, but as a force, one that was about to turn the tide.

*

In the aftermath of the chaotic clash at Morgan's hideout, the city was abuzz with whispers and wild speculation. Simon Fraser, the tenacious journalist known for his incisive reporting, had picked up the story, and the public's perception of the case began to shift like the tide.

Blake watched from his office as the news played on the screen, Fraser's voice narrating the recent events with a gravitas that demanded attention. "What began as a manhunt for a high-profile criminal has now revealed a network of shadows," Fraser reported, his face stern in the glow of the camera lights. "And at the heart of this darkness stands Detective Charlie Blake's team, a beacon of hope against the chaos."

The public, once sceptical, began to rally behind the police effort. Blake could feel the shift in the city's heartbeat, the pulse of community support that throbbed through the veins of the metropolis. This was more than just a criminal investigation; it had become a narrative of good versus evil, the people of the city becoming characters in a story they had once observed from a distance.

Fraser continued, his words painting a picture of a city united. "In the wake of the violence, a new sense of purpose has been ignited across the boroughs. Citizens stand in solidarity with the brave men and women who face the darkness to bring light."

Blake turned off the screen, his mind racing. Public opinion was a fickle thing—but for now, it was their ally. He knew the importance of this support; it was a shield against the scrutiny they were under, a validation of their sacrifices.

As he walked through the station, he could see the effect of Fraser's report on his team. There was a newfound spring in their steps, a lift in their spirits that had been absent before. The weight of the city's expectations was immense, but it was also an empowering embrace, a collective strength that bolstered their resolve.

Sarah Jennings caught Blake's eye, a smile playing on her lips. "Seems like we've got the city on our side now," she said, a note of pride in her voice.

Blake nodded, allowing himself a moment of pride. "Let's use this momentum," he said, his voice firm with conviction. "It's a rare thing to have the public's eye see the truth of our work."

The story was still unfolding, the narrative still being written, but for the first time in a long while, Blake felt that the city was not just a backdrop for their operations but an active participant in their quest for justice. The support was a tide that lifted all ships, and as they prepared for the next phase of their operation, they did so with the city at their backs.

The news cycle would continue, the public's attention would eventually drift, but for now, the tide was with them, and Blake intended to ride it all the way to Morgan's doorstep. The game was changing, and they were no longer the only players. The city had joined the fray, and together, they would face the fire that awaited them.

*

In the labyrinthine corridors of the station, the atmosphere was charged with a current of cautious optimism. The events of the day had taken their toll, yet Detective Charlie Blake's team was buoyed by a sense of accomplishment, a feeling that the tide was finally turning in their long battle against Alex Morgan's web of crime.

It was nearly midnight when the call came through.

Blake, who was poring over maps and surveillance photos, felt his phone vibrate with an urgency that matched his own pulse. The display showed an unrecognised number, but intuition urged him to answer. "Blake," he said, his voice the steady timbre of a man who had weathered many storms.

"You need to see this," came the crisp, unfamiliar voice on the other end. The line crackled with a static that spoke of encryption. "There's been a development. Something you didn't see coming."

Blake's grip on the phone tightened. "Go on," he urged, his eyes narrowing.

"Morgan has made a move that changes everything," the voice continued. "He's not just staying a step ahead; he's paving new ground."

A series of coordinates followed, numbers that Blake scribbled down with a hand steadied by years of experience. The call ended abruptly, leaving Blake with a silent handset and a new knot of intrigue in the pit of his stomach.

The coordinates led to an industrial area on the outskirts of the city, a place forgotten by progress and prosperity. Blake and his team arrived under the cloak of darkness, the only light emanating from their flashlights and the distant glow of the city skyline.

What they found was a scene that defied their expectations. An abandoned warehouse, presumed to be another of Morgan's many lairs, was instead a hub of activity. But not the criminal kind—instead, they stumbled upon a makeshift operation centre, buzzing with people Blake recognised as some of the city's most prominent figures in charity and social work.

In the centre of it all was a tableau that made Blake's

heart skip a beat: a wall covered with plans for community centres, housing projects, and rehabilitative programs—each bearing Morgan's unmistakable mark. It was a stark departure from the destruction and chaos they had associated with him.

The revelation was a chasm that opened beneath their feet. Had Morgan been a vigilante masquerading as a villain? Or was this yet another layer to his game, a ploy designed to throw them off the scent?

As they secured the area, Blake's second-in-command, Sarah Jennings, approached, her expression a mirror of his own bewilderment. "What does this mean, Charlie?" she asked, her voice barely above a whisper.

Blake didn't answer immediately. He was lost in the implications of this new development, the lines between ally and enemy blurring before his eyes.

"This means," he finally said, "that we've been looking at the board from the wrong angle. Morgan's not expanding the scope of his criminal empire—he's challenging the very foundations of our assumptions about him."

The team was silent, each member processing the staggering realisation that their adversary might not be the man they were chasing, but the hero they never expected to find.

As they left the warehouse, a new day was dawning, casting the first rays of light on a city that was, unbeknownst to its inhabitants, standing at the edge of a revelation. Blake knew the road ahead would be more complex than ever. Morgan's broader plans had expanded the scope of the threat, but they had also illuminated a path forward, one that required a keen mind and an open heart.

Chapter 17: Frayed Edges

Emotional Fallout

In the quiet sanctuary of a small, bare conference room within the station, Detective Charlie Blake's team sat in a loose semicircle, a collective portrait of exhaustion. The room, typically buzzing with strategy and theories, was now filled with a heavy silence, the kind that follows a storm. The emotional and physical toll of the case had woven its way through each member, binding them in a shared fatigue.

Blake observed his team, their faces etched with the strain of sleepless nights and relentless days. Elena, her eyes shadowed and distant, was the embodiment of their weariness. She had pushed herself beyond limits, her latest escapade into Morgan's world leaving her with more than just the physical scars that were now healing on her temple.

He cleared his throat gently, not to speak, but to remind them of his presence, his solidarity. "We knew this wouldn't be easy," he began, his voice carrying the warmth of empathy. "But knowing doesn't make it any easier to bear."

One by one, his team members raised their eyes to meet his. There was an unspoken understanding that they were not just colleagues but comrades who had seen the depths of human depravity and still chose to stand against it.

Sarah Jennings was the first to break the silence. "It's like we've been holding our breath," she admitted, her usually composed voice tinged with emotion. "Waiting for the next blow, the next move in Morgan's game."

Marcus, whose arm had healed enough to forgo the sling but still bore a stiffness, added, "And every move costs us. Not just in bruises or blood, but in pieces of who we are."

The room filled with murmurs of agreement, a chorus of vulnerability that had no place in the harsh light of the outside world but found its home here among those who understood.

Elena leaned forward, her hands clasped tightly. "We've given so much of ourselves to this case. Sometimes, I wonder what we'll have left when it's finally over."

Blake let their words hang in the air, a testament to their sacrifice. "This is more than a job, more than a case," he said. "It's a battle for something greater, and battles leave scars, both seen and unseen."

He stood, his gaze sweeping over his team, a captain steadying his ship in troubled waters. "We'll get through this together. We'll hold on to the reasons we started down this path. And when the dust settles, we'll still be standing, not because we're unbreakable, but because we're united."

As the team dispersed, the weight of their shared burden felt a little lighter, dispersed among them. They were frayed, certainly, but not severed. They would continue, they would fight, and they would do it together, for each other and for the justice that had called them to this life.

The emotional fallout of the case would linger, a silent echo of their journey, but it would not define them. Instead, it would be the resolve, the strength, and the unyielding spirit that would be their legacy, the story that would be told in the quiet rooms where they gathered, where they healed, and where they found the courage to face another day.

The solidarity of the team, a constant in the tumult of their high-stakes game against Alex Morgan, began to wane under the strain of a haunting suspicion. Blake could see it in the sidelong glances, the hesitations in conversation, a tension that twisted the very air of the incident room. Trust, the bedrock upon which they had built their unity, now seemed to be on the verge of a silent, insidious collapse.

It was Elena who voiced the dread that had wormed its way into their minds. "We're being outflanked... and I don't think it's just because Morgan is good," she said, her eyes scanning the room, alighting on each of her colleagues like a butterfly on a thorn. "Someone is feeding him our moves.'

The implication of her words was like a live wire dropped into water, sending shockwaves through the room. Suspicion was a wildfire, and once sparked it threatened to engulf them all.

Blake rose, his presence commanding the room into a reluctant calm. "We investigate," he stated firmly. "Quietly, methodically. We find this leak, this... betrayal within our ranks, and we seal it."

Sarah Jennings, ever the pragmatist, already had her laptop open, her fingers dancing across the keys. "I'll audit our communications, check for any discrepancies, any unauthorised access."

Dan Brooks, the youngest among them, looked around, his expression a mix of disbelief and hurt. "But we're a family," he protested, the word hanging heavily in the room, a reminder of what they were risking.

Blake's gaze met each of theirs in turn, a silent commander rallying his troops. "A family, yes. But even families have their secrets. We do this carefully—no accusations, no confrontations until we have hard evidence."

As they set to work, the camaraderie that had once defined them shifted, morphing into a wary dance of shadowed glances and unspoken doubts. But beneath the surface of their task lay an unyielding commitment to each other, to the justice they sought, and to the city they served.

The investigation into their own would be the harshest they had ever undertaken, for it was not a search for a stranger but a hunt for one of their own who had turned against them. The very thought was anathema to Blake, yet he could not deny the signs, the traces of treachery that seemed to lead back to the heart of his team.

The days that followed were a miasma of distrust and tension. Reports were scrutinised, alibis checked, every member of the team subjected to the same scrutiny they had so often applied to others. The irony was not lost on Blake; they had become their own suspects in a case that was as personal as it was painful.

As Blake watched his team, he felt the frayed edges of their bond tugging at his own resolve. They would find the traitor, he vowed, not just to preserve their mission, but to mend the fabric of their unity, to restore the trust that had been their greatest weapon against the darkness they fought.

*

Elena Martinez stood at the edge of the station's rooftop, the gusts of wind tugging at her jacket like warning whispers, imploring her to step back from the precipice—not just the physical one upon which she teetered, but the metaphorical one that loomed over her next decision. Below, the city stretched out, a tapestry of light and shadow, indifferent to the solitary figure above.

The risks had always been clear to her, but now they were tangible, the danger as real as the concrete under her boots. She had always been the one to volunteer for the undercover operations, to weave herself into the webs spun by those like Morgan. It was her talent, her curse, to blur the lines between law enforcer and lawbreaker in pursuit of a greater truth.

Blake had tried to dissuade her, his concern etched in the furrows of his brow and the tension in his voice. "You've done enough, Elena. Let someone else take the risk this time," he'd said, his hand on her arm a restraint she wasn't used to from him.

But Elena had seen the darkness in Morgan's network, had touched it, and she knew the pull it had. It was a gravity well of secrets and sins, and she felt inexorably drawn to it, compelled by a need to see their quest through, to end the nightmare that had consumed their city, their lives.

"I have to do this, Charlie," she had insisted, her resolve a steel thread. "There's something I need to find out, something only I can uncover. Morgan's network... it's not just about him. There's more, and I can sense it."

The silence that followed was her answer, Blake's reluctant nod a consent she had expected but wished she hadn't needed. There was trust there, but also resignation, a tacit acknowledgment of the path she chose to walk—a path that now found her shadowed in the anonymity of night, waiting for a contact that might lead her further into the labyrinth or might be a dead end.

The contact was a figure from the fringes of Morgan's network, a whisper of a name that had surfaced in one of the many tangled threads they had pulled. Elena had arranged the meeting with a few well-placed words and promises, her reputation as a chameleon within the criminal underbelly preceding her.

When the figure finally emerged from the darkness, their face obscured by a hood, Elena's pulse quickened. This was the moment of truth, the point of no return. She stepped forward, her voice steady despite the hammering of her heart. "You have information for me?"

The figure nodded, a hand delving into the folds of their cloak. What they produced was not a weapon, as Elena's instincts had braced for, but a small, encrypted drive. "Everything you need to know about Morgan's next move," they said, their voice a rasping whisper.

As Elena reached for the drive, she knew the risks were worth it. This was the break they needed, the key to unlocking the next piece of the puzzle. But even as her fingers closed around the cold metal, she couldn't shake the feeling that each step forward entangled her deeper into a web that might one day refuse to release her.

Back at the station, as she handed the drive to Blake, Elena's eyes met his, a silent conversation passing between them. They were in this together, come what may. But as she walked away, her mind was already racing, the drive in her pocket a burning question: was she stepping into the light, or further into the fire?

*

Detective Charlie Blake's reflection stared back at him— a gaunt mirror image etched with the signs of relentless pursuit. The office, quiet in the late hours, was a stark cell of solitude that echoed the relentless ticking of the clock, each second a reminder of the unsolved case that lay heavy on his shoulders.

The lines on his face had deepened, not just from the wear of time, but from the burden of a case that had consumed his life. The image of Alex Morgan was burned into his retinas, a spectre at the feast of his every waking hour. Blake's obsession with capturing the elusive figure had started to exact a severe toll on his health and his relationships.

Sarah Jennings, his longtime partner and confidante, had seen the change in him. "Charlie, you're chasing shadows at the expense of your own light," she'd said, her voice laced with concern. But her words, meant to be a lifeline, had felt like an anchor, dragging him further down into the depths of his fixation.

Blake's hands trembled as he reached for another file, his once-steady grip now betrayed by the tremors of exhaustion. Sleep had become a stranger, and food had lost its taste. The only hunger he knew was for the resolution of the case, for the peace that seemed an ever-receding horizon.

His phone vibrated, an incoming call from Emily Saunders, the forensic pathologist. He hesitated, knowing she would implore him to rest, to distance himself from the toxicity of the chase. But distancing was a luxury he could not afford, not when every moment brought Morgan the opportunity to strike again.

"Charlie, it's not just about catching him anymore," Emily's voice came through, strained with the effort of trying to reach him. "It's about not losing yourself to this. You have people who care about you, who need you to be whole."

Blake's eyes, red rimmed and tired, lifted from the desk and settled on a photograph of his team. They were more than colleagues; they were the family he'd chosen, the family he was now neglecting in his singular pursuit.

The call ended, and the silence returned, a deafening

void filled only by the creaks of the building and the low hum of the city beyond his window. Blake realised that the case had become his personal albatross, a weight around his neck that threatened to drag him into an abyss from which there was no return.

In a moment of rare clarity, he understood that this breaking point could either be his end or his salvation. With a heavy sigh, he pushed himself away from the desk, the files, the photographs—all the paraphernalia of the case—and made his way to the station gym.

As he pounded the treadmill, the adrenaline began to flush the fatigue from his limbs. The physical exertion brought a semblance of release, a small crack in the dam of his pent-up frustrations. And with each step, he felt a resolve solidifying within him, not just to catch Morgan, but to do so without sacrificing the man he was, the man he hoped to be once the storm had passed.

The breaking point was a test, a fire through which he must pass to emerge tempered and strong. For Blake, the chase would go on, but now he would run it with a newfound respect for the balance that had eluded him for so long. The obsession would remain, but it would no longer consume him. He would face the darkness, but he would not allow it to extinguish his light.

*

The station was a hive of quiet tension, the air thick with anticipation as Detective Charlie Blake and his team processed the latest piece of the puzzle—a set of cryptic clues left by Alex Morgan. The items were spread out on the evidence table, an enigmatic array, each seemingly disparate and yet undeniably interconnected by the thread of Morgan's dark design.

A series of photographs depicted historical landmarks

throughout the city, each overlaid with strange, arcane symbols. A set of coordinates had been scrawled across an old city map, pinpointing locations that, at first glance, appeared random. However, Blake knew better than to assume anything with Morgan was without purpose.

Elena, with her keen eye for patterns, was the first to speak up. "These aren't just random spots. They align with the historical events of the city—each one marked by some kind of tragedy or turning point."

Blake leaned over the photographs, his finger tracing the lines that connected the symbols to the landmarks. "He's taunting us, leaving breadcrumbs—or perhaps he's constructing a narrative, leading us to the next act of his play."

The cryptic nature of the clues left them with more questions than answers. Was Morgan laying out his plan step by step, or were these merely distractions meant to lead them astray? Every new clue seemed to deepen the enigma, painting a picture of a man whose mind was a labyrinth of complexity and darkness.

A handwritten note was among the items, its script elegant yet chilling in its brevity. *The past is prologue*, it read—a Shakespearean quote that resonated with a haunting significance. Blake felt a chill as he considered the implications. Morgan was a student of history, using the city's past as a canvas for his own twisted narrative.

Sarah Jennings approached, her face a mask of concentration as she pored over the clues. "It's like he's using the city's history as a stage—but to what end?"

Blake stood back, his gaze moving from the table to his team. "We need to think like him, get inside his head. He's left these for a reason. They're not just clues; they're a message."

The team worked into the night, piecing together the puzzle that Morgan had left for them. With each new discovery, the sense of urgency grew. They were not just hunting a criminal; they were delving into the psyche of a man who saw himself as an architect of narratives, with the city as his theatre and its citizens, unwitting actors in his drama.

The clues were cryptic, but the message was becoming clear: Morgan's plan was far from over. He was orchestrating a finale, and if they could not decipher the path he had laid out, the final act would be one of tragedy and bloodshed.

As Blake watched the dawn break over the city, the cryptic clues laid out before him, he knew that the race was on to prevent Morgan from bringing his macabre vision to fruition. The past may be prologue, but Blake was determined that this story would not unfold according to Morgan's script.

*

After days of chasing shadows and grappling with the truth that was as slippery as the darkness, Detective Charlie Blake summoned his team for a late-night gathering in the station's main conference room. The air was thick with tension and anticipation as each member filed in, their faces etched with a blend of determination and fatigue.

Blake stood at the head of the room, his eyes passing over each member of his team, his makeshift family. The recent revelations, the cryptic clues left by Morgan, they all pointed to one thing: the endgame was near, and it was time for a final push against the criminal mastermind's network.

"I know we're tired," Blake began, his voice carrying a

strength that belied the circles beneath his eyes. "We've been pushed to our limits, questioned everything we thought we knew, and we've been left with more questions than answers. But we've also uncovered truths we never expected to find."

He paused, letting his gaze rest on Elena, who had risked everything to bring them closer to Morgan's secrets. On Sarah, whose analytical mind had kept them one step ahead. On Marcus, who had worked tirelessly to piece together the digital puzzle that Morgan had scattered across the city.

"But we've come too far to let fatigue overcome us. Too far to let Morgan's games dismantle what we've built here. Together, we've faced more than just a criminal; we've faced our own doubts, and we've come out stronger for it."

The room was silent, every officer hanging on Blake's words, finding in them a spark to reignite their waning spirits.

"Morgan wants us to think that we're at the end of our rope," Blake continued, his tone hardening. "He's wrong. We're at the beginning of our victory. He's left us clues, breadcrumbs that he believes will lead us to our demise. But what he doesn't realise is that each clue is a step closer to his capture."

Blake reached for a map laid out on the table, its surface a tapestry of their long journey, marked with pins and strings that charted Morgan's movements, the sites of his chaos.

"This is our city," Blake declared, his hand sweeping over the map. "The people out there, living their lives in peace, they depend on us to keep the shadows at bay. We're the only thing standing between them and Morgan's brand of madness."

He looked around the room, meeting the eyes of his team, seeing in them the reflection of his own resolve. "So, we will take everything he's thrown at us, every challenge, every riddle, and we will turn it against him. We will be the storm he never saw coming."

A sense of unity filled the room, a collective strength that surged like a current through each officer. They nodded, ready to stand behind Blake, to follow him into the depths of the night where they would finally confront the chaos that had haunted their city.

"Tonight, we rally," Blake said, his voice rising with a call to arms that resonated in the hearts of his team. "We gather our strength, our courage, and our wits. And we end this. For the city, for the victims, and for ourselves."

The team rose, their chairs scraping against the floor in a chorus of solidarity. As they moved out, their steps were measured, purposeful, the weight of their task heavy but their spirits lifted by the promise of the dawn that would follow the darkest night of their careers.

As Blake stood at the forefront, a leader reborn in the crucible of the chase, his team a phalanx at his back, their eyes on the horizon and the battle that awaited them. The shadows would be chased away, the light of justice would prevail, and their dedication would be the herald of the dawn.

Chapter 18: The Web Widens

Expanding the Hunt

The dim glow of computer screens cast long shadows across the incident room where Detective Charlie Blake and his team delved into the night, unravelling the tangled threads of Alex Morgan's expansive web. The recent breakthroughs had not only shed light on Morgan's machinations but had also unveiled his connections to a criminal underworld far vaster than they had initially grasped.

Blake stood before a digital map pulsating with nodes and links, each representing the myriad ties of Morgan's reach. The network sprawled like a dark constellation across the city and beyond, its points connected by thin lines of illicit transactions, shared resources, and mutual conspiracies.

"This isn't just about Morgan anymore," Blake said, his voice a steady hum that filled the charged silence. "He's not the end; he's the nexus, a central hub in a larger system that feeds off the city's underbelly."

Elena, her eyes bloodshot but sharp, highlighted a series of offshore accounts on the screen. "These are just the financial arteries. There's a whole anatomy to this beast. Front companies, shell corporations, money laundering operations that span across continents."

The enormity of their task loomed over them, a Goliath to their David. But the sling in Blake's hand was his team's unwavering determination to bring justice to the shadows that had long thrived unnoticed.

"We expand the hunt," Blake continued, his gaze sweeping over his team. "We pull at every thread, lean on every informant, and turn every stone until this web unravels."

Sarah Jennings, her fingers flying over her keyboard, intercepted encrypted communications that hinted at the scale of their operation. "There's chatter all over the dark net. Morgan's associates are getting nervous; they're starting to make mistakes."

Marcus chimed in, his voice carrying the weight of resolve. "Let them. Every slip is a foothold for us. We'll use their network against them, turn their secrecy into our weapon."

The night aged as they worked, piecing together the puzzle with each clue they uncovered. It was a tapestry of crime that had insidiously woven its way into the fabric of society, hidden in plain sight yet invisible to the untrained eye.

Blake's hands clenched into fists as he considered their next move. "We're going to need more than just warrants and raids. We need to be as fluid and pervasive as they are."

Elena nodded, her previous forays into the criminal world lending her insight. "We hit them where it hurts. Their operations, their finances, their sense of security. We make it clear that nowhere is safe, no deal is secure, and no secret is kept from the law."

As dawn approached, the team's plan began to take shape, an intricate strategy designed to dismantle Morgan's network piece by piece. It was a campaign that would stretch their resources and test their limits, but the seeds of triumph lay within their grasp.

Blake looked out at the awakening city, its skyline a silhouette against the lightening sky. "This city has been in the dark for too long," he declared, his team's reflection in the window standing with him, a united front against the coming day. "It's time we bring the dawn."

*

Personal Sacrifice

As the hunt expanded, the burden of leadership weighed heavily on Detective Charlie Blake. It was in the quiet of his office, amidst the maps and evidence that littered his desk, that the personal cost of the case became undeniably clear. The lines on his face, once merely a testament to years of service, now told a story of nights spent in the grip of restless thought, the spectre of Alex Morgan always one step ahead.

Blake knew that to dismantle Morgan's network, it would require not just professional dedication but personal sacrifices. He reflected on a conversation he had with Dr Helen Zhao, the team's criminal psychologist.

"You're teetering on the edge, Charlie," Dr Zhao had warned him. "The line between obsession and commitment is a fine one. Make sure you don't cross it."

Her words echoed in his mind as he reached for his phone. With a deep breath, he dialled a number he knew by heart, the one that connected him to his estranged wife, Laura. The call went to voicemail, as he had expected, but this time he left a message.

"Laura, it's Charlie. I... I want you to know that I'm sorry. This case, it's taken more from me, from us, than I ever intended. I've made a decision. I'm stepping back from the field after this is over. For our family, for you. Whatever happens, that's a promise."

The silence of the room settled around him like a shroud as he ended the call. Blake knew that his words were more than a mere apology; they were a commitment to a future he had neglected, a promise to reclaim the life that his work had overshadowed.

The following days were a flurry of activity as the team followed leads and surveilled potential connections within the criminal underworld. Blake, while orchestrating the operation, felt the pull of the promise he made, a promise that was now a beacon in the tumultuous sea of the case.

And then came the moment that tested his resolve. A high-stakes operation was underway, a chance to ensnare key figures in Morgan's network. As the team prepared, Blake handed the reins to Sarah Jennings, his most trusted colleague.

"I'll be in command, but from a distance," Blake said, his eyes meeting hers. "It's time I start keeping my promises, beginning with this one."

Sarah nodded, understanding the weight of what he was entrusting to her. "We'll bring them down, Charlie. You've laid the groundwork. We'll finish it."

As the operation unfolded, Blake watched from the sidelines, his heart racing with every radio transmission that crackled through. The team moved like a well-oiled machine, their precision a reflection of the years of training and leadership he had instilled in them.

The bust was a success, a significant blow to Morgan's operations. As the team celebrated, Blake stood back, a slight smile gracing his lips. He had made a personal sacrifice, stepping back from the action, from the direct line of fire, but in doing so, he had gained something invaluable—a step towards redemption, towards the life he had promised to rebuild.

The case was not over, but as Blake watched his team work, he felt a shift within him. The obsession that had driven him was now tempered with the knowledge that the strength of his team was his legacy, a legacy that would continue to fight the darkness, even as he sought the light of his own path.

*

The conference room was bathed in the blue glow of the projector, casting a ghostly light over Detective Charlie Blake and his team as they delved deeper into the criminal network surrounding Alex Morgan. The walls were lined with photographs, documents, and digital renderings of a vast and insidious empire that sprawled like a dark web through the city's underbelly.

"Each of these threads is a story," Blake began, pointing to a complex diagram of interconnected nodes. "Stories of greed, power, and fear. But also, stories of people—their weaknesses exploited by Morgan and his ilk. To dismantle his network, we must understand the narrative behind it."

Elena, her face set in grim determination, traced a line from one node to another. "These are not just criminals; they're cogs in a larger machine. Each has a role, a function in Morgan's grand design."

The team's collective gaze followed her movements as she highlighted the flows of money, the paths of communication, and the patterns of influence that painted a picture of a network more intricate and entrenched than any they had encountered before.

Sarah Jennings chimed in, her analytical mind dissecting the complex web. "It's like a dark economy, operating on its own set of rules, its own perverse supply and demand. Morgan's not just a kingpin; he's a market maker."

Blake nodded, the realisation sinking in. "Exactly. And we've been too focused on the nodes, on the individual

213

players. It's the connections between them where the real power lies. Break those, and the whole structure begins to crumble."

The room fell into a contemplative silence as the magnitude of their task dawned on them. They were no longer simply pursuing a criminal; they were unravelling an underworld that had, for too long, operated in the shadows.

Marcus, his eyes weary but resolute, broke the silence. "So, we keep pulling on the threads. We find the weak links, the vulnerable points. We turn their secrecy into our weapon."

Elena's voice was low but fierce. "And we use their fear. The same fear they instil in their victims, we instil in them. We show them that no one is untouchable."

The team worked through the night, piecing together the profiles of associates, tracing the flow of illicit funds, and mapping out the hierarchy of the network. With each layer they uncovered, the more formidable the task appeared—yet the more driven they became to see it through.

As dawn broke, casting a soft light through the blinds, Blake stood and addressed his team. "We are on the brink of a breakthrough. The insights we've gained tonight have given us a map through this underworld. We know the players, the places, and now, the patterns. It's time to take this knowledge to the streets, to the courts, and to the people."

The team's response was a unified nod, a silent pact made in the early morning light. They were no longer just hunters; they were warriors stepping into the fray, armed with the knowledge that could topple an empire of darkness.

With a new day came a new resolve. The web had widened, but so had their understanding of it. They were ready to take the fight to Morgan's doorstep, to shine a light into the darkest corners of his world. And as they left the conference room, the maps and charts that adorned the walls stood as testament to their dedication, a promise that justice would find its way through the web, no matter how wide it had become.

*

In the waning light of the operations room, a sense of urgency hung over Detective Charlie Blake and his team. The plan they were about to execute was risky. a dangerous gambit that could either ensnare a significant portion of Morgan's associates or leave them with nothing but the bitter taste of failure.

The large city map on the wall was now marked with a constellation of red dots, each representing a node in Morgan's criminal network. Their strategy was to strike simultaneously, a coordinated series of raids that would leave the network too rattled to regroup quickly.

"Everyone knows their part?" Blake asked, his eyes locking with each member of the team. Assured nods were his answer, the team's confidence in stark contrast to the churning in his gut.

Elena, who had infiltrated the deepest, spoke up. "We're going to hit them where it hurts, but we must remember that they're most dangerous when cornered."

Blake acknowledged her with a grim nod. "We have the element of surprise on our side. We strike fast, hard, and without mercy."

The team dispersed to their designated positions, leaving Blake and Sarah Jennings in the control room, monitoring the operation from a bank of screens. Each screen displayed a different location, a different team lying in wait for the signal.

Sarah looked over to Blake. "You sure about this, Charlie?"

"We're as ready as we'll ever be," Blake replied, though the doubt he felt was a cold hand around his heart.

The clock struck the hour, and Blake gave the command. The screens erupted with activity as the teams moved in. Blake's heartbeat matched the pulsing blue lights of the police vehicles converging on their targets.

Then, the unexpected happened. On one of the screens a group of Morgan's associates was seen escaping through a hidden exit, a contingency they hadn't anticipated.

Cursing under his breath, Blake dispatched additional units to the location, but he knew the crucial moment had passed. The trap had been sprung prematurely, and the prey was slipping through their fingers.

In the aftermath, as the teams reported in, the extent of their success and failure became apparent. They had apprehended several key figures, but the biggest fish had escaped. Blake's dangerous gambit had paid off, but not as well as he had hoped.

Back in the operations room, Blake and Sarah reviewed the operation, the tension between them palpable. "We knew it was a long shot," Sarah said, trying to ease the sting of disappointment.

Blake's eyes never left the screen, where the last of the teams were clearing the scenes. "A long shot, yes, but it was a shot worth taking," he said, his voice firm. "This is a war of attrition, and tonight, we made them bleed."

As the adrenaline faded and the weight of the operation's toll settled in, Blake knew that this was just one battle in a larger war. They had shaken Morgan's network, but the man himself remained at large, his web still wide and dangerous.

But Blake also knew that every victory, no matter how small, brought them closer to the endgame. They would regroup, reassess, and come back stronger. Morgan's days were numbered, and Blake would see to it that justice would be served, no matter the cost.

*

The station was a cauldron of silent tension as Detective Charlie Blake and his team faced the inevitable revelation that one of their own had betrayed them. The traitor's identity had surfaced like a wound revealed—a name that had once commanded respect but now spelled treachery: Marcus Levine.

In the quiet aftermath of the sting operation, Marcus sat across from Blake, the room between them charged with a betrayal that was almost appreciable. The evidence was irrefutable, the trail of deception leading back to the very desk where Marcus had plotted alongside colleagues he had secretly undermined.

"Why?" Blake's voice was a low growl, a mix of hurt and incredulity.

Marcus met Blake's gaze, his eyes a tumult of remorse and defiance. "I believed I was protecting us," he began, his voice a raspy whisper. "Morgan... he threatened my family. I thought I could play both sides, keep everyone safe."

The silence that followed was suffocating, as if the very air had been robbed of trust.

Blake's fist clenched and unclenched as he processed the confession. "You risked everything we've worked for, everything we are. You risked the very lives you swore to protect."

"I know," Marcus uttered, "and I'll spend the rest of my life making amends. But right now, I can help you end this. I have information that can lead us to Morgan, to the heart of his operations."

It was a desperate gambit, a plea for redemption from the depths of dishonour. Blake stood motionless, the lines of his face hardening as he considered the offer.

"Tell me," he said finally, the decision to trust once more a burden heavier than any verdict.

Marcus disclosed locations, names, plans that he had kept from the team, each revelation a thread that could lead them to Morgan's undoing. As the web of betrayal began to unravel, it revealed the possibility of redemption, of a path back to the light.

The team, once fractured by suspicion, found new unity in the face of Marcus's betrayal. They rallied, not with the brittle tension of before, but with the solid resolve of those who had faced their demons and emerged stronger.

Together, they crafted a plan that would use Marcus's inside knowledge to their advantage, setting a trap for Morgan's associates that would draw the elusive mastermind out of the shadows.

As they set the trap, the city held its breath, the night pregnant with the promise of justice or the peril of failure. And in the midst of it all stood Marcus, the betrayer, offering himself as bait for the trap he had helped to design.

The operation was fraught with the chaos of confrontation, the team moving as a singular force against the darkness they sought to vanquish. In the end, it was Marcus's intel that tipped the scales, leading them to a victory that was as cathartic as it was costly.

In the aftermath, as the team gathered in the dim light of the station, the weight of their sacrifice lay heavily upon them. But there, amidst the shadows of their triumph, glimmered a flicker of redemption for the man who had once betrayed them.

Marcus Levine, traitor, had found a way to atone for his sins, his redemption etched in the ledger of justice that Blake and his team had fought so hard to balance. And as dawn approached, the first light of morning casting a soft glow on the city they had sworn to protect, they knew that the web had not only widened but had been woven anew with threads of trust restored.

*

In the quietude that followed the storm of activity, Detective Charlie Blake's team gathered, the air heavy with the aftermath of their recent victory. They had struck a decisive blow against Alex Morgan's network, the culmination of countless hours of surveillance, sacrifice, and tenacity. But the triumph was not without its price.

As Blake surveyed the weary but resolute faces of his team, he acknowledged the cost. "We've achieved something monumental today," he began, his voice carrying the weight of their shared journey. "We've dismantled a significant part of Morgan's network. But our success came at a high price, and it's one we must bear together."

The room was suffused with a sombre reflection as they considered their fallen colleagues—brave souls who had given their all in the name of justice. Blake's eyes momentarily darkened with the pain of loss, a sentiment echoed in the faces around him.

"We honour their sacrifice by continuing the fight," Blake continued, his gaze lifting with a spark of resolve.

"Morgan is reeling from our strikes, but he's not defeated yet. We must remain vigilant, for the web we've uncovered is wider than we ever imagined."

Elena Martinez, who had once again proven her mettle in the field, spoke up, her voice steady despite the shadows beneath her eyes. "There's a glimmer of hope now. People who were once under Morgan's thumb are coming forward, offering information. We're no longer fighting in the dark."

The information they had uncovered in the raid had provided them with new leads, threads that, if followed, could finally lead them to Morgan himself. The criminal underworld was beginning to unravel, the veil of fear lifted by the promise of protection and justice.

Blake nodded at Elena's words, pride and gratitude evident in his expression. "Your courage has given us that hope, Elena. All of you," he said, encompassing the entire team with a sweeping look, "have shown what it means to stand on the side of right, even when the odds are against us."

The team's analyst, Sarah Jennings, brought up the latest data on the screen, lines of communication and financial transactions that they had intercepted. "We're tracking the fallout. Some of Morgan's associates are scrambling, others are in hiding. It's only a matter of time before they lead us to him."

Blake approached the screen, studying the web of data that represented their next steps. "We'll use everything we've learned, every tool at our disposal. This is far from over, but today, we've struck a blow that will echo through the underworld for years to come."

As the team dispersed to their respective tasks, fortified by their leader's words, the station felt like a bastion of hope amidst the chaos that had once threatened to engulf it. They had taken back the night, piece by piece, and now they stood ready to face the new day, not as mere detectives, but as guardians of a city that had placed its trust in them.

Blake sat at the window, looking out over the city he had sworn to protect. The skyline, bathed in the golden hues of dawn, was a reminder of the fragile line between darkness and light. They had paid a significant cost, but the glimmer of hope on the horizon was a testament to their resolve, a beacon guiding them towards the final confrontation that awaited.

Chapter 19: The Calm Before the Storm

Reflection and Regrouping

In the quiet hours of the early morning, Detective Charlie Blake's team gathered in the station's solemn conference room, the walls now a familiar collage of the case that had consumed their lives. The room, once buzzing with the energy of pursuit, was now infused with a reflective stillness as they prepared for what could be their final confrontation with Alex Morgan.

Blake watched as his team, a microcosm of determination and resilience, silently reviewed the case files. The photographs, the maps, the endless notes—they were not just evidence; they were reminders of the journey they had endured, the sacrifices made, the small victories, and the painful setbacks.

"It's been a long road," Blake began, his voice resonating with the gravity of their shared experience. "We've seen the best and the worst of what this city can hide. We've been tested, both as a team and as individuals."

The team members lifted their eyes to meet Blake's steady gaze. Elena, whose role had been pivotal in infiltrating Morgan's network, nodded silently, her expression one of sombre acknowledgment.

Blake continued, his words carefully chosen. "We started as investigators, seeking justice in the wake of chaos. But we've become so much more. Guardians, warriors, and yes, survivors. We've learned that the line between light and dark is thin, and it's our duty to walk it."

Sarah Jennings, her analytical mind always a step

ahead, spoke up. "We've pieced together a puzzle that many would have abandoned, found order in the chaos. It's not just about catching a criminal anymore; it's about healing a city."

The team members exchanged glances, their bonds fortified by the trials they had faced. They were no longer just colleagues; they had become the threads in a tapestry of resilience, woven through the very fabric of their mission.

Marcus, whose betrayal and subsequent redemption had been a crucible for them all, added quietly, "And now, we stand at the precipice of the final act, the culmination of everything we've worked for. We go into this together, with the knowledge that we've done everything we can to prepare."

Blake acknowledged the sentiment with a nod. "Today, we regroup. We reflect not on the fear of what's to come, but on the strength we've gained from what's passed. We rest, we plan, and we focus on the task at hand. Morgan is still out there, but now, he's the one who should be afraid."

As the meeting disbanded, each member took a moment to themselves, collecting their thoughts, steeling their nerves. They had become a phalanx against the darkness, a shield against the encroaching shadows that Morgan had cast over their city.

The calm before the storm was a necessary respite, a time to breathe, to steady their hearts for the tumult to come. And as they left the conference room, the rising sun cast a golden light through the windows, a herald of the dawn that promised an end to the long night of their ordeal.

*

Detective Charlie Blake's hands lay flat on the cool surface of the conference room table; myriad case files before him whispered a silent testament to the arduous journey they had travelled. He lifted his eyes, meeting the gaze of each member of his team in turn. Their faces were a mosaic of resolve and quiet anticipation, united by the journey they had shared and the battle that loomed on the horizon.

Blake cleared his throat, breaking the hush that had settled over the room. "We've been through hell and back," he began, his voice steady and sure. "We've seen the worst of what this city hides in its shadows. We've been tested, bent—but not broken."

He paused, letting his words sink in, allowing the weight of their shared experiences to fill the space between them.

"Morgan has been a spectre haunting us, a constant reminder of the evil that dwells among us. But we've turned every haunt into a lead, every whisper of his presence into a shout in our pursuit," Blake continued, his hands now forming fists, the physical manifestation of his inner resolve.

"This man has taken much from us. From me," Blake admitted, a rare crack in his stoic armour showing through. "But we've gained something invaluable in return. A unity forged in the fires of adversity. And it's that unity that will see us through to the end."

Blake's eyes were fierce now, burning with a renewed determination that seemed to ignite the same fire in the eyes of his team.

"We stand on the precipice of the final confrontation. And I have never been more certain of our victory. Not because we are infallible or invincible—but because we have justice, righteousness, and each other on our side."

Blake straightened, his stature commanding the room with an almost palpable intensity. "I have led you to this point, and I ask you now to stand with me one last time. To face this storm not as subordinates, not as colleagues, but as warriors of light against the encroaching dark."

A murmur of assent rippled through the team, a wave of solidarity that swelled into a tide of collective strength.

"We prepare now, knowing the dangers that await. But we will not waver; we will not falter. We are the beacon that will draw Morgan out, and we will be the storm that eradicates his reign of terror from our city."

Blake's declaration was more than a vow; it was a clarion call that resonated in the hearts of his team, a pledge that bound them to the path ahead, come what may.

The meeting concluded not with the silence that had begun it, but with the sound of chairs pushing back, of determined footsteps, of resolute hearts beating in unison. They left the room not as a group of individuals, but as an unbreakable front, ready to face the calm before the storm that awaited them.

*

In the deep hours of the night, where the shadows were long and the city held its breath, Detective Charlie Blake's team assembled in the solemnity of the Special Operations room. This was the calm before the storm— the final gathering where strategies were honed, and the air was thick with the resolve of warriors on the brink of their defining battle.

The room brimmed with a silent intensity as Blake surveyed his team. Their faces were stoic masks, but their eyes betrayed the adrenaline that thrummed just beneath the surface, the collective heartbeat of a unit ready to face the culmination of their relentless pursuit.

Blake's voice cut through the quiet. "This is the moment we've trained for, the fight we've been gearing up to since the first day Morgan slipped through our fingers. We know the risks, and we know what's at stake." His eyes met each of his team members', a silent acknowledgment of the dangers that lay ahead.

Elena Martinez, standing slightly apart, was a statue of focused energy. She checked her gear one last time, her movements precise, a dance of preparation that she had performed countless times, yet none as critical as this. Blake approached her, his hand resting on her shoulder, the unspoken language of solidarity passing between them.

"We rely on each other out there," Blake said softly. "Watch your corners, keep the lines of communication open, and remember, we do this together."

The team echoed his sentiment, a chorus of muffled affirmations as they checked their weapons, secured their bulletproof vests, and synchronised their communication devices. Each action was charged with the urgency of the impending dawn.

Blake turned to Theo Wallace, the man whose insights into Morgan's network had been a wildcard, now a crucial part of their arsenal. "Your intel has given us the edge we needed," Blake stated, offering a nod of gratitude that was mirrored by a subtle lift of Theo's brow.

The makeshift war room was a hive of activity as maps were consulted, routes were confirmed, and contingencies were set. Marcus Levine, his betrayal and redemption now woven into the team's fabric, worked silently at his station, his focus a razor's edge.

The clock on the wall ticked down the minutes, a relentless march toward the inevitable confrontation. With each passing second, the weight of their shared journey—the losses, the victories, and the haunting spectre of Morgan's game—seemed to press down upon them.

Blake stepped back, allowing his team the space to embrace their individual rituals. Some were silent, others whispered to loved ones, and a few bowed their heads in personal reflection. These were the moments that fortified their souls for the trials to come.

As the first light of dawn began to seep into the room, it cast an ethereal glow over the team, painting them as spectral avengers against the darkness they sought to dispel. It was a fitting tableau for what would come, a testament to their unity and their unwavering commitment to the cause.

The final preparations were complete, and the team stood ready. They were the spear tip of justice, the hope of a city that slumbered in ignorance of the darkness that had almost consumed it. Blake's final words to them were a quiet storm, a promise of the retribution that was to come.

"We go out there as the shield against the coming storm," he said, his gaze fierce. "We go as the bearers of dawn's light. For the city, for the innocents, for us. Let's end this."

The silence that followed was one of understanding, of a shared destiny about to unfold. The team moved out, their steps a collective march into the heart of the storm, the calm now behind them, the tempest ahead.

*

The hushed tone of the operations room was a stark contrast to the high stakes that played out in the field.

Elena Martinez, her recent endeavours as an undercover agent having taken her deep into the underbelly of the city's crime network, was about to reveal the culmination of her dangerous gambit.

As the team gathered around, the air crackled with anticipation. Blake, his features betraying the first signs of hopeful expectation they had seen in weeks, gave Elena a nod to proceed. She connected a secured drive to the main computer, and a series of encrypted files cascaded onto the screen, each one a potential key to unlock the mystery of Morgan's intricate plan.

"This," Elena began, "is the result of every risk, every moment I spent in the shadows. These are Morgan's communications, his transactions. They're coded, but they hold the answers we need."

The team leaned in as the encryption began to unravel under the expert hands of Dan Brooks. Lines of code transformed into messages, numbers into accounts, and aliases into real names. The web they had been tracking now started to reveal its true form—a sprawling and complex network that Morgan had orchestrated with meticulous precision.

Blake's eyes sharpened as he absorbed the information. "This could be it," he murmured. "The breakthrough we've been waiting for."

Elena's gaze met his, a fire of vindication burning in her eyes. "There's more. I was able to track down a meeting, a gathering of the key players in Morgan's network. It's happening soon, and if we play this right, we could take down the entire hierarchy."

The room erupted into a buzz of strategic planning. The team, rejuvenated by the prospect of a definitive end to their long and arduous hunt, was suddenly alive with energy. They pored over the new intel, drawing connections, plotting out the next steps.

Blake stepped back, allowing his team the space to work, but his mind was on Elena. She had walked a razor's edge, danced with danger in its purest form, and had emerged not just unscathed but triumphant.

As the preparations for the impending sting operation went into high gear, Blake pulled Elena aside. "You've done more than we could have ever asked for," he said, his voice laden with a respect that went beyond their professional bond.

Elena's response was tinged with the weariness of the road she had walked. "We do what we must," she said. "Morgan has taken enough from this city, from us. It's time we take back."

They returned to the group, a united front against the darkness they were about to dispel. The team's morale was at an all-time high, their movements precise, each person playing their part with the assurance that came from trust and the promise of impending victory.

As the night wore on and plans solidified into action, Blake knew that this triumph was more than a strategic win; it was a testament to their resilience, to Elena's courage, and to the unyielding spirit of every person in the room. They were more than a team; they were the bearers of hope in a fight that many had deemed hopeless.

*

As the day waned into the early hours of dusk, Detective Charlie Blake sat alone in his office, the walls closing in with every tick of the clock, each sound a harbinger of the impending psychological warfare that awaited. The room was still; the only movement came from the occasional flutter of papers as the ventilation system hummed its monotonous tune.

Blake's hands were clasped tightly in front of him, his knuckles white with the grip of a man holding onto the last vestiges of control. Across from him, the empty chair seemed to take on the form of his adversary, Alex Morgan, invisible yet omnipresent, a ghost in the room.

He had always known that capturing Morgan was as much a mental endeavour as it was physical—a chess game with human lives as the pieces. Now, as the final showdown loomed, Blake felt the weight of every move, every decision, pressing down on him with the gravity of the lives lost and those still at risk.

The phone rang, shattering the silence like a gunshot. Blake's hand was steady as he answered, his voice betraying none of the tumult that raged within. "Blake."

The voice on the other end was distorted, the electronic modulations failing to mask the unmistakable tone of Alex Morgan. "Hello, Detective. I hope you're looking forward to our game's end as much as I am."

Blake's eyes narrowed, his mind racing to place Morgan's location, to catch any background noise that might give away a clue. But there was nothing—just the sterile, cold modulation of a voice masking device.

"Your games are over, Morgan. It's time to face justice," Blake replied, his voice a steel blade cutting through the tension.

Morgan's laugh was a distorted, hollow sound. "Justice? Is that what you call it? We both know this is about more than that. It's about understanding, about seeing the world for what it truly is."

Blake leaned forward, his instinct telling him that this conversation was more than just taunts. It was a window into Morgan's psyche, a chance to understand the man behind the monster.

"You think you have the world figured out, but you're just a man, Morgan. A man who's made some very bad choices."

There was a pause, and when Morgan spoke again, there was something new in his voice—a note of respect, perhaps, or something akin to camaraderie. "We're not so different, you and I. We both want to see the truth come to light. But only one of us will be standing when it does."

The line went dead, leaving Blake in the silence of his office, the psychological battle lines drawn. This conversation was Morgan's way of asserting control, but Blake knew better. He knew that fear was Morgan's weapon, and understanding it was the shield against whatever was to come.

Blake stood, his resolve fortified by the exchange. He had entered the mind of Alex Morgan and emerged unscathed, his path clearer. The psychological game had begun, but he would not play by Morgan's rules. He would end this on his terms, with the truth as his compass.

He left the office, the pieces of the puzzle now forming a clearer picture, the psychological profile of Morgan taking shape. It was a shape Blake intended to shatter, to bring closure to the victims and their families, to a city that had been held in the grip of fear for far too long.

The stage was set, the players in place, and as Blake joined his team, his heart was steady. This was the calm before the storm, but they were the storm, and Morgan was directly in their path.

The fluorescent lights of the incident room hummed a low dirge, a stark contrast to the charged silence that blanketed the room. Detective Charlie Blake's team, a portrait of grim determination, clustered around the central table. They had been through the crucible, their edges sharpened by the ordeal of betrayal and the relentless pursuit of the spectre known as Alex Morgan.

Blake's eyes, once the guiding beacon for his team, now reflected the gravity of what lay ahead. They had uncovered Morgan's patterns, but it was the deviations, the unexpected moves, that had led them here, to the precipice of the final act.

"We've dissected his plans, anticipated his moves," Blake began, the map of the city spread before them dotted with markers. "Now, we set the stage for the final showdown. Morgan's made this personal, and he expects us to crumble. We will not give him that satisfaction."

The team's response was not in words but in the collective tightening of fists and the resolute nods that followed. They had each other's backs, a unity forged in fire, ready to face the tempest Morgan would unleash.

Elena Martinez, fresh from her harrowing encounter, her spirit undimmed, spoke up. "He's been the puppet master, pulling strings from the shadows. It's time we cut those strings."

Blake, bolstered by her tenacity, turned to the map, his finger tracing the routes they had charted, the trap they had meticulously set. "We've identified his likely lair," he declared, "an old theatre in the heart of the city, abandoned and forgotten, much like the victims he chose."

The room shifted as they absorbed the significance.

The theatre was a fitting arena for Morgan's penchant for the dramatic, a place where he had controlled the narrative from behind the curtains.

"Today, we change the script," Blake continued, his tone a resonant command. "We take control of the narrative. This ends on our terms."

Dan Brooks, the young tech genius whose keen eyes had spotted the anomaly that led them to this moment, looked up from his monitors. "All surveillance is in place. He won't see us coming."

The room stirred as the team readied themselves. Vests were strapped, weapons checked, each action a beat in the rhythm of preparation. Blake watched them, pride swelling in his chest for the men and women who stood ready to walk into the storm with him.

The sun had begun to peek over the skyline, casting a golden hue that seemed to light the fire of dawn in their eyes. The city they protected lay out there, a sprawl of steel and stone that held its breath, unaware of the showdown that was to come.

Blake's voice, when he spoke again, was a hushed vow. "This theatre, this stage we set, it will be Morgan's last. We'll draw him out of the shadows and into the light of justice."

As they filed out, the incident room emptied of its occupants but filled with the echoes of their resolve. The theatre awaited them, its archaic majesty a silent witness to the final act that was about to unfold.

Blake was the last to leave, his hand lingering on the map, his eyes tracing the streets that led to the heart of the labyrinth they were about to enter. The trap was set, the players ready, and the storm that had been brewing on the horizon was now upon them.

With a final glance back at the room where plans had been laid and alliances formed, he stepped out to join his team. The city was waking, the calm before the storm now just a memory as they moved into the light of the new day, ready to bring an end to the darkness that had haunted them.

Chapter 20: The Eye of the Storm

The Final Showdown

The skies above were a brooding canvas of greys, mirroring the sombre mood of Detective Charlie Blake as he stood, concealed in the shadows of the derelict warehouse that was to be the stage for the final showdown. The air was thick with tension, an electric prelude to the storm that was about to erupt.

Alex Morgan's taunting messages had led them here, to a place that felt like the heart of the tempest itself. The building loomed large and silent, its walls scarred with the passage of time, a mute witness to the impending clash of wills.

Blake's team was positioned strategically, their presence hidden by the cloak of the building's vastness. Every exit was covered, every potential ambush point secured. The trap was set, but Blake knew that Morgan was no ordinary prey. He was the storm personified: unpredictable and devastating.

As if on cue, a figure emerged from the darkness of the warehouse, the echo of his steps a measured beat in the hush that had fallen over the area. Morgan, clad in his trademark coat, his face a mask of calm that belied the chaos he wrought, stopped at the centre of the open space inside the warehouse.

Blake stepped forward, his own movements deliberate, his senses attuned to every slight sound, every shift in the shadows. This was it—the culmination of months of pursuit, of a game of cat and mouse that had taken its toll on the city and his team.

"Morgan!" Blake's voice, though controlled, carried

the weight of authority and the promise of retribution.

Morgan turned, his eyes finding Blake in the dimness. "Detective Blake," he greeted, his voice smooth, almost affable. "I wondered when we would finally have this conversation."

"It ends tonight, Morgan," Blake stated, his hand resting on his weapon, though he did not draw it. This was not yet a battle of bullets; it was a confrontation of ideals, of justice against anarchy.

Morgan's laugh was soft, a sound that danced with the shadows. "Ends? Oh, Charlie, you see an end where I see evolution. You see justice where I see the game."

The stand-off was material, two forces of nature squared off in the silence that was the eye of the storm. Blake's team awaited his signal, ready to close in. But Blake held them back with a subtle gesture. This encounter was personal, a duel that needed to play out.

"You've caused enough chaos, spilled enough blood. It's over," Blake said, his voice a sharp edge against the softness of Morgan's.

Morgan spread his arms wide, as if to embrace the darkness around them. "Chaos? Blood? They are but the ink with which the stories of civilisations are written, Charlie. I merely chose to be the author rather than a character."

Blake felt the coiled spring of tension tighten. "And how many more chapters do you intend to write with the lives of those I've sworn to protect?"

"For as long as the story demands," Morgan replied, his gaze unwavering.

It was then that Blake realised the truth of the game. Morgan would not be swayed by words or by the threat of capture. He was a man who lived by his own code, a code that was anathema to the order Blake upheld.

With a nod that was almost imperceptible, Blake signalled his team. The final act was set in motion, the storm unleashed as his officers moved in. Morgan stood still, a statue in the eye of the hurricane, as Blake approached, his weapon now drawn.

The clash, when it came, was not of gunfire but of wills, a dance as old as time itself. And as the two men faced each other, the fate of the city hanging in the balance, the storm raged around them, a tempest that would only calm with the conclusion of their deadly waltz.

*

The grim aftermath of the confrontation with Alex Morgan was like the silence after a fusillade; stark, deafening, and laden with sorrow. Detective Charlie Blake's team had made it through the fire, but not unscathed. The warehouse, a tableau of their most desperate battle, was now a mausoleum of their greatest sacrifice.

In the midst of the chaos, they had lost one of their own. Officer James "Jimmy" Bennett, the team's liaison with the city's emergency services, had been caught in the crossfire—a moment that replayed in Blake's mind with cruel clarity. Bennett had been with them since the beginning, his easy smile and unshakeable calm a balm to the frenetic pulse of their operations. Now, his badge lay atop a folded flag on Blake's desk, a stark reminder of the cost of their crusade.

The team gathered, not in the sterile light of the station, but in the dim comfort of a local bar that had become their refuge from the storm of their duties. The clink of glasses punctuated the sombre murmur, a toast to their fallen comrade. Blake looked around at the faces of his team, etched with the pain of loss and the fatigue of battle. Each one carried the weight of the night's events, the shared burden of sacrifice etched into their collective soul.

Sarah Jennings, her analytical mind always seeking the logic in chaos, struggled to make sense of the randomness of Bennett's death. "He was just... it wasn't supposed to..." Her voice trailed off, the words lost in the futility of trying to rationalise the irrational.

Elena Martinez, her arm bandaged from a graze wound, reached across the space between them, her touch a silent solidarity. "We knew the risks," she said, her voice a whisper of steel wrapped in velvet. "But knowing doesn't make it any easier."

Blake's gaze settled on the empty stool at the bar, Bennett's usual spot. The jovial stories and laughter that usually emanated from that corner were now a haunting absence. "He believed in what we were doing," Blake said, his voice steady despite the storm of emotions within. "He believed that we could make a difference. And we will—his sacrifice won't be in vain."

The promise hung in the air, a vow that bound them as tightly as any oath. They were more than a team; they had become a family forged in the fires of adversity. And like any family, they would mourn their loss, remember the joy, and then continue the fight with renewed vigour in honour of the one who had fallen.

As the night drew on and the bar emptied, the team lingered. They shared stories of Bennett, each tale a thread in the tapestry of his memory. Laughter mingled with tears, the catharsis of grief giving way to the resilience of remembrance.

When Blake finally stood to leave, the first light of

dawn was creeping across the sky, painting the world in shades of hope and renewal. The storm had passed, but its echoes would linger in the hearts of those who had weathered it together. They would return to the field, to the hunt, carrying with them the legacy of those who had made the ultimate sacrifice—their loss a constant reminder of the stakes for which they battled every day.

*

The cold light of dawn seeped through the blinds of the operation room as Detective Charlie Blake and his team processed the aftermath of their narrow victory. The room, usually abuzz with the electricity of active pursuit, was now a solemn ground, thick with the weight of reflection.

Morgan's downfall had come at a steep cost. Blake looked around at his team, each member nursing the kind of wounds that were as much mental as they were physical. They had won, yes—but the price paid in blood and tears could never be refunded.

Blake cleared his throat, breaking the silence. "We need to piece together the full extent of Morgan's plans," he said, his voice a firm command that seemed to pull the room back into focus. "Every scrap of data we've collected, every piece of evidence we've secured—it all leads us here, to understanding the why behind his madness."

Elena, still sporting the remnants of her last undercover operation, stepped up to the digital board, her fingers deftly moving through the information. "It's all connected," she began, "the patterns, the victims, the locations. Morgan wasn't just lashing out; he was sending a message with every move."

The team listened, rapt, as the horrifying tapestry of

Alex Morgan's mind was laid bare. His motivations were a dark mirror to their own; where they sought to protect and serve, he sought to punish and enslave. His methods were chaos, but his reasoning was coldly, terrifyingly logical. He was a man who saw the system as a beast, and himself as the hunter necessary to cull the herd.

Marcus Levine, the digital analyst, patched into the database, drawing up myriad hidden accounts, encrypted messages, and dark web activities that Morgan had orchestrated. "He had plans within plans," Marcus said, shaking his head in disbelief. "Even now, we're uncovering layers of contingencies he had in place."

Blake stepped forward, his eyes tracing the web of Morgan's making. The clues they had been chasing were not just breadcrumbs; they were a trail leading to a deeper, more sinister operation than they had imagined. Morgan had been building an army in the shadows, one that was ready to rise at his command.

"His goal wasn't just fear or revenge," Blake concluded, the realisation dawning on him like the morning light. "He wanted to topple the entire system, to watch the world burn and dance in the ashes of the aftermath."

The room was quiet, each member of the team lost in their thoughts, the gravity of what could have been hanging over them like a guillotine blade. They had stopped Morgan, but the echoes of his grand plan would resonate for years to come.

Blake knew that the closure of this case would not bring an end to the threats that lurked in the darkness. But the truth they had unveiled provided not only a grim understanding of the enemy they faced but also a testament to their resilience. They were the thin blue line, and today that line had held.

As the day broke and the city awoke, ignorant of the storm that had just passed, Blake and his team stood as the silent guardians who had weathered the onslaught. They were the ones who stared into the abyss so that others could live in the light. The truth of Alex Morgan was a burden they would carry, a reminder of the cost of vigilance and the price of peace.

*

The ruins of the theatre lay silent, a mausoleum to the night's events, as Detective Charlie Blake and his team gathered amidst the debris. The dust had settled, but the air was still thick with the acrid scent of smoke and the faint echo of chaos. In the grey light of pre-dawn, Blake's team, though battered, stood resolute—the embodiment of the victory they had narrowly secured.

Their target, Alex Morgan, had eluded capture by mere moments, a ghost slipping through the fingers of the law once again. But this time, the chase had yielded something invaluable: evidence. Amidst the shattered glass and twisted metal, they had found Morgan's personal effects, a trove of data drives, and scribbled notes that lay scattered like the puzzle pieces of his twisted psyche.

Blake crouched among the ruins, his fingers brushing over a charred photograph. It was an image of Morgan, younger, unscarred by the deeds that would later define him. The eyes in the photograph stared back with an intensity that Blake felt in his bones—an echo of the man who had become the storm they were chasing.

"Sir?" It was Elena Martinez, her voice cutting through Blake's reverie. She held up a drive, its casing singed but intact. "This could be it—the key to his plans."

Blake's eyes met hers, and in that glance was the exchange of a thousand words. They had come so close to losing everything, their very lives a breath away from being extinguished. But here, in the detritus of their confrontation, lay the seeds of their hard-fought hope.

The team rallied around Blake as he stood, the drive clasped in his hand like a talisman against the darkness they had yet to vanquish. They were wounded, yes, but not in spirit. Their resolve was a tangible thing, a force that the flames could not consume.

"We've taken a hit," Blake admitted, addressing the circle of expectant faces. "But we've also struck back. This"—he raised the drive—"is Morgan's downfall."

The path to victory had been a gauntlet, each step fraught with danger and sacrifice. But as the sky lightened to a pale blue, a symbolic lifting of the night's shadow, Blake felt a stir of triumph amidst the weariness that clung to his limbs.

Their victory was narrow, the cost high, but the war was not over. Blake knew that the fight would go on until Morgan was behind bars, or until the storm he had conjured consumed him.

As the team began to sift through the rubble, their movements methodical and their determination undimmed, Blake allowed himself a moment to watch the sunrise. It was a new day, a new beginning in the aftermath of the night's tempest—a new dawn that promised the end of Alex Morgan's reign of terror.

*

The dust settled slowly after the climactic confrontation, the silence a stark contrast to the chaos that had reigned moments before. Detective Charlie Blake and his team were scattered around the remnants of what had once been Alex Morgan's last stand, each member processing the victory and its cost.

The warehouse, now a scene frozen in the aftermath of the storm, bore the scars of the battle. Evidence markers dotted the landscape, attestation to the final showdown that had taken place. Blake stood amidst the ruin, his heart heavy with the weight of what had transpired.

They had secured their victory, but the cost was written in the faces of his team. Losses had been suffered, sacrifices made that could never be reclaimed. Blake's gaze lingered on the spot where one of their own had made the ultimate sacrifice, a brave act that had turned the tide but had left a void no success could fill.

The team moved with a sombre efficiency, collecting evidence, documenting the scene, but their movements were shadowed by the losses they had endured. Blake felt each loss as if it were his own, a burden he would carry as the leader who had guided them into the eye of the storm.

As the sun began to rise, casting a soft light over the scene, Blake called his team together. They formed a circle, a band of warriors who had faced the darkness together and had emerged—not unscathed, but victorious.

"We did what we set out to do," Blake began, his voice steady but filled with emotion. "We brought down one of the greatest threats this city has ever known. But our victory came at a price, a price paid in blood and sacrifice."

The team bowed their heads, a moment of silence for those they had lost, for the innocence that had been a casualty of their war against Morgan.

"But let this not be in vain," Blake continued, lifting his head to meet the eyes of his team. "Let the sacrifices made be the foundation on which we build a safer future.

Our battle against the darkness does not end with Morgan's fall. It is a fight that continues, a vigil we must maintain."

The aftermath of their confrontation was more than just the physical clean-up of the warehouse. It was the beginning of the healing process, of rebuilding the bonds that had been tested, of honouring the sacrifices by continuing the fight.

Blake knew that the days ahead would be filled with challenges, with the echoes of the battle they had fought. But as he looked around at his team, at the faces of those who had stood by him, he knew they were ready for whatever came next. They were not just a unit; they were a family, forged in the fire of their shared ordeal.

As they left the warehouse, the rising sun a symbol of the new dawn they had fought for, Blake felt a resolve settling over him. The storm had passed, but their duty remained. The city they had sworn to protect would always need its guardians, and Charlie Blake and his team would be there, standing watch at the edge of the storm.

*

The dawn after the tempest found Detective Charlie Blake and his team amidst the ruins of their final confrontation with Alex Morgan. The warehouse, once a labyrinth of Morgan's making, now stood silent, its secrets laid bare in the light of the new day. The city beyond remained unaware of the night's events, of the storm that had raged in the shadows.

Blake stood looking out over the scene, the weight of the night's victories and losses heavy on his shoulders. The battle was over, but the war, he knew, would continue in other forms, other places. Yet, this morning, there was a sense of closure, of a chapter concluded.

"We did it," Blake said, turning to face his team. Their faces, though marked by fatigue and the scars of battle, were alight with the soft glow of triumph. "Morgan's reign is over. His network is dismantling, and the city can breathe easier because of what you've all accomplished."

The team gathered, their unity a testament to the trials they had endured together. They were more than colleagues; they were comrades bound by a shared purpose and the sacrifices they had made.

Sarah Jennings stepped forward, her analytical mind always seeking to understand the broader implications. "What now, Charlie? Morgan was just a part of a larger problem. The underworld he tapped into, the corruption... it's still out there."

Blake nodded, acknowledging the truth in her words. "We keep fighting," he declared. "We've shown that no one is untouchable, not even Alex Morgan. We continue to stand as the barrier between the city and those who seek to harm it."

The conversation turned to those they had lost, the heroes who had made the ultimate sacrifice. Their names were spoken aloud, a roll call of honour that would be remembered not just in medals or commendations, but in the continued dedication of the team to their mission.

As the sun climbed higher, casting a warm light over the weary team, Blake knew that this was not just an end, but a beginning. A new dawn not just for the city they protected, but for each of them personally. They had faced the darkness and emerged not unscathed, but undeterred.

"The work continues," Blake said, his voice firm with resolve. "But today, we take a moment to reflect, to mourn, and to celebrate our victory. Tomorrow, we face whatever comes with the same courage and determination that brought us here."

The team dispersed, some to file reports, others to find solace in the company of loved ones. Blake remained a moment longer, his gaze lingering on the horizon where the light of the new dawn met the shadows of the city.

This was their victory, hard-won and costly, but it was also a promise—a vow to continue the fight, to stand against the tide of darkness with unwavering resolve. As Blake finally turned to join his team, the light of the dawn at his back, he knew that whatever challenges lay ahead, they would face them together, as guardians of the light in the heart of the storm.

Part 3: The Final Act

Chapter 21: The Storm Breaks

Resurgence

The digital clock struck 3 a.m. in the shadow-clad office of Charlie Blake. The world outside lay cloaked in the stillness of the predawn hours, but inside, the soft glow of the computer screen painted Blake's face in hues of blue and white. It was a canvas of concentration, his eyes flickering across streams of data, seeking the aberration in the digital landscape that would lead them to Morgan.

Blake had always possessed an intuition for patterns, an almost preternatural ability to spot the needle in the data haystack. Tonight, that skill bore fruit. A sequence of transactions, a subtle, almost imperceptible anomaly, drew his attention. It didn't belong, a stark deviation from Morgan's modus operandi. He leaned forward, the cogs of his mind whirring, decoding the implications.

"That's it," Blake whispered to the silent room, a triumphant edge to his voice. The breakthrough was more than a lead; it was the thread that, once pulled, would unravel Morgan's entire plan. He reached for his phone, the urgency imbuing his fingers with haste as he typed out a message to his team: *Meeting, 8 a.m. Breakthrough.*

The response was immediate, a series of affirmations from his weary team. Despite the hour, despite the exhaustion that clung to their bones like the city smog, this was the moment they had been chasing. This was the resurgence of their campaign against the shadow that had eluded them for too long.

The dawn was breaking as Blake stepped out of his

building, the first golden rays of sunlight cutting through the retreating night. He could feel the city stirring around him, a sense of kinetic energy that matched the newfound vigour in his veins. Today, they would not chase shadows but become the harbingers of the storm that was set to break upon Morgan's world.

Blake arrived at the station, the early morning bustle already beginning to swell. His team was assembled, the air ripe with anticipation and freshly brewed coffee. He laid out the discovery, the digital breadcrumbs that led to a series of offshore accounts, encrypted messages, and ultimately, to a location that was previously invisible in the maze of Morgan's digital trail.

"It's a front," Mike, the digital forensics expert, concluded, tapping at the keyboard with a renewed fervour. "A business listed under so many shell companies it might as well be a ghost."

"A ghost we're going to chase right out of hiding," Blake declared, his voice the command of a general rallying his troops.

Sarah Jennings leaned over the table, her eyes tracing the web of connections. "Morgan's getting bolder. This hubris could be his downfall."

Blake nodded, his mind already racing ahead. "We need to move fast. He's slipping up, and we have to catch him before he realises it."

The meeting adjourned with a new objective etched into the day's agenda. Blake could sense the shift in the air, the electric charge of the hunt. It was a game of cat and mouse, and they were on the prowl.

As the team dispersed, Blake lingered, his gaze falling upon the cityscape visible from the station windows. Morgan's days of lurking in the shadows were numbered.

The storm was breaking, and justice was the thunder that would follow.

*

The walls of the conference room seemed to pulsate with a newfound energy, each member of the task force carrying the weight of Blake's revelation. They gathered around the scarred oak table, a symbol of their relentless pursuit, its surface a testament to cases past and present. Here, they stood not just as colleagues, but as comrades bound by a shared oath to serve and protect.

Blake watched as his team settled into their seats, the early morning light casting a resolute glow upon their faces. They had all felt the sting of frustration, the nights of dead ends and the bitter taste of elusive justice. But this morning was different: it was a harbinger of change, a promise of a tide turning in their favour.

He caught Elena's gaze across the table, her eyes ablaze with the fire that had first drawn him to recruit her. Undercover work had etched lines of steel into her resolve, and now, it was about to pay dividends.

"We've been chasing phantoms in the fog, but now, we have a chance to bring the fight to Morgan's doorstep," Blake began, his voice a steady timbre that resonated with authority.

Elena nodded, the corners of her lips turning upwards in a fierce smile. "Morgan's been a step ahead, but he left a trail of breadcrumbs this time. We're going to follow it straight to the witch's house." Her metaphor elicited a round of chuckles, breaking the tension that had cocooned the room.

Mike tapped away at his laptop, his fingers a blur. "The digital trail is just the beginning. We need to start thinking like him, anticipating his moves. It's a chess game, and he just put us in check."

"It's time to checkmate," Sarah interjected, her profiler's mind already outlining the psychological profile that would be their map through Morgan's labyrinth.

The room buzzed with strategy, each member contributing pieces to a puzzle that was slowly forming a coherent picture. The unity was palpable, a testament to the countless hours they had spent in each other's company, learning the silent language of glances and half-spoken thoughts.

As plans were laid and roles assigned, Blake felt the invisible threads that tied them together strengthen. This alliance was their armour against the chaos Morgan had sown, and it was impenetrable. They were not just a unit; they were a force, each individual's strength magnified by the trust and camaraderie that united them.

The meeting concluded with a shared sense of purpose, their resolve echoing in the firm handshakes and determined glances. As they filed out of the conference room, Blake stayed back, allowing himself a moment to bask in the quiet confidence that filled the space.

The storm was no longer a distant rumble of thunder; it was here, electric and imminent. They were ready to face it head-on, an alliance strengthened by the fires they had walked through together. Morgan would soon learn that a storm could be both harbinger and harbinger of doom, and they were the tempest he had not anticipated.

*

The glow of early morning sun filtered through the blinds, casting lines of light and shadow across the room where Mike Hanover was already immersed in his work. The digital forensics lab had become his domain, a sanctuary of screens and data where he could listen to the subtle whispers of cyberspace. Today, those whispers had grown into a chorus as he unravelled the digital trail that Blake had uncovered.

The rest of the team had dispersed, each with their own piece of the puzzle to solve, but Mike remained, the keystrokes his steady drumbeat against the quiet of the room. He'd been working on Morgan's encryption for weeks, a maddening dance of algorithms and dead ends. Yet, as he sifted through the data, a pattern began to emerge, a consistent anomaly in the code that he hadn't noticed before. It was the breakthrough they needed.

"Got you," Mike muttered under his breath, his fingers moving with renewed purpose. Morgan's digital trail had always been a labyrinth of complexity, but this... this was the thread that could lead them out of the maze.

The digital breadcrumbs led to an encrypted server hidden behind layers of security that would take a normal person months to penetrate. But Mike wasn't normal; he was a digital savant, and as he deployed a series of custom scripts, the walls protecting Morgan's secrets began to crumble.

Hours passed, the sun climbed higher, and the lab's air grew thick with tension. Mike's focus was absolute, the world reduced to the screens before him and the puzzle they contained. Then, with a final stroke, he was in. The server's contents spilled out before him, a treasure trove of data that Morgan had never intended for them to see.

Mike's heart raced as he navigated the files, his eyes scanning rapidly. Financial records, communication logs, plans for operations yet to unfold—it was all there. But one document caught his eye, a file simply labelled *Phoenix*. He opened it, and, as the words came into focus, he realised they had underestimated the scope of

Morgan's vision. This wasn't just about the crimes they'd been investigating; it was bigger—a plan years in the making.

The sound of the lab door opening pulled Mike from his reverie. It was Blake, his face expectant, a silent question hanging in the air.

"We've got him," Mike said, unable to keep the triumph from his voice. "We've got everything."

Blake approached, his gaze falling upon the screen. As Mike explained what he'd found, Blake's expression shifted from anticipation to awe. They had known that Morgan was planning something monumental, but this... this was a revelation.

"This changes everything," Blake said, the weight of the discovery evident in his voice. "We need to act fast."

Mike nodded, already compiling the data they needed. "I'll get everything to the team. We'll need everyone on this."

As Blake left to coordinate their next move, Mike couldn't shake the feeling that they had just uncovered the tip of an iceberg. Morgan's plan was vast, and they were only just beginning to understand its true scale.

The document titled *Phoenix* hinted at a resurgence, a rebirth from the ashes of the chaos Morgan aimed to unleash. It was a plan designed to be untraceable, unassailable, and unstoppable. But with this breakthrough, Mike had done the impossible: he had given the team a fighting chance.

The room was silent now, save for the hum of machines and the quiet tapping of Mike's keyboard as he sent the data to his colleagues. The storm Blake had spoken of was indeed upon them, but they were no longer floundering in the darkness. They had a beacon, and its light was cast from the depths of Morgan's own machinations.

Mike leaned back, allowing himself a rare moment of stillness. The code had been deciphered, the veil lifted. Now it was up to them to use this knowledge, to turn the tide in a battle that had just become their own to lose.

*

Elena Martinez's heart thudded in her chest, a rhythmic echo to the steady click of her heels as she navigated the labyrinthine corridors of Morgan's headquarters. Her role was a chameleon, a master of disguises, and now she wore the mask of confidence, an employee among sharks. The hidden recorder pressed against her skin was a comforting weight; it was proof that she wasn't alone in this den of iniquity.

The deeper she delved into the belly of the beast, the more the air seemed to grow colder, the walls whispering secrets of the deals made in the dark, of lives bartered for power. She could almost feel the ghostly fingerprints of Morgan's elusive presence, his influence a tangible force that permeated the very fabric of the building.

Turning a corner, she entered what was known as 'The Hub', a nerve centre where Morgan's acolytes conducted their dubious affairs. Computers beeped and phones rang in a symphony of subterfuge, while screens displayed a kaleidoscope of surveillance feeds. Elena's gaze was drawn to a flurry of activity at one of the terminals. A group huddled around, their focus absolute, their hushed tones slicing through the hum of technology.

She edged closer, the pretence of checking a nearby printer cloaking her true intent. The fragments of conversation she caught were laced with urgency.

"...secured the shipment," one murmured, the words

heavy with meaning.

"It's the last piece," another replied, a note of triumph barely contained.

Elena's pulse quickened. This was it, the pivot she had been searching for, a lead that could unravel the threads of Morgan's plan. She committed every face to memory, knowing that soon she would be pouring over the footage, identifying each player in this deadly game.

A sudden silence fell upon the group, and Elena's instincts screamed a warning. She feigned a yawn, turning away nonchalantly, but not before she caught the icy stare of a man whose eyes had lingered on her just a second too long. The hairs on the back of her neck stood on end; the predator had sensed an anomaly in his midst.

She needed an exit strategy, now.

With casual grace, she left the room, her mind racing. The elevator would be too obvious, the stairs too exposed. Her training took over, guiding her to an unassuming door marked *Maintenance*. Inside, the claustrophobic embrace of a service corridor offered a concealed route, a passage woven into the building's skeleton.

As she moved through the dimly lit space, Elena allowed herself a moment to breathe. The information she had gathered was vital, a key to unlock the enigma of Morgan's operation. But more than that, she had confirmed the existence of a shipment that could provide the leverage they needed to topple his empire.

Reaching the endpoint of her clandestine journey, she stepped out into the daylight, the mask of anonymity back in place. Elena knew that the real work would begin now, as they deciphered the clues she had risked everything to obtain. The lion's den had not been kind, but she had emerged not as prey, but as the huntress.

With a determined stride, she headed back to the task force, her mind already weaving the fabric of their next move. Morgan's hubris had led him to believe he was invincible, but he hadn't counted on the tenacity of a team led by Charlie Blake, nor the silent threat of Elena Martinez, the woman who walked through the shadows with eyes wide open.

*

Back at the station, the air was charged with a kinetic energy that seemed to buzz through the very walls. Blake's team, now scattered across different rooms, were each engrossed in their tasks, yet united by a shared pulse of anticipation. The breakthroughs had been coming in waves, but it was the latest find that could signify a turning point.

In the evidence room, the sound of shuffling papers and clicking keyboards provided a steady backdrop as Detective Sarah Jennings laid out the newly unearthed financial records. The numbers and transfers painted a stark picture of Morgan's operation—both its scale and its potential vulnerabilities.

"These transactions," Sarah began, her finger tracing the lines of figures on the screen, "they're repetitive, cyclic. It's a pattern. Morgan is meticulous, but even he can't cover every trace."

Blake leaned in, his eyes narrowing as he followed her explanation. The numbers indeed told a story, one of a vast network of resources being funnelled towards a singular, unknown point.

"Could this be related to the 'Phoenix' file Mike found?" Blake pondered, the gears in his mind turning.

"It's more than related," Sarah affirmed. "It's the blueprint of Morgan's resurgence. He's been moving assets, consolidating power, all for whatever this 'Phoenix' is meant to be."

The room grew silent as the gravity of the discovery settled over them. Blake's team had been chasing the wake of Morgan's chaos, but now they had a chance to pre-empt his next move.

"It's not just a blueprint," a new voice chimed in. Dan Brooks, stepped into the light with a sheaf of papers in hand. "I cross-referenced the financial data with the digital breadcrumbs Mike pieced together. There's a convergence happening in real time. Money, digital traffic, personnel—all pointing to one place."

Blake's eyes lit up with a fusion of adrenaline and resolve. "That's our target," he said, his voice steady with the promise of action. "We need to move, and fast. Morgan's 'Phoenix' is about to rise, and we're going to be there to clip its wings."

As the team mobilised, there was a palpable shift in the atmosphere. It was the kind of moment that every law enforcement officer trains for, a culmination of investigation and instinct. The turn of the tide wasn't just in the evidence they had uncovered; it was in their step, their gaze, their unified purpose.

The operations room became a hive of activity, each member of the team a vital component in a larger organism that was now poised to strike. Blake's voice cut through the din, clear and commanding. "Positions, people. We're going to hit Morgan with everything we've got."

The plan was set into motion with the precision of a well-oiled machine. Surveillance teams were dispatched, tactical units briefed, and every available resource was directed towards the culmination of their investigation.

The storm that had been building was about to break, and it was their hands on the lightning rod.

As Blake watched his team spring into action, the tension that had been his constant companion began to morph into something else: hope. They were no longer chasing the storm; they were summoning it, directing its fury, its potential for cleansing. And at the heart of the tempest, they would find Morgan, the eye of the chaos, now vulnerable to the winds of justice they were about to unleash.

As Blake looked out over the city from his office window, the sky now painted with the hues of dawn. The promise of light on the horizon was not just a new day, but the dawn of retribution. The tide had turned, and it was their currents that would now reshape the landscape of the city they vowed to protect.

*

Blake's office was a fortress of solitude as he sat, ensconced behind mountains of files and screens displaying constellations of crime scene photos and maps. The faint buzz of fluorescent lighting above was the only sound, a monotonous hum that had become the soundtrack to their countless hours of strategizing and analysing. He leaned back in his chair, the creak of the leather a stark contrast to the stillness, and closed his eyes. The room faded away, and he allowed himself to listen to the intuition that had so often been his compass in the murky waters of criminal investigation.

The pieces were all there, laid bare in front of him. Mike's digital foray had unearthed the 'Phoenix' file, Elena had infiltrated the very heart of the beast, and the financial trails had converged on a singular, ominous point. Yet, there was something more, a niggling at the edge of his consciousness, a premonition that told him they were on the precipice of something far greater than they had anticipated.

His phone vibrated, snapping him back to reality. The message was brief: *Something's off. Meet me.* It was from Elena, her words echoing the disquiet in Blake's gut.

Gathering his team, he relayed his intuition. "We're not waiting for the next move. We make it," he announced, his voice a blade cutting through the tension. "Elena has a hunch, and it's time we trust the instincts that have gotten us this far."

The team was an embodiment of controlled urgency, each member moving with purpose. Blake's premonition had now become a shared sentiment, a collective sixth sense that had each of them glancing over their shoulders, anticipating the storm that was to come.

They convened in the incident room, the epicentre of their operation. Elena stepped in, her presence commanding attention. "The Hub's activity has spiked," she reported, her voice laced with gravity. "I have a source who confirms Morgan is accelerating his timeline. Whatever 'Phoenix' is, it's happening soon."

Blake's eyes swept over his team, their faces a mosaic of resolve and relentless determination. "We strike tonight," he declared. "We use the cover of darkness, not just as concealment, but as an ally. Morgan thinks he's the night's master, but we are going to turn his world upside down."

The room erupted into a flurry of activity. Dan and Sarah dove back into the financial records, seeking any last scrap of insight. Mike's fingers danced across his keyboard as he synchronised with law enforcement databases, pulling up real-time feeds, and tapping into city surveillance systems.

In this orchestra of anticipation, Blake was the conductor, his team the players, each note of their movement building towards the crescendo that would be Morgan's undoing.

The premonitions Blake felt were not of dread, but of the approaching justice. They were the harbingers of a storm that had been brewing since the first day Morgan decided to play God with the lives of the innocent. Now, the reckoning was upon them, the prelude to the final act.

As the night embraced the city, the task force moved out, shadows among shadows. They were the silent tempest, the embodiment of the storm Blake had promised. This was their city, their fight, and the darkness that had once been their adversary now bore witness to the unity and might of those sworn to dispel it.

Blake stood by the armoured vehicle, his gaze fixed on the building that housed the heart of Morgan's operation. The premonitions had led them here, to this moment where every second was a step closer to the confrontation they had all been waiting for. The rain began to fall, a gentle patter that soon grew into a torrential downpour, the heavens opening to wash away the grime of the pursuit.

"Let's end this," Blake whispered, almost inaudibly, as he gave the signal to advance. The storm had broken, and they were its fury.

Chapter 22: The Heart of Darkness

Descent into Madness

The storm had passed, leaving the city with the hush of a world washed clean. But beneath the surface, the waters of chaos churned, driven by the machinations of a man who had long since abandoned the shores of sanity. Morgan's madness was not the kind born of frenzied delusion but a meticulous, methodical descent into a darkness of his own design.

Blake sat in the quiet aftermath, poring over the 'Phoenix' file, its contents displayed across the screen. It was more than evidence; it was a window into the soul of a madman. The plans, the contingencies, the sheer breadth of Morgan's vision were laid bare, each more diabolical than the last. The deeper Blake delved, the more the grim realisation settled upon him—Morgan's psyche was a labyrinth with no exit, every turn a reflection of his twisted convictions.

Across the city, in a nondescript building that seemed to swallow light whole, Morgan paced in his study, the darkness around him a mere echo of the void within. The screens that lined his walls were a mosaic of surveillance, each feed a string in the web he had woven through the underbelly of the metropolis.

He stopped before a canvas, an expansive piece that dominated the room. It was a chaotic swirl of colour, a storm captured in oil and pigment. This was the eye of his tempest, the heart of his darkness. To any other, it was an abstract piece—but to Morgan, it was a map, a blueprint of the chaos he would unleash.

His hand reached out, fingers tracing the lines that

only he could see, the paths of destruction that would culminate in his 'Phoenix' rising. The city that had once been his playground would become the stage for his final act, a descent not into madness, but into legend.

Blake's team gathered, the 'Phoenix' file open before them, the silence a heavy shroud. They each understood the task that lay ahead, the descent they must undertake to bring an end to Morgan's dark dream. The madness on display was not just a man's mind unravelling, it was a calculated plunge into an abyss that threatened to consume all it touched.

"It's not just about stopping a criminal," Blake said, breaking the silence. "It's about pulling someone back from the edge of an abyss so deep, it has its own gravity."

The team nodded, their faces set in grim determination. They were not just law enforcers; they were the keepers of sanity in a world that Morgan sought to drown in darkness.

As they left the room, each sensed the gravity of the journey they were about to embark upon. To stop Morgan, they would need to understand him, to walk the razor's edge between order and the madness he had succumbed to. The descent would be perilous, but they were resolved. For in the heart of darkness, it was not the light that would guide them, but their unwavering resolve to end the nightmare that Morgan had conceived.

*

In the quiet of the task force's office, the storm's aftermath lingered not in the skies but in the minds of Blake's team. Each member found themselves at a crossroads, the case's unyielding pressure fracturing the facade of professional detachment to reveal the personal demons they fought alongside the real ones.

Detective Sarah Jennings sat at her desk, the flicker of

her computer screen illuminating the conflicted contours of her face. The reflection staring back at her from the darkened window was a woman changed by the hunt for Morgan, her once unshakeable composure now punctuated with the fatigue of sleepless nights and the gravity of too many lost.

Next to her, Mike Hanover scrolled through lines of code, each string a reminder of the digital battleground where he had chased Morgan's ghost. The glow of the monitor cast shadows over his features, giving him the appearance of a man split between the light of his convictions and the darkness of the cyber realm he navigated.

Across the room, Elena Martinez trained her gaze on the wall of evidence, each photograph a milestone in their descent into the heart of Morgan's darkness. She could feel the responsibility of her undercover work clinging to her like a second skin, the lines between her true self and the personas she had adopted blurring dangerously.

Dan Brooks, the financial analyst, sat with his head in his hands, the enormity of Morgan's network sprawled out before him in a web of transactions and transfers. The numbers that had once made sense now danced mockingly before his eyes, a reminder of the chaos that lay just beneath the surface of the city's veneer.

The silence was finally broken by Blake's voice, resonant and resolute. "We all joined this force to make a difference, to chase down the shadows and stand up to the monsters," he began, his reflection a steadfast anchor amidst the sea of doubt. "But sometimes, it's about facing the ones within us: the doubts, the fears, the fatigue. That's what makes us human, and that's what gives us the edge. Morgan may not be bound by conscience, but we *are*—and that's our strength."

The team lifted their heads, drawn to Blake's conviction. His words, a beacon in the dark waters they navigated, brought a sense of unity, of shared purpose. The fractured reflections began to coalesce, forming not just images of wearied detectives but of warriors steeled for the battles ahead.

"We've come too far to let the darkness win," Blake continued, his eyes meeting those of his team. "We face our demons, we embrace them, and then we use them to drive us forward. Morgan is counting on us to crumble, to falter. We will not give him that satisfaction."

The room came alive with a renewed sense of determination, the shadows of doubt retreating to the corners where they belonged. The reflections that stared back from the darkened glass no longer appeared fractured but whole, the visages of a team bound by more than duty—bound by the shared scars of a journey through the night.

As they turned back to the evidence, to the screens and papers that held the keys to unlocking Morgan's endgame, they did so not as fragmented individuals but as a collective force. The reflections of their journey, however fractured, had forged them into something formidable, something unbreakable.

With the echoes of Blake's words uniting them, the team set back to work, the reflections of their past hardships a mosaic of motivation. They were the light in the heart of darkness, and together they would see the dawn.

*

The night air was fraught with tension as Blake's team donned their tactical gear, each piece a familiar weight against the backdrop of pounding hearts and steady breaths. The industrial site loomed ahead, a dark silhouette against the city skyline, an edifice of Morgan's empire and the stage for their direct assault.

"This is the gauntlet," Blake said to his team, his voice cutting through the static of radio checks and last-minute equipment inspections. "We run this, we take down a cornerstone of Morgan's operations."

Elena, clad in Kevlar and determination, checked her firearm, her mind a tapestry of the undercover work that had led them here. The infiltration had provided them with blueprints, guard rotations, and, most crucially, Morgan's reliance on this nerve centre.

Mike was a step away, his laptop open, the glow of the screen casting an ethereal light on his focused expression. "All surveillance systems have been looped. We've got a window, but it won't stay open for long," he informed, tapping a final command into the keyboard.

The team assembled, a phalanx of resolve, as Blake reviewed the plan. "Elena and Dan, you take point. Sarah, you're with me. Mike, you cover our tech flank. We move in two waves. The first disables their comms, the second secures the site. We do this by the numbers."

Nods were exchanged, a silent language of shared history and unified intent. They moved out, a shadow against shadows, the site growing ever larger as they approached.

The first sign of resistance was a barely perceptible shift in the night's chorus, a whisper of motion. But it was enough. The team sprang into action, each movement choreographed by countless drills and an intimate knowledge of each other's tactics. The guards were neutralised swiftly, efficiently, with a professionalism that was the hallmark of Blake's unit.

They breached the perimeter, a breach into the depths of Morgan's labyrinth. The corridors echoed with the sound of their advance, a symphony of purpose amidst the silence of potential traps and lurking dangers.

The central hub was a cavern of activity, screens and equipment casting a kaleidoscope of light across the faces of Morgan's operators, now stunned into inaction by the intrusion. Blake's team worked with surgical precision, dismantling the web of surveillance and control that Morgan wielded like a weapon.

A shout rang out, the first real sign of organised resistance, but it was met with the unwavering force of the task force. Blake found himself at the forefront, exchanging gunfire with the shadows that defended Morgan's dark vision. Each shot, each command he issued, was a defiance of the madness they sought to end.

The skirmish was brutal but brief. The team's preparation and unity overcame the chaos, a testament to their training and resolve. As the last of Morgan's men were secured, and the site was declared clear, Blake allowed himself a moment to survey the conquered hub.

They had run the gauntlet and emerged victorious, but the cost was etched on the faces of his team. This victory was not without sacrifice, a prelude to the final confrontation they all knew was still to come.

"We hold here," Blake commanded, his gaze sweeping over his team. "We've struck a blow, but the fight isn't over. Morgan is still out there, and we will be the ones to end his reign. For now, we fortify and prepare. The storm isn't over, but we are its eye."

As the team set to work securing the site, the weight of their task, the gauntlet they had just run, was palpable.

But so too was their resolve, hardened in the crucible of battle, ready for the storm that awaited.

*

The sombre mood at the station was a stark contrast to the flurry of activity that had defined the previous hours. As Blake's team regrouped, the weight of their recent victory was tempered by the cost it had exacted. The hollow echo of a hero's footsteps resonated through the halls, a reminder of the sacrifice made.

Detective Dan Brooks sat in the corner of the room, his normally stoic demeanour giving way to a rare display of emotion. He had taken a calculated risk during the assault, drawing the enemy's fire to allow his teammates to secure the objective. The bullet had found its mark, and though it had not been fatal, the close call had left an indelible mark on him and the team.

Blake stood before his team, his eyes surveying the faces of those who had become more than colleagues—they were a fellowship forged in the fires of shared trials. "We knew the risks when we took this on," he began, his voice steady despite the storm of emotions within. "Dan's bravery today is the kind that doesn't get medals or parades, but it's the kind that keeps this city safe."

Sarah Jennings approached Dan, placing a hand on his shoulder with a nod of gratitude and respect. "You did good, Dan. You gave us the edge we needed." Her voice was a low murmur, but it carried the weight of the team's collective sentiment.

Elena, still clad in her tactical vest, her expression sombre, spoke up. "We've come far, seen too much. But it's the sacrifices we're willing to make that bind us, that give us the resolve to see this through."

Blake turned his gaze to the window, watching the city

lights flicker against the night sky. "Morgan is still out there, and he'll be reeling from this loss. We've struck at the heart of his operation, but the beast isn't dead yet."

The team's resolve had been cemented by Dan's sacrifice, their purpose clear. They would bring an end to Morgan's reign of darkness, not for glory or accolades but because it was the fight worth fighting, the cause worth bleeding for.

As the team disbanded to rest and recuperate for the battles ahead, Blake lingered in the room, his thoughts with the wounded and the weary. The heart of darkness that was Morgan's legacy would be confronted, and in the end it would be their unwavering resolve that would shine the brightest.

"Rest up," Blake finally said, his words directed at those departing and those who remained, vigilant and steadfast. "Tomorrow, we end this, once and for all."

The station grew quiet as the team members found solace in their own ways, some in the company of family, others in the solitude of their thoughts. But the silence was not empty—it was full of the promise of justice, the vow of peace restored, and the honour of sacrifices not in vain.

As Blake turned off the last light, the shadows of the office seemed to retreat, as if in deference to the resolve that had been strengthened within its walls. The darkness outside was not daunting—it was a canvas, and they were the artists who would redraw the lines between light and shadow.

*

The hushed sounds of the city night provided a stark canvas as Elena Martinez made her way toward the epicentre of Morgan's web. The intel gleaned from their recent victory had provided them with the key they needed—an introduction to Morgan's inner circle.

Elena slipped into the role they had carefully crafted for her: a disillusioned law enforcement officer seeking a new master. It was a guise that felt uncomfortably close to the bone, reflecting the darkness she'd witnessed these past months, but it was her conduit into Morgan's world.

The meeting place was an old theatre, its grandeur faded to a mere whisper of what it once was. Here, the remnants of Morgan's elite gathered, cloaked in the anonymity that the night afforded. Elena felt the eyes upon her as she entered, the burden of their scrutiny like hands upon her skin. Yet, she walked with purpose, her demeanour calm, betraying none of the tension that coiled within her.

As she was ushered through the corridors, lined with cracked plaster and the ghosts of performances past, she could hear the low hum of conversation from the main hall. The air was thick with the smell of old wood and older secrets. This was the sanctuary of Morgan's most trusted, and as she stepped into the light, she met the gazes of those who held the strings to the city's underworld.

The man at the centre of the room was a figure she knew only from fleeting glances and the edges of overheard conversations. He was the gatekeeper, the one who would decide if she was worthy to be brought into the fold. His eyes locked onto hers, a silent challenge issued and accepted.

"What brings you to our gathering?" His voice was smooth, like velvet draped over the rough edges of suspicion.

Elena's response was measured, her fabricated story

woven with enough threads of truth to be convincing. "I'm tired of the fight on the losing side. I want to be where the real power lies."

There was a moment of silence as her words hung in the air, the tension rising like a tide. Then, the gatekeeper smiled, a serpent baring its fangs, and the room relaxed into murmurs of approval. She was in.

Over the next hour, Elena listened and observed as Morgan's inner circle spoke of logistics and influence, of pieces moved on the city's chessboard. Each revelation was a piece of the puzzle, and she committed it all to memory, knowing that the information was a lifeline to her team and their mission.

As the meeting came to an end, Elena made her exit, her mind racing with the details she needed to convey. Morgan's network was vast and tangled, but now they had a map—and with it, the means to unravel his empire from within.

Outside, the night had relinquished its hold to the first light of dawn. Elena felt the weight of the recorder against her skin, the conversations it held a testament to her success. But more than that, it was proof of the trust she had earned, a trust she would betray for the greater good.

She made her way back through the sleeping city, her shadow long in the morning light. Today, they infiltrated the heart of Morgan's inner circle. Tomorrow, they would use what she had learned to bring his kingdom of shadows to ruin.

*

The air was still in the task force's command centre, the tension like a silent drum roll before the crescendo. Detective Charlie Blake and his team were gathered around the table that had become their altar of strategy, the surface littered with maps, photographs, and reports. They were the sentinels on the precipice of battle, the quiet force before the storm that would envelop them all.

"Tonight, we have the chance to end this," Blake stated, his eyes locking with each member of his team. "We know Morgan's next move, thanks to Elena. We've seen into the heart of his darkness, and now we're going to use that knowledge to shine a light so bright it'll burn it all to the ground."

Elena stood by the window, the light casting her shadow long and resolute across the room. Her infiltration into Morgan's inner circle had been the turning point, and now the team was poised to strike with the precision of a surgeon's blade. "His network is expecting to rise from the ashes," she said, her voice a harbinger of the storm to come. "But we're going to ensure it's consumed by the very fire they sought to control."

The team moved through their final preparations with a calm efficiency. Weapons were checked and rechecked, bulletproof vests strapped on with the finality of armour donned for an ancient battle. Mike Hanover's fingers flew across his keyboard one last time, ensuring their communication lines were secure and their digital eyes were open and watching.

Sarah Jennings, the profiler who had delved into the abyss of Morgan's mind, stood beside Blake. Her insight had often been the compass that guided them through the twisted psyche they were up against. "Remember, Morgan thrives in the chaos he creates," she reminded them. "Stay focused, stay together, and remember who we are and what we stand for."

Blake nodded, the weight of command settling on his

shoulders like a mantle. He looked over the team, a mosaic of determination and duty. "We are the storm he never saw coming," Blake said, his voice low but filled with the thunder of their collective resolve. "We are the ones who stand in defence of those who can't defend themselves. Tonight, we bring an end to the fear he's spread through our city."

The room's atmosphere was an alchemy of fear, anticipation, and courage as the team shared silent nods of understanding, the kind that needed no words, forged in the fires of trials overcome together.

Blake stepped toward the door, pausing to glance back at the tableau of his team, a tableau of warriors in the calm before the storm. "Let's bring the thunder," he said. And with that, they moved out, leaving the silence of the room behind for the chaos that awaited them.

The city was quiet, the deceptive peace before the deluge, the streets unaware of the reckoning that was to approach with the dawn. As they moved towards their vehicles, the first drops of rain began to fall, a soft whisper that heralded the tempest to come.

Chapter 23: Shadows and Light

Final Preparations

In the grey light of predawn, the command centre was alive with the quiet buzz of focused energy. Detective Charlie Blake's team moved with a precision that spoke of the countless hours they had dedicated to this moment, the final act in their pursuit of Morgan. The room was a chessboard, and they were the pieces poised for the endgame.

Blake oversaw the final preparations, his eyes tracing over the maps and photographs that told the story of their long campaign. Each member of his team was a specialist, a unique set of skills that, when combined, formed the perfect machine for justice.

Elena Martinez was double-checking her equipment, the lines of her face set in a mask of calm determination. Her role had been critical in uncovering the depths of Morgan's network, and now she would be instrumental in bringing the man himself to light.

Mike Hanover was at his station, his fingers dancing across the keys with an intensity that matched the stakes of their endeavour. He was their eyes and ears in the digital world, ensuring that Morgan's technological web would not ensnare them as they made their final move.

Sarah Jennings was with Blake, her insights into the criminal mind of their quarry more important than ever. They were not just hunting a man; they were dismantling an ideology, a perverse vision that had bled into the city's veins.

The final piece was Dan Brooks, now recovered from his earlier brush with mortality. He was the backbone, the steady hand that had guided them through the financial maze that was Morgan's empire.

Blake gathered them, his gaze sweeping over the team, his voice a low rumble of command. "This is it. Everything we've worked for comes down to today. We know Morgan's patterns, his weaknesses. We've dismantled his network, and now we take him down."

He laid out the plan with meticulous detail, each phase interlocking with the next. The capture of Morgan would be the culmination of all they had sacrificed, all they had learned. It was a tapestry of strategy and skill, woven with the threads of their collective resolve.

"We move out in two hours," Blake concluded, the finality of the statement hanging in the air. "Check your gear, run through the plan. When we next step foot in this room, it will be with Morgan in custody."

The team dispersed to make their final preparations, the air around them charged with the gravity of their task. As they checked their weapons and communications equipment, there was a sense of unity that transcended the words of any pep talk.

This was more than a mission; it was the culmination of a journey that had taken them to the edge of their own darkness, only to find the light that lay beyond. They were the barrier against the night, the guardians who would bring the dawn.

As they donned their bulletproof vests and loaded their firearms, each member of the team felt the weight of the approaching confrontation. They were ready, not just in body and mind, but in spirit. The shadows that Morgan had cast over the city would soon be dispelled, and they would be the ones to usher in the light.

*

The stage was set, and the team was ready. Detective Charlie Blake, however, knew that capturing Morgan was not just a matter of strategy and manpower; it was also a psychological battle, a war of the mind where the winner would be determined by wit as much as by force.

In the dim light of his office, Blake reviewed the file that laid bare Morgan's psyche, a complex tapestry of intelligence, ruthlessness, and a deeply ingrained need for control. To shake Morgan, to truly unsettle him, Blake would have to strike at the heart of what Morgan held dearest—his sense of superiority and invincibility.

"Mike, are we ready?" Blake's voice cut through the quiet.

Mike nodded, a headset in place, fingers poised above his keyboard. "The broadcast is set. On your word."

Blake gave a curt nod, his gaze hard as flint. "Do it."

The screen flickered to life, and the face of Charlie Blake filled every monitor in the room, and—more importantly—it infiltrated the screens across the city, hijacking the airwaves, usurping the digital throne Morgan had built for himself.

"Citizens of our city," Blake began, his voice a calm, resonant force, "you have been living in the shadow of a man who believes himself to be a puppeteer, a man who thinks he can control the very threads of our society. But he is mistaken."

Blake's eyes seemed to pierce through the screen, as if looking into the eyes of every viewer, every citizen, and directly into the eyes of Alex Morgan.

"Morgan," Blake continued, the name a bullet shot into the heart of the city's fear, "your reign of manipulation ends today. We are not your pawns; we are not your playthings. We are the force that will dismantle the chaos you've sown."

It was a bold move, one that would surely draw Morgan's attention, force him to react. Blake was counting on it.

The city, so long held in the grip of Morgan's terror, watched as Blake's broadcast played out. In homes and on devices, in the very den of Morgan himself, the message was clear: the hunter had become the hunted.

As the broadcast ended, the team waited in a tense silence. Blake stood, eyes fixed on the map of the city spread out before him. The psychological seeds were sown; now it was time to see what fruit they bore.

A call came in, the voice of an officer stationed near one of Morgan's known hideouts. "Detective Blake, we've got movement. Looks like your message hit a nerve."

Blake allowed himself a small smile. "Good. Keep eyes on it. He'll be looking to regain control, which means he'll make a mistake. And we'll be there when he does."

The psychological edge they needed had been gained. The message had been a gambit, a play that laid bare Blake's own understanding of the man they were up against. It was a declaration that they were not afraid, that they would stand against the darkness with the light of truth.

The team rallied around Blake, their own resolve steeled by the conviction of their leader. They were ready to follow him into the heart of the storm, into the battle that awaited.

Blake's voice was the last sound in the room before they moved out. "Let's bring him into the light."

*

The air of the operations room was thick with an unspoken dread, a silent miasma that clung to each member of

Detective Charlie Blake's task force. They stood as a spectacle of vigilance, their eyes betraying the heavy burden of knowing that among them walked a traitor.

Blake had always prided himself on his ability to read people, to anticipate the bends in human nature. But this betrayal cut deep, not just into the fabric of their mission but into the very heart of their bond as a team.

The room, usually abuzz with the low hum of strategy and determination, was now a cavern of tension. They had gathered to finalise their plan to capture Morgan, but first, they had to confront the rot within.

"Marcus," Blake's voice was a blade, sharp and direct, as he addressed the man they had once counted as their own. "Why?"

Marcus, the man they had trusted, now stood with his head bowed, the shame of his betrayal a heavy cloak. "It was my sister," he confessed, his voice a whisper of defeat. "Morgan... he has her. I didn't have a choice."

The team absorbed the blow, the realisation that their campaign against Morgan had been compromised from within by a threat more insidious than any they had prepared for—a threat to family.

Sarah Jennings stepped forward, her eyes hard as steel. "We understand loyalty, Marcus. But you should have trusted us to help you."

Blake's gaze shifted to the rest of his team, his eyes locking with each in turn. "This is the price of betrayal," he announced, his voice resonating with a cold finality. "The price is trust, and the cost... the cost is our unity."

The silence that followed was a chasm, bridged only by the unspoken resolve that filled the space. Blake would not allow the fracture to spread; they were stronger than the forces that sought to divide them.

He turned back to the map, his finger tracing the lines that represented streets and lives, the city that was counting on them. "We adapt, we overcome," he stated with renewed resolve. "We will bring Morgan to justice, and we will do it together. Marcus, you will help us. It's time to make this right."

Marcus nodded, a broken man seeking redemption. He divulged everything he knew, every detail that Morgan had forced from him, turning his betrayal into their advantage.

The team worked with a feverish intensity, reshaping their strategy around the new information. Elena fortified their tech defences, Sarah reassessed Morgan's psychological profile, and Dan recalculated the financial implications.

Blake watched his team, a sense of pride welling within him. They were more than a team; they were the embodiment of resilience, a phoenix rising from the ashes of deceit.

As they set out, the gravity of their mission anchored each step. The betrayal had been a wound, but in its healing, they found a renewed strength. They were ready to step into the fray, ready to face the darkness with a light that was all the brighter for the shadows it had endured.

*

The city lay quiet as the first light of dawn crept across the skyline, but beneath the serenity, a storm brewed, ready to break. Detective Charlie Blake's task force, clad in tactical gear, stood assembled in the muted glow of early morning. This was it—the decisive battle that would determine the fate of Alex Morgan's reign of terror.

Blake surveyed his team, a silent affirmation of the trust and camaraderie that had been their armour in the fight against the darkness. "Remember," he said, his voice a steady undercurrent beneath the adrenaline that charged the air, "we're not just dismantling an operation; we're dismantling a philosophy. Stay sharp, stay focused."

The team nodded, each member a coiled spring of readiness. Elena Martinez, her face a mask of stoic resolve, checked her weapon one final time. Mike Hanover's eyes were alert, his fingers poised to disrupt any digital offensive Morgan's forces might launch.

They moved out, a stealthy procession of shadows converging on the coordinates that would lead them to Morgan. The industrial complex loomed ahead, a maze of metal and concrete that had been Morgan's fortress. But today, it would witness his downfall.

As they breached the perimeter, silent alarms were triggered, invisible signals that sang out into the morning. Mike's handiwork ensured their approach remained a ghostly whisper, giving them the precious element of surprise.

They split into teams, each moving with the precision of a well-rehearsed play. Blake and Elena led one group, their path a calculated advance through the complex's spine. Mike and Dan took another route, cutting off any escape that Morgan might attempt.

The first sign of resistance met them in the form of Morgan's guards, but they were quickly and quietly subdued, a testament to the team's efficiency and Morgan's underestimation of their resolve.

Blake's team reached the central hub, the heart of Morgan's operation, where the final stand would take place. The room was a cavernous space, a cathedral to Morgan's ego, where monitors displayed the breadth of his network.

They didn't have to wait long. The sound of heavy doors sliding open heralded Morgan's entrance, a dramatic display meant to intimidate. But Blake's team was beyond such tactics; they were the embodiment of the storm Morgan had so often fancied himself the master of.

Morgan stood there, a smirk playing on his lips as he took in the sight of the encircling law enforcement. "Detective Blake," he greeted, his voice a calm sneer. "You think you've won?"

Blake stepped forward, his own expression unyielding. "It's over, Morgan. Your network is dismantled. Your reign ends here."

What followed was a maelstrom, as Morgan's forces, hidden within the complex, emerged in a last, desperate offensive. But Blake's team was relentless, a force of retribution that met each attack with unflinching courage.

Bullets flew, shattering the silence of dawn, as the team engaged in a ballet of gunfire and strategy. Elena moved with lethal grace, her aim true, while Mike's hands flew over his portable tech, jamming signals and disarming traps with digital mastery.

The battle raged, echoing through the halls of the complex, a cacophony of justice clashing with the remnants of anarchy. Blake himself moved through the fray, a figure of unwavering resolve, his focus solely on bringing Morgan to justice.

And then, as swiftly as it had begun, the tide turned. Morgan, realising the futility of his position, attempted to flee—but Blake was there, anticipating the move. They faced off, the detective and the criminal mastermind, the final confrontation between light and darkness.

As the team secured the remaining forces, Blake

approached Morgan, who was now cornered, the realisation of his defeat sinking in. "You never understood," Blake said, his voice resolute. "It's not about control or power. It's about protecting those who can't protect themselves."

With Morgan in custody, the team exhaled a collective sigh of relief. The fray had ended, but their resolve remained, the knowledge that they had faced the darkness and emerged victorious a testament to their unwavering spirit.

*

The aftermath of the battle was not just one of smoke and debris but of a stark revelation of the human condition. As Blake's team secured the perimeter of Morgan's last stronghold, the air was heavy with more than just the remnants of gunfire; it was laden with the weight of lives intertwined in the chaos of a man's dark vision.

In the midst of the controlled chaos, a small, incongruous sound pierced the veil of concentration—a soft, rhythmic whimpering that drew Elena's attention. She followed the sound, her steps measured, her weapon at the ready, until she came upon a door, slightly ajar. Pushing it open, the sight that met her eyes was a jarring counterpoint to the world outside.

Huddled in the corner of the dimly lit room was a young girl, no more than seven, her eyes wide with the terror of the unknown. Elena's heart clenched at the sight, the child's fear a palpable thing that seemed to call out to her own maternal instincts. She holstered her weapon and knelt, her voice a soft whisper meant to soothe.

"It's okay, you're safe now," Elena murmured, her hand extended in a silent offer of peace.

The girl's response was hesitant, a tentative reach that

spoke of a trust that had been shattered by the events she had been witness to. As Elena enveloped the child's small hand in her own, the bond was formed—a connection that was a beacon of light in the lingering darkness.

Blake, having been alerted to the discovery, joined Elena, his expression softening as he took in the scene. "We'll get her to safety," he promised, the unspoken vow to protect the innocence that had survived the storm evident in his tone.

As they escorted the young girl out, her hand clutching Elena's with a quiet strength, the team gathered around, their battle-hardened facades melting away to reveal the compassion beneath. This moment, this small victory of humanity, was a light in the darkness, a reminder of why they fought, why they bore the weight of the badge.

The girl, now safe in the arms of the paramedics, turned to look at her saviours, her eyes reflecting a depth of understanding far beyond her years. In that gaze was the acknowledgment of the monsters they had vanquished and the heroes they truly were.

Blake watched as the ambulance drove away, the light of its tail lamps a receding promise in the night. He turned to his team, their silhouettes outlined by the first light of dawn breaking on the horizon.

"This is why we do it," he said, his voice carrying the conviction of their shared creed. "Not for the takedowns or the accolades, but for the lives we touch, for the hope we bring."

The team stood in silent agreement, their resolve fortified by the truth that had been laid bare in the aftermath. They were the guardians of the light, the sentinels standing watch at the boundary where shadows gave way to the dawn.

As they prepared to leave the scene, each carried with them the image of the child they had rescued, a symbol of the light they had fought to restore to a city that had been held in the grip of fear for far too long.

*

The final pieces of Blake's plan clicked into place with the precision of a well-crafted timepiece. The trap for Morgan had been meticulously laid out, each component resting on the other, a cascade of events that would lead to the inevitable capture of a man who had fancied himself untouchable.

In the subdued lighting of the makeshift command post, the air hummed with a silent charge, a collective breath held in anticipation. The team was dispersed, each member in their position, ready to spring the trap that Blake had orchestrated. They were shadows within shadows, an unseen force encircling Morgan's last known stronghold.

"Positions," Blake's voice was a soft command over the radio, a conductor's cue to a symphony of justice. "Stand by."

Elena, her senses heightened by the adrenaline coursing through her veins, nodded from her vantage point. Mike, his gaze locked on the bank of monitors before him, gave a silent thumbs up. Sarah and Dan, each poised for the takedown, waited for the moment to strike.

Blake's trap was not one of brute force: it was a chess game, and they were moments away from checkmate. Morgan, unaware of the net closing in around him, continued his machinations, a spider in the centre of a web that was about to be unravelled.

And then, with the suddenness of a lightning strike, it began.

Mike's hand flew to his keyboard, sending the signal that breached Morgan's digital defences, a Trojan horse that infiltrated and brought down the surveillance network that had been Morgan's eyes and ears.

Simultaneously, Elena and Dan moved in, their approach silent but swift, the element of surprise their greatest ally. As they breached the door to Morgan's lair, a flood of light from their tactical flashlights sliced through the darkness, the beams converging on the figure of Alex Morgan.

Morgan's expression, one of shock and disbelief, was the canvas upon which the realisation of his downfall was painted. His arms raised slowly as the team closed in, the instruments of his capture a symphony of precision and planning.

Blake stepped into the room, his presence the final note in the opus that had been their pursuit. "Alex Morgan," he said, the name an epitaph for the empire of shadows that was now nothing but dust. "You are under arrest."

The words were not just a statement; they were the closing of a chapter that had held the city in its grip of fear. The team moved in, their movements a dance of efficiency as they secured Morgan, the man who had thought himself a god now just a man in cuffs.

As Morgan was led away, his empire crumbling around him, the team allowed themselves a moment of quiet triumph. The trap had been sprung, and it had held fast. The shadows that had once loomed so large were now dispelled, the light of justice shining through.

Blake watched as Morgan disappeared into the waiting vehicle, his eyes reflecting not just the light of dawn that was now breaking but the light of a battle won, a city saved, and a future reclaimed from the darkness.

The trap had been sprung, and it had captured more than a criminal; it had captured hope.

Chapter 24: The Endgame

Convergence

The city was a chessboard once again as dawn cast its first rays over the skyline, the golden light touching the tops of buildings like a benediction for the battle to come. Detective Charlie Blake stood before his team, their faces set in a grim determination, ready for the convergence of all paths in the final showdown with Alex Morgan.

The station had become a war room, maps and screens alive with the flow of information as the last threads of Morgan's empire were traced and targeted. Today would see the end of Morgan's machinations, the final moves in a game that had spanned the darkest corners of the city.

Blake's eyes met those of his team, each member a vital piece in the strategy that would bring Morgan to justice. "This is where everything we've done comes to a head," Blake said, his voice the calm before the storm. "Today, we end this."

Elena Martinez stood by the monitors, her posture betraying none of the fatigue that fought for a foothold in her bones. Mike Hanover was ready at his station, the digital maestro prepared to counter any last-minute cyber offensives. Sarah Jennings and Dan Brooks were a united front, their expertise a cornerstone of the day's critical movements.

The team moved out, a synchronised force descending upon the locations that formed the sinew of Morgan's remaining power. The city began to wake, the normalcy of its routine a stark contrast to the silent battle being waged in its shadows.

In a nondescript building that had served as Morgan's

fortress of solitude, Blake and his team prepared to breach. This was where Morgan would be, surrounded by his most loyal protectors, those who had not yet realised the futility of their allegiance.

The door gave way under the weight of the ram, and the team surged forward, a singular entity driven by the collective will to see justice served. The halls of the building echoed with the sounds of confrontation, the staccato rhythm of a final stand.

They found Morgan in his inner sanctum, a room that was a testament to his ego, walls adorned with the trappings of power and control. But his empire was crumbling, the walls figuratively falling around him as Blake's team dismantled the last vestiges of his network.

Morgan's eyes, cold and calculating, met Blake's, a silent acknowledgment passing between them. This was the convergence, the point where the hunter and the hunted met, where the game would reach its conclusion.

Blake stepped forward, his team fanning out behind him. "Alex Morgan, it's over," he declared, the words a gavel pronouncing judgment.

And with those words, the endgame began.

*

The chamber was cold and sterile, its walls echoing the emptiness of the victories and defeats that had transpired within its confines. This was the theatre where the final act of Blake and Morgan's intricate dance would unfold, a culmination of strategy, intellect, and sheer human will.

Detective Charlie Blake entered the interrogation room, the door closing behind him with a decisive click that marked the threshold between justice and the moral abyss Morgan had created. Across from him, Alex Morgan sat cuffed, yet his posture remained defiant, almost regal, as if the steel table between them were his court and the handcuffs his sceptre.

Blake's eyes were unforgiving, the lines on his face etched by the countless hours spent in pursuit of the man before him. He placed a dossier on the table, the sound sharp in the silence, a prelude to the verbal sparring to come. "Alex Morgan," he began, his voice carrying the weight of the law and the burdens of the innocent. "Your game ends here."

Morgan's gaze met Blake's, unwavering, a smile playing on his lips as if he savoured the moment. "Detective," he replied, his tone laced with chilling amusement. "Do you truly believe you've won?"

Blake leaned forward, the shadow of the room's single light casting a stark contrast on his features. "It's not about winning or losing, Morgan. It's about justice," he stated, sliding the dossier toward the man who had eluded and challenged him at every turn.

Within the dossier lay the evidence of Morgan's heinous acts, the stories of lives he had shattered, and the web of deceit he had woven through the city's underbelly. As Morgan flipped through the pages, his smirk faded, replaced by the realisation that the walls he had built around him had crumbled.

Blake watched, his analytical mind dissecting Morgan's reactions: each flicker of emotion, every subtle shift. This was more than a clash of ideals; it was a confrontation between two men who had shaped each other's destinies in their relentless chase.

"Look at them, Morgan. Every victim, every life you thought you could take without consequence," Blake continued—each word deliberate and calculated to unravel Morgan further.

Morgan's composure began to crack, the facade of the untouchable mastermind slipping. "You think you understand, Blake? You see this as a black-and-white world of crime and punishment. But it's all grey, Detective. I am but a shade within it."

Blake's response was a cold laugh, devoid of humour. "Grey is just a mixture of light and darkness, Morgan. And I'm here to bring you into the light."

The room fell silent, the tension a palpable force that seemed to suffocate the space between them. Blake stood, his chair scraping against the floor, a herald to the closing of this chapter. "You will face the consequences of your actions. You will see how the system you so despise dispenses justice."

Morgan leaned back, the chains of his cuffs rattling against the table, a discordant melody to his defeat. "We shall see, Detective. We shall see."

The door opened, officers ready to escort Morgan to his cell, but the true battle had been fought and won here, in this room, with words and wills as weapons. Blake didn't look back as he left; his mind was already on the aftermath, the healing that the city and his team would need.

But, in this moment, he allowed himself a small, private victory. The battle of wits had ended, and the will of justice had prevailed.

*

The walls of the interrogation room seemed to close in, the very air charged with the electricity of impending finality. Detective Charlie Blake, the embodiment of relentless pursuit, stood resolute as his team, weary yet unbroken, mustered around him. They were at breaking point, on the precipice of culmination, each one pushing beyond their known limits to support their leader, their comrade-in-arms.

Sarah Jennings, her eyes shadowed but sharp, watched through the two-way mirror as Blake paced like a caged lion before Morgan, who sat with deceptive calm. Mike Hanover's hands, though steady, betrayed a tremble as he manned the surveillance equipment, ensuring not a single word was lost. Elena Martinez stood at Sarah's side, her posture rigid with tension, testament to the emotional and physical marathon they had endured.

Their collective breath seemed to hold as Blake stopped pacing and leaned in towards Morgan, his voice a low growl of determination. "You can't outlast the law, Morgan. You think you've designed an intricate web, but we've been unravelling it strand by strand."

Morgan's only response was a slow, taunting clap. "Bravo, Detective. But the question remains: how much has this 'unravelling' cost you and your team? How far have you stretched before breaking?"

Blake's fist slammed onto the table, a punctuation in the silence. "This is not about us. This is about every life you've darkened with your schemes. And that... that gives us the strength to break you."

Outside, the team flinched at the sound, each feeling the reverberation as if it were a crack in their own armour. But it wasn't a crack of weakness; it was the fissure that would break the dam, allowing the waters of justice to flood through.

They watched as Blake continued the psychological onslaught, dismantling Morgan's defences with each pointed word, each shred of evidence laid bare. The team's role was silent but pivotal, their support the fortress from which Blake launched his final assault.

As the hours ticked by, the stand-off in the interrogation room mirrored the internal struggle within each team member. They grappled with their own fatigue, their own doubts, their own fears. Yet, with each passing moment, with each revelation from Blake's lips, their spirits were bolstered.

This was the breaking point—not of surrender, but of breakthrough. It was the moment when the tide shifted, when the last walls guarding Morgan's psyche began to crumble, when the team, bound by a shared resolve, stood unwavering against the tempest.

The chapter would close not with the snap of a breaking will but with the roar of a breaking wave, the triumph of a team standing shoulder to shoulder, their resolve turning the tide in the final act of their long and arduous journey.

*

The sun was high now, its midday glare reflecting off the glass and steel of the city, a beacon of light that seemed to pierce through the shadows that had so long been cast by Alex Morgan's network. In the relative calm of the station, Detective Charlie Blake and his team stood amidst a warren of papers, digital displays, and corkboards laced with strings and pins—a physical manifestation of the intricate web they were now unravelling.

Sarah Jennings, her eyes weary yet unwavering, traced the connections on the board, her mind dissecting the network with the precision of a surgeon. "Here," she said, pointing to a cluster of pins tied to a series of offshore accounts, "these are the financial nodes. If we sever these, the rest will wither."

Mike Hanover nodded, his fingers flying across his

keyboard as he brought up account after account on his screens, each one a strand of the web that had ensnared the city. "I can freeze these accounts, redirect the funds back to the legitimate channels. It will cause chaos in Morgan's ranks; they won't be able to move without tripping alarms."

Elena Martinez, her face a mask of determination, studied the layout of a building that had served as Morgan's command centre. "I've got teams ready to move on this location. Once we take this down, it will send a clear message: Morgan's empire is collapsing."

Blake watched his teamwork, a sense of pride swelling within him. They had been through the crucible, faced their own darkness, and now stood on the precipice of victory—not just for themselves, but for the city that had placed its trust in them.

The web was unravelling rapidly now, each move they made causing it to disintegrate further. Blake could almost hear the echoes of Morgan's network as it fell apart, the sound of justice that had been so long in the making.

But it was more than just taking down a criminal empire; it was about restoring faith, about showing the city that the web that had once seemed so impenetrable was nothing before the light of truth and the resolve of those who served it.

As the day wore on, the team dismantled Morgan's network piece by piece. They arrested key players, seized assets, and shut down operations that had plagued the city for too long. With each move, they could feel the tide turning, the balance shifting back to the side of order and peace.

And then, amidst the sea of activity, Blake received

the call. The voice on the other end was crisp, definitive. "It's done, sir. The last of Morgan's safe houses has been cleared out."

Blake hung up the phone, allowing himself a moment of quiet satisfaction before turning to his team. "We've done it," he announced. "Morgan's web has unravelled. The city can breathe again."

The room erupted into subdued cheers; the exhaustion of their long campaign tempered by the sweet taste of victory. They had pushed beyond their limits, and now, as they counted the high cost of their pursuit, they knew it had been worth it.

The web had unravelled, and in its place stood a team, a city, ready to move forward into the light.

*

The clock in the station's operations room ticked on, marking the passage of time in a place where it had stood still for too long. Detective Charlie Blake and his team sat in a circle of chairs, no barriers between them, no rank—just human beings facing the toll of their triumph. The room was silent, save for the occasional shuffle of a foot or the soft clearing of a throat, as each member grappled with the cost of their victory.

Blake looked around the circle, his eyes resting on each of his team members in turn. They were more than colleagues; they were comrades who had traversed the darkest paths together. Each face told a story of sacrifice, of sleepless nights and personal tolls, of relationships strained and sacrifices made for the greater good.

Sarah Jennings, her fingers laced tightly together, spoke first. "We did what we set out to do," she said, her voice steady but soft. "But I can't help but think of those we couldn't save, the ones caught in Morgan's web that we couldn't reach in time."

Elena Martinez nodded, her eyes reflective. "And the danger we faced... It wasn't just our lives on the line, but our families', our friends'. We've won, yes, but at a cost that I'm still trying to comprehend."

Mike Hanover leaned forward, his elbows on his knees. "The lines we had to walk, the decisions we had to make. I'm proud of what we've done, but there are moments I wish I could erase from my memory."

Dan Brooks, usually the most stoic among them, allowed a crack in his armour. "I've been chasing numbers, assets, and shadows for so long," he admitted. "Now, we have to rebuild, not just the city's financials but the trust that was broken."

Blake listened, his heart heavy with the weight of their words. He knew all too well the price they had paid. The victory they had achieved was not just in capturing Morgan or dismantling his network; it was in standing up against an evil that sought to corrupt the very soul of their city.

"We've paid a high price," Blake finally said, his voice resonant in the quiet room. "But remember this: our city sleeps peacefully tonight because of what we've done. The peace we've given them... it's worth every hardship we've endured."

The team fell into a contemplative silence, each lost in their thoughts, their emotions a tangled web as complex as the one they had unravelled. They had paid a high price, but in their hearts they knew that they would pay it again, without hesitation, for the safety and peace of the streets they had sworn to protect.

As they rose from their chairs, there was a sense of closure, of a chapter ending. They had faced the darkness, and though it had exacted its toll they had emerged into the light—not unscathed, but undefeated.

The cost of victory was high, but the reward—a city saved, lives changed—was higher still. And as they walked out of the operations room, they carried with them not just the weight of their sacrifices but the knowledge that they had made a difference, that they had stood on the side of light against the shadows.

*

In the sterile chill of the holding facility, Detective Charlie Blake stood before the cell that held Alex Morgan. The din of the station was a distant murmur here, the silence a canvas for the final encounter between two men whose lives had become inexorably intertwined.

Morgan sat on the edge of the steel cot; his usual arrogance replaced by a quiet contemplation. His hands were clasped, his eyes following Blake with a mix of resentment and something that might have been respect.

Blake stepped closer, the bars between them a symbolic divide that ran deeper than the physical. "Alex," he began, his voice echoing slightly in the stark expanse, "it's not often we see the full consequence of our actions, but here we are."

Morgan tilted his head slightly, the ghost of a smirk on his lips. "Detective, even now, you seek some sort of poetic justice?"

"It's not about poetry, it's about truth," Blake replied, holding Morgan's gaze. "You built an empire on fear and corruption, but look around you—this is where it ends. Not with a bang, but a whimper."

Morgan's expression hardened. "You think this cell holds me? Ideas, Detective, are far more difficult to incarcerate."

Blake nodded, acknowledging the point. "Ideas can be powerful, but so is the law. And the truth it upholds. Your ideas will fade, but the truth will remain."

For a moment, there was silence, the two men locked in a final stand-off, not of guns or fists but of ideals.

Then, Blake turned to leave, pausing briefly to add, "Your trial will be fair, Morgan. Justice will be served, and the city will move forward. That is the truth you cannot escape."

As Blake walked away, the sound of his footsteps receding, Morgan sat back on his cot, the reality of his situation settling upon him like the weight of the walls around him. The empire he had built, the power he had wielded—it had all come to this, a moment of truth in a cold cell.

Outside, Blake allowed himself a deep breath, feeling the burden of the case lifting. The city would indeed move forward, and so would he, carrying with him the lessons learned, the battles fought, and the truth that had been his guiding star.

The endgame was complete, and in this final moment of truth the light of justice shone clear and undimmed.

Chapter 25: Aftermath

Reflection

The night air hung heavy over London, a stark silence settling where sirens had once screamed. Charlie Blake stood alone on the roof of the Metropolitan Police headquarters, overlooking the city's expanse—a chaotic tapestry of lives and stories, of secrets buried deep within the shadows. It was over. Alex Morgan, the spectre from his past who had morphed into the city's most feared nightmare, was now confined behind the iron bars of justice.

Blake's mind replayed the final confrontation, each moment etched into his memory with painful clarity. There had been a look in Morgan's eyes—something beyond hatred, beyond vengeance. It was as if, in that final breath before surrender, Morgan had passed on a weight, an invisible torch that Blake now carried alone.

Around him, the team was processing the victory in their own ways. Some found solace in quiet solitude, others in the clinking glasses at the pub down the street. But each of them, like Blake, carried the marks of their journey—some visible, others buried beneath a facade of strength.

Sarah Jennings, Blake's steadfast partner, had approached the aftermath with a quiet grace. She understood the cost of their victory more than most. In the dim light of her office, her eyes scanned the case files that had consumed their lives. Each photograph, each piece of evidence, was testament to their resilience. Yet as she packed them away, one by one; she couldn't shake the feeling that something remained unfinished, that

Morgan's shadow might never fully recede from their lives.

Michael Hanover, the digital forensics specialist, sat before his monitors, the glow casting an eerie light across his focused expression. He delved into the digital footprints they had traced, the web of connections Morgan had spun across the city. Despite the closure, his search continued, driven by the nagging thought that they had only seen the surface. *What else lay hidden in the digital depths?*

Lieutenant Grace Hudson, once a soldier beside Blake, now stood as a reminder of the world he had left behind. Their last conversation lingered in his thoughts—a blend of military brevity and an unspoken understanding that some wars never truly end. She had saluted him, not just for the victory, but for the battles he continued to fight within himself.

Blake's gaze shifted to the streets below, where life moved on, indifferent to the scars left in the wake of justice. The chase had ended, but the reflection had only just begun. Each step they had taken, each choice made in the darkness, had led them here—to a victory that felt as much a loss as a triumph.

As the city's heartbeat pulsed beneath him, Blake realised the journey was far from over. The path to healing was just another road to travel, winding and uncertain. But for now, he allowed himself a moment to simply breathe, to feel the weight of what they had accomplished, and what it had cost them all.

The reflection was not one of triumph, but of survival. And as the dawn began to break, spilling light over a city that had seen too much darkness, Charlie Blake and his team were left to ponder the immeasurable depth of their sacrifice, and the resilience of the human spirit that carried them through.

*

The halls of justice echoed with the footsteps of the weary as Alex Morgan was led in shackles, a stark contrast to the shadow he once cast. The courtroom was a theatre where the final act of his macabre play would unfold. Blake watched from the gallery, his eyes never leaving Morgan, seeking an answer in the man's calm demeanour. He wondered what justice would look like for a man who had redefined the very concept of crime in the city.

Blake wasn't alone in his search for meaning. The families of the victims, the press, the public—they all sought closure from the trial. Dr Helen Zhao, the criminal psychologist, had spent countless hours profiling Morgan, yet even she sat with bated breath as the charges were read. There was a collective need to see the man behind the monster, to understand the why behind the horrors.

The trial was a reckoning, not just for Morgan, but for the entire city. His crimes had touched so many lives, had altered the very fabric of London. Simon Fraser, the journalist who had doggedly covered Blake's cases, tapped away at his laptop, his fingers capturing the weight of the moment. Each click of the keys was a reminder that the story wasn't over; it was simply entering a new chapter.

As the evidence was presented, a chilling silence fell over the room. Photos, videos, testimonies—each piece a fragment of the darkness that had once lurked unseen. Blake's team, who had pieced together this puzzle, now watched as the full picture was laid bare for all to see. Sarah's eyes were fixed forward, her expression unreadable. Hanover's face was a mask of concentration, his mind already analysing the proceedings with a detective's detachment.

The prosecutor, Fiona Barrett, presented the case with precision and resolve. Her words were sharp, each sentence meticulously crafted to ensure that justice would be served. She knew the legal system was not just about punishment; it was about restoration, about the community's collective healing.

Morgan's influence had indeed been deep, and questions lingered in the air like the remnants of a bad dream. How had he remained a step ahead? What secrets did he still hold? Blake felt the weight of those questions, but he also felt something else—a sense of responsibility, to learn from the past, to prevent such a force from ever rising again.

The judge's gavel fell, and, with it, a chapter in Blake's life closed. But as Morgan was led away, his eyes met Blake's one last time, a silent exchange that spoke volumes. In that look, Blake saw the end of one story and the seeds of another. The reckoning had been delivered, but the echoes of Morgan's deeds would resonate long after the cell door locked.

As Blake stepped out into the sunlight, the city breathed around him, a living organism that had survived its illness. He knew that the healing was only just beginning, both for those who had suffered at Morgan's hands and for himself. The road to recovery would be long, but it was a path that they could now start to walk.

*

The dust had settled in the squad room, but the air still carried a charge, the echo of urgency that had thrummed through its walls now replaced by a subdued hush.

Detective Sarah Jennings manoeuvred through the desks, her steps careful, as if the floor were littered with the remnants of the past months' chaos. Each desk, each chair held a story of late nights, of cold coffee sipped in desperation, of theories debated until dawn.

At her desk, she found a small pot of chrysanthemums, their yellow blooms bright against the grey backdrop. A card leaned against it, the handwriting unmistakably that of Emily Saunders, the team's forensic pathologist. *For healing*, it read. It was a small gesture, but it spoke volumes of the solidarity that had fortified them.

She glanced across to where Charlie Blake stood, his gaze lingering on the empty space where Morgan's file had once been an omnipresent weight. He seemed to be in conversation with himself, a silent debate that required no other participant. Blake had always carried his burdens internally, but now, with the case closed, those burdens demanded to be acknowledged, if not shared.

"You okay?" she asked, breaking the silence.

Blake's eyes met hers, a tumult of reflections passing through them before he nodded slowly. "Yeah. Just... thinking about the next steps."

"The wounds are still fresh, Charlie. It's okay to take a moment to heal," she reminded him, her voice a soft undercurrent of concern.

He sighed, running a hand through his hair. "Healing isn't something we're trained for, Sarah. We chase, we catch, we move on. But this..." He gestured vaguely around the room, encompassing all that had transpired, "it's different."

"It is," she agreed, setting the flowers on her desk. "But we did more than just chase and catch, didn't we? We looked after each other. We'll keep doing that."

Natalie Chen, the newest recruit, approached hesitantly, her youthful features etched with a question. "Detective Jennings, I... I was wondering if..." She trailed off, unsure.

Sarah turned to her with an encouraging nod. "What is it, Natalie?"

"Is it always like this? The aftermath, I mean. Does it always feel like there's something left unfinished?"

Sarah considered the question, aware of Blake's attention now fixed on the young detective. "Sometimes it does," she said truthfully. "But that feeling—that's where growth happens. It's where we learn how to be better detectives, and more importantly, better people."

Blake stepped forward, adding his perspective to the mentorship unfolding before him. "Morgan's gone, but the echoes of what he did will stay with us. That's the nature of our work. We carry the echoes, so the city doesn't have to."

Michael Hanover chimed in from his desk, where he'd been eavesdropping with a light-hearted grin. "And if we're lucky, those echoes turn into wisdom. Right, boss?"

Blake cracked a small smile, the first genuine one in what felt like an eternity. "Let's hope so, Mike."

The conversation drifted into a comfortable lull, each member of the team lost in their reflections, their shared experience binding them in silent understanding. They were wounded, yes, but not broken. Together, they would find a way to mend the fractures, to smooth the jagged edges left by the case. The process would be gradual, with setbacks and victories in equal measure, but they would endure.

As the afternoon sun cast long shadows across the room, it seemed to paint the space with a promise—a promise that while the wounds of the past might never fully disappear, they would, in time, become less of a scar and more of a badge, a testament to their strength and their unwavering commitment to justice.

*

The city's underbelly, once a thriving nexus of unspoken deals and shadowed meetings, felt the tremors of change. In the wake of Morgan's capture, the criminal world was in disarray. Power vacuums opened like wounds, and the dark corners where fear had reigned now flickered with uncertainty. Detective Charlie Blake, from his vantage point within the Met. Police, could sense the shift—a tectonic realignment of the landscape he knew so well.

In the aftermath, the team gathered in the now too-quiet war room, the hum of monitors a soft backdrop to their introspection. "It's like cutting the head off a snake," mused Detective Tim Carter, his voice a low rumble in the stillness. "The rest of them are all scattering, trying to find some dark hole to hide in."

Sarah Jennings nodded, her eyes on the city map that sprawled across the wall, its web of digital pins and strings a testament to their long struggle. "They're scared," she observed. "Morgan wasn't just a leader; he was a symbol. His fall... it's shaken the foundations."

Lieutenant Grace Hudson, her military posture somewhat relaxed in this familiar setting, chimed in. "And it's not just the criminals. There's a ripple effect. The public's perception, the pressure on political offices, other departments... Everyone's watching to see what moves we'll make next."

Charlie Blake, leaning against the table's edge, felt the weight of those words. The case had been more than a pursuit; it had been a crusade, altering the very fabric of their reality. The victory was not without its cost, and the landscape they were left with was unfamiliar territory that needed navigating with care and foresight.

Dr Helen Zhao, the criminal psychologist who had delved deep into the mind of Morgan, understood the psychological impact of such a shift. "The void left by Morgan will create a power struggle. There will be those who attempt to rise, to take what they perceive as theirs," she said, her voice steady. "Our work has, in some ways, just begun. We must be vigilant, as the chaos of transition can be as dangerous as the reign of a tyrant."

The team absorbed her words, each lost in thought. Blake knew the challenges ahead required a new strategy, a new way to police a city that was redefining itself in the wake of their most significant victory.

Elena Martinez, who had been instrumental as an undercover operative within Morgan's network, spoke up. "We've disrupted the ecosystem. It's going to take time for a new order to establish itself."

Blake looked at his team, their faces a mixture of fatigue and quiet satisfaction. "We'll adapt, as we always do," he stated with a resolve that had carried them this far. "We'll continue to protect this city, no matter what form the threat takes."

As they filed out of the war room, the screens continued to flicker, the only witnesses to the silent promise that hung in the air. The landscape had changed, but so had they—tempered by fire, bound by a shared purpose, they were ready to face whatever new challenges the city held in its depths.

*

The stillness of the station was a stark contrast to the cacophony that had once filled its corridors. Charlie

Blake, a sentinel of justice, paused at the threshold of the office he had known as his command centre. The walls, once lined with the frenetic energy of crime-solving, now harboured the silence of completion. His team had dispersed, some to desks piled with new cases, others to the respite they had earned.

Detective Sarah Jennings was among the former, her eyes scanning the burgeoning files on her desk. Each represented a thread of the city's complex tapestry, a new story to unravel. She felt the pull of the chase, the seduction of the unsolved, but the shadow of their recent victory tempered her eagerness with a newfound sobriety.

Michael Hanover had turned his attention to mentoring the next wave of digital forensics experts. The echoes of his keystrokes were a different kind of music now, one that spoke of legacy and the transfer of invaluable wisdom. His humour, once a shield against the dark, had matured into a tool for inspiring others.

Lieutenant Grace Hudson found herself at a crossroads, her military discipline and police experience coalescing into a role that bridged the gap between the two worlds. She was constructing a new programme designed to prepare soldiers for transitions into law enforcement, inspired by her own journey and that of Blake's.

Elena Martinez, her cover now abandoned, was adapting to life in the daylight. She had taken to training in negotiation tactics, her undercover experiences lending authenticity to scenarios that rookies might one day face. The thrill of the covert had given way to the pride of shaping the force's future.

Blake watched them all, the bittersweet knowledge that their shared crucible had changed each life irrevocably. He felt the undercurrent of transformation, not just in his team but within himself. The weight of leadership had both grounded him and granted him flight, and now it was time to soar into uncharted skies.

His gaze fell upon the empty chair of James Carter. The grizzled detective had opted for retirement, the case's end a bookend to a storied career. Blake could still hear Carter's gruff wisdom in the quiet, a guiding echo that would remain with the team forever.

And there was Natalie Chen, the youthful optimism she had brought to the team now tempered with the steel of reality. She had chosen to specialise in victim liaison, her empathy and resilience finding a home in the healing of others.

For Blake, the future was a blank canvas. The scars he bore were maps of the past, each line charting a course of trials and triumphs. He knew the path ahead would be fraught with new challenges, but the taste of victory had rekindled a flame that no darkness could extinguish.

As he stepped out into the city, its cacophony a symphony of the living, he felt the pull of a new beginning. The story of Charlie Blake and his team was far from over, their next chapter whispered by the winds of fate, ready to be written in the ink of their indomitable spirit.

*

The sun dipped below the skyline, casting long shadows across the city that had been the battleground for justice. In the relative peace of the evening, Detective Charlie Blake stood by the window of his office, the files of closed cases stacked neatly on his desk, a stark contrast to the turmoil that had once reigned there. The city was quiet, but the silence was deceptive, a thin veneer over the uncertainty of the future.

Sarah Jennings broke the silence, her voice tentative. "What now, Charlie? After all this, where do we go from here?"

Blake turned from the window, his eyes reflecting the fading light. "We did what we set out to do. We brought a monster to justice, but the world doesn't stop turning. There will be others, and we'll be ready."

Mike Hanover piped up from his corner, where the glow of computer screens couldn't hide his weary yet determined expression. "It feels like we've been through a war," he said.

"We have," Blake replied, "and wars change people. They change the world. What we've done, it matters. It's reshaped the landscape of crime and justice in this city."

Lieutenant Grace Hudson entered, her presence as commanding as ever. "This team," she began, looking at each member, "has shown what it means to stand against chaos. You've set a precedent, but the real challenge is maintaining it."

Blake nodded in agreement. "We've been in the dark for so long, chasing Morgan and his shadows. Now, it's time to step into the light and face whatever comes next."

Elena Martinez leaned against the doorframe. "We've all changed," she observed. "We're not the same people who started on this case. We're stronger, more connected. Whatever the future holds, we face it together."

The room filled with a sense of camaraderie and a quiet strength. Each person carried the scars of their ordeal, physical or otherwise, but there was an unspoken resolve that they would not be defined by the past.

Blake's gaze lingered on a photo on his desk, one of the entire team, taken on a rare day of celebration.

"Morgan's downfall... it's not the end of our story. It's just a part of it. We've turned a page, but there are many chapters left to write."

Natalie Chen, the youngest member, spoke up. "So, what's the next chapter then?"

Blake offered a small, knowing smile. "That, Detective Chen, remains to be seen. But rest assured, the pen is in our hands, and we'll write it with the same dedication we've always had."

As they left the station, the team looked out at the city—their city—with a newfound perspective. They had protected it from a monster, and now they stood ready to guard it against the next storm on the horizon. The future was uncertain, full of potential threats and unseen challenges, but one thing was clear: Detective Charlie Blake and his team would face it head-on, with the resilience and courage that had become their hallmark.

The story of Charlie Blake might have found a moment of closure, but it was far from over. The end of Morgan's reign was just the beginning of a new legacy— a legacy of bravery, sacrifice, and the relentless pursuit of justice in the face of an uncertain future.

Chapter 26: Reflections in the Aftermath

The City's Breath

London exhaled. The tension that had gripped the city's heart had finally eased, and its citizens began to embrace the mundane tapestry of everyday life once more. The newspapers, once emblazoned with grim headlines and the terror that Alex Morgan's spree had wrought, now turned to stories of hope, community, and the ordinary heroes walking the streets.

Detective Charlie Blake watched from his favourite coffee shop, a little nook that overlooked the bustling High Street. Parents with strollers, teenagers laughing with carefree abandon, couples meandering hand in hand; these were the scenes that painted the true picture of the city. This was the lifeblood that flowed through London's veins, a rhythm that spoke of resilience and an enduring spirit.

A child's balloon escaped upward, dancing towards the sky, and Blake followed its ascent with a soft smile. It was a vibrant splash of red against the grey canvas of the city, a symbol of life continuing in defiance of the darkness that had once threatened to swallow it whole. The release of that balloon seemed to mirror the collective release of the city's breath, a visual sigh that things were going to be okay.

The coffee in his hand was a comforting warmth, a simple pleasure that he had learned to appreciate all over again. There was a richness to the aroma that seemed to say that while the world could be a harsh and unforgiving place, there were still simple, good things to be found. Things worth protecting.

As the thrum of life swirled around him, Blake felt a connection to the city that went beyond duty. He had fought for it, bled for it, and seen its darkest corners, but now he was witnessing its light. It was a tapestry woven with countless threads, each one a story, a life, an existence that deserved the peace he and his team had fought so fiercely to protect.

Today, London breathed easier—and so did he. The weight of the past months had lifted, and in its place was a quiet affirmation of his purpose, a reminder that the fight, the sleepless nights, the sacrifices—all of it was for this: the simple, unremarkable beauty of a city's breath returning to normalcy.

*

The room was silent, save for the occasional creak of the old leather chair that Blake had insisted on keeping, despite its age. Here, in the sanctity of his home, surrounded by walls lined with bookshelves filled with literature and case files alike, Blake found solace. It was his haven, a place untouched by the chaos that often consumed his professional life.

He sat there, a solitary figure, the golden hue of the desk lamp casting a warm glow over the pages of an open book. But tonight, the words blurred before his eyes, his thoughts adrift on the tide of reflection that the quiet inevitably brought.

The investigation had taken more from him than he liked to admit. It had stripped layers off his soul, revealing parts of himself he had long since buried under the veneer of the stoic detective. Morgan had been a mirror in many ways, a dark reflection of what Blake could have become if life had dealt him a different hand.

His gaze shifted to the window, where the night

painted the world in shades of silver and shadow. The city's breath might have returned to normalcy, but he knew the scars it bore were much like his own—hidden beneath the surface, aching reminders of the past.

The cost of the investigation was not just measured in time or resources but in the pieces of himself he had left behind in the pursuit of justice. Yet, as he sat there, the weight of solitude felt strangely comforting. It was in these quiet moments that Blake allowed himself to feel— to acknowledge the pain, the loss, and the rare instances of fear that had crept in when the darkness seemed too dense to navigate.

But with the pain came growth, an evolution of character forged in the fires of adversity. He had emerged not unscathed, but changed, tempered by the trials he had faced. Blake knew the journey was far from over, that there would be others like Morgan in the future, other reflections of the human condition's darker side. However, he also knew that he was not the same man who had started this journey. He was stronger, more compassionate, and with a deeper understanding of the fragile balance between light and dark.

Blake closed the book and stood, stretching the stiffness from his limbs. He moved to the window, pressing a hand against the cool glass. The city was out there, breathing and living, because of the sacrifices made by those who dared to stand against the tide.

Tomorrow would bring new challenges, new cases, new battles to fight. But for now, in this moment of solitude, Charlie Blake allowed himself the space to heal, to reflect, and to prepare for whatever lay ahead, with the quiet assurance that he was ready for it all.

*

In the quiet sanctum of the conference room, the members of Blake's team assembled, a tableau of survival and perseverance. The air hummed with a soft echo of chairs scraping against the floor, papers shuffling, and the weighty silence that precedes a storm of emotions.

Blake stood at the head of the table, his eyes scanning the faces of his team—each one a story of triumph and trauma, unity and resolve. "I know it's been a long road," he started, his voice the familiar baritone that had guided them through their darkest hours, "and I can't say it enough—I'm proud of what we've achieved together."

One by one, they began to share their reflections. Sarah Jennings spoke first, her voice steady but her eyes betraying the toll the case had taken. "We dove into the abyss, and we came out on the other side. But we brought a piece of it back with us," she said, a quiet strength in her words.

Michael Hanover, the man who fought battles in cyberspace, leaned back in his chair, his fingers drumming a staccato rhythm on the table. "In all the bytes and bits, I saw the worst and the best of what people can be," he mused. "It changes you, knowing that."

Lieutenant Grace Hudson, her military discipline ever-present, added a strategic perspective. "We adapted; we overcame. But the landscape has changed; the threat matrix is different now. We need to be ready for what's next."

Emily Saunders, the forensic pathologist, rarely one for group discussions, spoke up with a soft-spoken conviction. "Every victim told a story, and in those stories, we found the truth. It's a heavy burden, carrying their last words, but it's our duty to speak for them now."

The youngest among them, Natalie Chen, offered a

fresh insight. "I came into this team looking for mentorship, for experience. I found a family, and a purpose that's larger than any of us."

Blake listened, his heart full for the team that had become his second family. "Each of you brought something unique to this fight," he acknowledged. "It wasn't just skill or knowledge, but the heart. You reminded me why we do this job."

There was a pause, a collective breath as they all shared in the weight of the moment. Then Blake continued, "We've been through the fire, but we've also seen the sparks that can start a new fire. Our job isn't just to put out flames but to make sure that what rises from the ashes is better than what came before."

As the debriefing wound down, the team was not just recounting the past but knitting a narrative for the future. They stood at the cusp of a new beginning, aware that the echoes of what they had endured would ripple outwards, shaping their paths forward.

The meeting concluded with a silent agreement, an unspoken pledge to carry forward the lessons learned, the camaraderie forged, and the resolve strengthened. They were the vanguard of a city's hope, the writers of a narrative that would continue to unfold in the streets they had sworn to protect.

And as they filed out, there was a renewed sense of purpose in their strides, a readiness for the next chapter, for the next challenge. They were the sentinels at the gates of dawn, and they were resolute.

Chapter 27: Legacies and New Beginnings

Changed Lives

The investigation had concluded, but its echoes resonated in the lives of those who had seen it through. Detective Charlie Blake's apartment now housed more than just his collection of jazz records and case files; it held the quiet reflection of a man who had been through the storm and was still standing. His mornings began not with an immediate plunge into work but with moments of solitude on his balcony, where he contemplated the city he had sworn to protect. The case had changed him, lent a softer edge to his once rigid adherence to the job. There was a new resolve in his steps, a determination to not just solve cases but to understand the human condition that lay beneath them.

Sarah Jennings found herself at the cusp of a decision that once would have seemed unthinkable—taking a sabbatical. The case had taken a toll, and she now understood the value of stepping back, of healing not just the mind but the soul. Her desk, once cluttered with the debris of tireless investigation, was an organised space, a reflection of her need for order amidst the chaos that had once reigned.

Michael Hanover had turned a corner too. The man who once lived behind screens, a barrier between him and the world, now volunteered his time teaching kids about cybersecurity. He wanted to build, to educate, to prevent the kind of darkness they fought from reaching the next generation.

Lieutenant Grace Hudson, always the soldier, found a new battlefield—advocacy. She worked with veterans, ensuring their sacrifices weren't forgotten and that their transitions to civilian life were not as turbulent as hers had been. Her leadership skills found new avenues, and her once cold efficiency was now tempered with an understanding warmth.

Emily Saunders, the forensic pathologist, dedicated a portion of her time to lecturing, sharing her knowledge and the grim realities of her work to eager minds in university halls. Her experiences had instilled in her a sense of duty to educate, to prepare the future pathologists for the world they would step into.

For the younger detectives like Natalie Chen, the case had been a crucible, a rite of passage that had instilled in her a wisdom beyond her years. She was more confident now, her contributions more assertive, her insight sharper. The case had carved out her place in the team, and she embraced it with a quiet pride.

Each member of the team carried the legacy of the investigation within them, shaping their lives in ways they could never have anticipated. The journey had been arduous, but out of the fires of their shared trial, new aspirations and paths had been forged. They were no longer just detectives and colleagues; they were the bearers of change, both within the force and in their personal lives.

*

As the city moved forward, so too did the lives of those who served to protect it. Yet, within the walls of the Metropolitan Police headquarters, there were unspoken acknowledgments of the unfinished business lingering in the air, like the faintest trace of smoke after a fire has been extinguished.

Detective Charlie Blake found himself at his desk,

staring at the sparse remnants of the Morgan case. The puzzle was ostensibly complete, yet the edges seemed not to align perfectly. There were loose threads, subtle hints that not all was as neatly tied as the records would claim. It nagged at him, this sense of incompletion, a symphony with an unresolved final note that kept the mind wary.

Sarah Jennings, too, felt the disquiet. It came to her in quiet moments, a whisper of doubt that perhaps they had been too eager to close the book on Morgan. The underworld was like a hydra: cut off one head, two more would sprout forth. Had they been thorough enough? Had they mistaken the end of a chapter for the end of the story?

Michael Hanover would spend nights poring over data trails that seemed to dissipate into the ether. There were accounts that had been left untouched, digital footprints that led to encrypted doors he couldn't open. "The internet never forgets," he would mutter to himself, the glow of the screen making spectres of his usually vibrant features.

Even as the team moved on to other cases, other pursuits, there was a collective understanding that the echoes of Alex Morgan might resurface in ways they couldn't predict. They had unravelled the web he had woven, but the silk of such webs was often stronger than anticipated, and its reach was long.

Lieutenant Grace Hudson's words during one of their briefings echoed this sentiment. "Remember, the absence of evidence is not evidence of absence. Stay sharp, we're not out of the woods yet."

And so, as they stood on the cusp of new beginnings, the team also balanced on the knife-edge of vigilance. They were changed, not just by their successes but by the realisation that their fight against the darkness was perennial. It was a truth they accepted as the cost of the badges they bore, a truth that bound them together in their unending watch over the city they called home.

*

In the intimate glow of the low-lit pub that had become their unofficial refuge, the members of Blake's team gathered around a secluded table, their faces reflecting a camaraderie that only those who have weathered great storms together could understand. Glasses raised, they paused for a moment, letting the silence speak volumes of the journey behind them and the horizon ahead.

"To us," Blake began, his voice steady and sure, "to the ones who aren't here to share this drink, and to the future—no matter what it may hold."

"The future," they echoed, the word hanging between them, a beacon of hope and a challenge yet to be met.

Sarah Jennings, her eyes brighter than they'd been in months, raised her glass higher. "To healing, to growth, and to the new roads we'll travel," she added, her gaze touching each person at the table.

Mike Hanover, with his ever-present wit, chimed in. "To the bytes and bits, the clues and the hunches, and to the humanity behind all the tech."

Grace Hudson offered a respectful nod, her toast short but laden with meaning. "To the battles ahead and the peace we fight for."

Each member of the team took their turn, words of gratitude, of remembrance, of anticipation for the challenges and the victories yet to come. They spoke of personal aspirations and professional goals, of lessons learned and wisdom gained.

Natalie Chen, her voice no longer tinged with the

naïveté of a rookie, added softly, "To the family we've become and the differences we make every day."

As the evening wore on, the conversation turned from solemn reflection to hopeful anticipation. They speculated on the nature of the new threats that awaited them, the personal endeavours they would undertake, and the unshakable bond that would continue to unite them.

The pub's old walls, steeped in the memory of a thousand such gatherings, seemed to lean in, listening to the pledges of a team that had once operated in the shadows and now stepped into the light. There was a sense that, although one chapter had closed, their story was far from finished.

As they finally stood to leave, their shadows long in the flickering candlelight, there was a sense of completeness, but also a collective understanding that the world outside would always hold more for them. More cases, more threats to the peace they held so dear, and more opportunities to affirm the oath they took as guardians of the city.

Their toast to the future was more than just words. It was a promise, a declaration that they were ready for whatever lay ahead. They would meet it with the same tenacity, the same integrity, and the same unwavering commitment to justice that had defined them from the start.

In that moment, the future was not a spectre to be feared, but a challenge to be met—a new beginning that they would face together, as they always had.

Chapter 28: New Horizons

The Unseen Threat

London had returned to its usual rhythm, the city's pulse strong and vibrant as ever. But beneath the surface, beneath the everyday bustle of life, something was stirring. Detective Charlie Blake felt it—a dissonance in the city's symphony, a note out of place.

As he walked through the crowded streets, his trained eyes scanned the faces around him. People from all walks of life went about their day, oblivious to the undercurrent of something amiss. Blake, however, was all too aware that peace was often a precursor to the storm.

It was a message waiting on his desk that solidified his instincts. An unmarked envelope, the contents cryptic—a single photograph and a note with nothing but a date and a time. No signature, no explanation, but the implication was clear: someone was reaching out from the shadows.

The photograph was of a place, nondescript and seemingly innocuous, but Blake knew better. He could read the subtext, the underlying threat that was veiled within the ordinary. It was a challenge, one that carried with it the thrill of the hunt and the chill of potential danger.

This was how it began, not with a bang but with a whisper—a nudge that set the dominoes of a larger game in motion. And Blake, along with his team, would be the ones to play it.

The threat was unseen, its shape unknown, but it was there, lurking at the edge of perception. It was a promise that the peace they had fought for was merely a temporary respite. A new adversary had emerged, one that dared to pull at the threads of the fabric they had so meticulously woven.

As Blake studied the photograph, his mind already piecing together the puzzle, he felt the stirrings of anticipation. The game was afoot once again, and the stakes were as high as ever. This unseen threat would not remain hidden for long; not if he had anything to say about it.

*

In the quiet of the early morning, before the city awoke, Charlie Blake was already at his desk, the photograph from the unmarked envelope spread out before him. The image was nondescript—a cityscape, buildings that could be anywhere in London—but to Blake, it was a canvas waiting for a stroke of insight to bring it into focus.

The hints of a new threat, the shadow of an unseen adversary, they all culminated here in this silent moment. Blake's mind was a whirlwind of strategy and intuition, honed by years on the force and countless encounters with the city's darkest elements. Yet, there was something invigorating about the unknown, about the challenge that was now taking shape in the murky edges of his city.

He thought about his team, about the bonds they had formed under pressure, in the heat of pursuit. They were his strength, each bringing unique skills and perspectives to the table, each as committed as he was to safeguarding the city they loved. He knew that whatever this new challenge was, they would face it together, with the same unbreakable spirit that had seen them through the storm of Morgan's chaos.

Blake's resolve was a beacon, a steadfast light that would guide his team through the uncertainty that lay ahead. He was the anchor, the unwavering leader whose resilience and dedication had become the backbone of their collective purpose. His determination was not just to face the upcoming challenges but to overcome them, to continue the relentless pursuit of justice.

As he sat there, the first rays of dawn breaking the horizon, Blake felt a surge of clarity. The path forward might be shrouded in shadows, but his will to protect the city from emerging threats was as bright and as sharp as the morning light. It was this resolve that would lead them, that would define the legacy of their work, and that would illuminate the path forward, no matter how treacherous it might become.

*

The final meeting room was awash with the soft glow of the evening sun, casting long shadows across the walls lined with whiteboards and case photos. The team gathered around, a sense of closure palpable in the air, but with eyes clearly set on the horizon ahead.

Blake leaned against the edge of the table, his presence as much a pillar in the room as the very columns that held the building up. "We've been through the gauntlet," he acknowledged, his voice carrying the weight of their shared experiences, "but it's what comes next that will define us."

His team, a mosaic of resilience, nodded in agreement. They had been tempered by the fires of their past trials, and now, they looked towards the future, ready for the next call to action.

Sarah Jennings, who had once contemplated a sabbatical, now found renewed purpose in her work, the idea of stepping away no longer holding the same appeal. Her analytical mind was already piecing together the fragments of the new puzzle they had been handed.

Michael Hanover, the man behind the monitors, cracked his knuckles with a grin. "Whatever this new threat is, it's just another set of data waiting to be decrypted," he said, the excitement for the challenge sparking in his eyes.

Elena Martinez, whose undercover work had been crucial, stood firm. "We have a bond that goes beyond the badge," she said. "It's that bond that will carry us through whatever comes our way."

And Natalie Chen, no longer the rookie but a seasoned detective in her own right, added, "We're more than just a team. We're a force. And we're ready."

Blake surveyed the room, his gaze lingering on each member of his team. "We've faced down the darkness before, and we'll do it again. Our path forward is clear. We walk it together, as guardians, as seekers of truth, and as symbols of hope for this city."

The meeting dispersed, but the feeling of unity remained. They had each other, a bond forged in adversity, a shared commitment to stand against the coming tide.

The city outside continued its ceaseless hum, a never-ending cycle of life and motion. But within the walls of the Metropolitan Police headquarters, a quiet determination settled over Charlie Blake and his team. They were the watchmen, the unsung heroes holding the line between order and chaos.

As the sun dipped below the skyline, night began to blanket the city. The team left the station, each member carrying with them the knowledge that tomorrow's challenges would be met with the same tenacity and resolve that had become their hallmark.

A new horizon awaited, and Detective Charlie Blake and his team were ready to face it: together.

END

About The Author

Andrew Janes (A C Janes)is an author whose passion for storytelling emerged during his travels for work in 2018. Inspired by the reflective solitude of his downtime, he began weaving intricate narratives that explore the complexities of human nature and the profound psychological impacts of life's challenges on individuals and those around them.

With a keen eye for detail and a deep appreciation for the multifaceted nature of human emotions, Andrew strives to create immersive stories that resonate with readers. His writing delves into the intricacies of his characters, offering layered perspectives and rich emotional depth. Through carefully crafted plots, he takes readers on journeys filled with tension, introspection, and moments of raw humanity, ensuring they are fully engaged with every turn of the page.

Andrew brings a fresh perspective to the literary world, combining his love for detailed narratives with an understanding of the emotional landscapes that shape us. He is committed to crafting stories that linger in the minds of readers long after they've closed the book.

www.blossomspringpublishing.com